"I CAN IMAGINE THAT YOUR TEAMS ARE SPREAD PRETTY THIN," THE PRESIDENT SAID

"Law enforcement agencies in eight nations are running themselves ragged dealing with riots orchestrated by this group, the Fist of Heaven," Brognola explained. "If anything, our boys are right where they need to be."

"And you've confirmed that this is an international amalgamation of white-supremacist groups?"

"There's a violent Christian identity organization in the U.S. called the United Legion of Messianic America," Brognola answered. "We have also encountered elements of ODESSA, the Jakkhammer Legacy, the Justice Coalition of Argentina and a Japanese pseudo-Christian cult called Masa Minori."

The President sighed. "All those crazies would have to come out of the woodwork on my watch."

Brognola managed a weak smile. "They say the caliber of a man is judged by the scope of his enemies."

"Is that a good thing or a bad thing with all these psychotic bigots?" the President asked.

Brognola looked out the window of the office, his gaze settling on the map of the world. The President waited a moment before the big Fed heaved his shoulders with a sigh, returning his attention to the conversation. "Ask me after this is over, sir."

Brognola left the Presiden~~t~~ contemplate the worldwi~~de~~

DON PENDLETON'S

STONY

AMERICA'S ULTRA-COVERT INTELLIGENCE AGENCY

MAN ®

ORBITAL
VELOCITY

A GOLD EAGLE BOOK FROM
W RLDWIDE ®

TORONTO • NEW YORK • LONDON
AMSTERDAM • PARIS • SYDNEY • HAMBURG
STOCKHOLM • ATHENS • TOKYO • MILAN
MADRID • WARSAW • BUDAPEST • AUCKLAND

Recycling programs
for this product may
not exist in your area.

First edition April 2011

ISBN-13: 978-0-373-61996-2

ORBITAL VELOCITY

Special thanks and acknowledgment to
Doug Wojtowicz for his contribution to this work.

Printed in U.S.A.

ORBITAL
VELOCITY

PROLOGUE

In the jungles of the Congo, in the border region between the Republic of the Congo—ROC—and the
Democratic Republic of the Congo—DRC—life was
especially cheap. In the ROC, slavery was still a very
real and modern threat, while the Kiva conflict in the
DRC continued to claim lives the way only an ethnically
charged civil war could. Right now, though, an African
American man tried to move as fast as he could without
aggravating the injury of his companion, also American
but several shades lighter than his friend and growing
more wan by the moment. The Latino's normally tan
features were now clammy, his black hair stuck to his
forehead.

John Carmichael struggled to keep David Arcado
moving, one hand hooked under his armpit with
Arcado's limb drawn across Carmichael's shoulders.
Arcado's face was pale, his eyes sunken, his forehead
soaked with sweat. Carmichael looked down at the
bullet wound in Arcado's side, his hand clamped around
the injury. Blood painted the hand bright red, meaning
that he was losing oxygenated blood. No wonder Arcado
was wheezing.

"Let me sit," Arcado rasped. "You can get the hell
out a lot faster alone than lugging me along."

"Fuck that shit," Carmichael replied. "We don't leave soldiers behind."

Carmichael glanced back at the game trail they'd tromped along. He could see where dark, drying blood had smeared on leaves, which meant that the guards of the illegitimate launch facility wouldn't have too much trouble following them. "If we stop now, there'll be all manner of arrows aimed at you."

Arcado swallowed hard, eyeing the bloody trail he'd left behind. "Which is why you need to dump me."

"No," Carmichael growled. "We ride together, we die together."

"Not with the information in your head," Arcado told him, trying to wrestle his arm away from the black man. "You've got to get moving."

"Stop fighting me," Carmichael complained. Suddenly he felt something hard jammed into his ribs. Carmichael looked at the snub-nosed .357 Magnum locked in Arcado's fist. "You shoot me, you're defeating your own purpose."

Arcado gritted his teeth, then lowered the .357. "You see that streak rising from the ground?"

Carmichael didn't want to look, but through the gap in the forest canopy roof, he could see it: the cottony column of smoke that spiraled up into the clear blue skies above. His shoulders fell as he knew what was at the top of that pillar of expended liquid oxygen fuel. He didn't know the payload atop, but it was an orbital launch missile, akin to an Atlas IV, reverse engineered from old American designs. Whatever was riding into the heavens on millions of pounds of concentrated thrust, it was nothing good, not when it was being rocketed out of Earth's atmosphere from a forsaken, hidden corner of the world.

"I see it," Carmichael answered. He took a deep breath.

"And what was that shit you kept telling me? Your country before everything else?" Arcado told him, gripping a fistful of Carmichael's BDU shirt, twisting it to bring Carmichael's ear closer to his mouth.

"If you stay here, then we need to give you as much of a chance as you can get," Carmichael whispered harshly. "Give me a spare bullet."

Arcado nodded as Carmichael withdrew his folding multitool. "Want mine, too?"

"Yeah," Carmichael answered. Taking the .357 Magnum round between the two folding pliers, the black agent pried the bullet from its casing. With a shell full of fast-burning, high-intensity powder, he had what he needed. "Move your hand."

Arcado grit his teeth. "This is going to suck."

Carmichael poured the powder into the wound, then pulled his stainless-steel lighter. It fired on the first flick, and when the flame touched the gunpowder, it flared. Arcado's fingers dug into Carmichael's biceps, his eyes clenched tightly shut as the bullet-torn flesh cauterized under the flashing heat. The pain was horrendous, if the muscle-squeezing grip Arcado inflicted on him was any indication. When the wound was seared closed as the powder burned out, Arcado finally loosened his clawlike clutches on Carmichael.

"I was right," the Latino gasped.

"You usually are, damn it," Carmichael replied. "Even when you say I need to leave you behind."

Arcado nodded. "You left me a round short."

"So you're not looking to die nobly?" Carmichael asked.

"Fuck that noise," Arcado answered. He leaned back, gulping down a fresh breath. Carmichael sorted through his gear, pulling four extra magazines from his reserve for his partner. Arcado reached out weakly to add them to his stash. With shaky hands, the Latino drew his Beretta and worked the slide to make certain it had a round in the breech.

Carmichael tried to ignore how physically weakened his partner was. The two men had a duty to get information to the outside world, and one man could travel more quickly through the heavy jungle than one healthy man escorting an injured companion. Arcado was far from suicidal, but he knew that here in the jungle, without medical attention and a bullet lodged in his abdomen, he was only going to be engaged in a delaying action. Arcado's real role was to give Carmichael space, wiggle room to get to civilization.

It wasn't going to be a short journey, either. Carmichael was on foot, without high-tech communications and only a small amount of ammunition. Arcado was going to stem the tide of a small army, from the looks of the launch facility. They didn't know who had been sent out after the two, and Carmichael couldn't give his friend any odds that were worthwhile.

"You'll be all right here?" Carmichael asked, the words catching in his throat.

"If I say no, you still ain't sticking around," Arcado growled. He leaned on his rifle and pushed to his feet.

Carmichael reached out to brace his friend, but the Latino shook him off.

"You'll need all your strength to do your job," Carmichael told him. "Being a stubborn asshole isn't going to help you with anything. Or do you want a bunch of gunmen to run my ass down?"

Arcado grimaced, then held out his hand. "Me, me, me. That's all you ever whine about. Don't you ever think of anyone else?"

Carmichael held him up, but held his tongue. Arcado was joking, trying to cut through his worries. "Shut up."

"Don't get serious on me now," Arcado whispered. "I need a few laughs."

Carmichael kept quiet, not wanting to demoralize his friend any further. He helped Arcado into a position that allowed for decent cover and concealment along their trail. The spy settled into a nest.

"Get running, John," Arcado whispered. "I don't know how much time I'll buy you, but I'll pay for as much as I can."

Carmichael nodded, giving his friend's shoulder a squeeze.

He turned, cursing himself for doing his duty at the expense of a friend.

ILYA SORYENKOV LOOKED at the threat matrix list on his desk. He was the Moscow bureau chief for the federal security service, or FSB. Though he had to deal with the FSB's rivalry with the CSR, which was the central intelligence service, he was fairly certain that he wasn't cheated out of any information from the daily threat matrix. Details of the CSR's operations would be kept from the FSB, but if there were rumors of trouble, the agency that held back information about an impending crisis would be scalped in the press. Soryenkov dropped into his chair and picked up the file of accumulated data.

For all the problems that had been going on for years, through a particularly corrupt administration that pounced at any chance for a return to the bad old days, Soryenkov had felt a little hope. The new president was willing to make some deals to alleviate some of the tensions that were threatening to draw Russia and her sister states into civil war, Chechnya especially. Soryenkov's work was never really going to be done. Since the collapse of the KGB, lots of old grudges were being settled, and trouble in the form of organized crime was steadily worsening with the addition of trained espionage and special operations veterans flooding the ranks of the Russian *mafiya*.

He looked at the top sheet in the file. The envoys to the latest G8 conference were returning home today. Soryenkov had spent the past couple of days coordinating the Moscow police and FSB in setting up security for their return. It had been a fairly sedate conference, protestors more peaceful than usual. The Russian was glad for that. The Iraq war was winding down, and Chechnya was no longer being used as a tool to reinforce the need for the old, harsh methods by a would-be hardline revivalist.

Soryenkov looked at a printout of a recently received bit of chatter. Several Moscow news sources had received an ominous yet anonymous threat. Conventional radio and television had received the same line, as well as several Moscow-area blogs. The message was short and to the point.

"For failure to humanity, the Fist of Heaven smites thee."

Soryenkov rubbed his forehead as he read it. He had operatives looking for any prior indications of a group called the Fist of Heaven. There were only half-whispered rumors regarding the Fist, but there had been mention of a similarly named group, the Celestial Hammer, which had threatened the whole world with satellite-launched dirty bombs. However, that group had threatened far more than just Russia, causing damage in Cuba with a weapon that had triggered a deadly tidal wave. The man-made tsunami had destroyed a fishing village near the U.S. Marine base at Guantanamo Bay.

Soryenkov looked over his notes about potential missing nuclear waste, then thought the better of it. If one organization had experienced a catastrophic failure of agenda by bombarding the Earth from low orbit, he didn't feel that it was likely another group would try such a tactic so soon afterward. That kind of a mistake would set their plot back even before it began due to the nature of the international response. The now-defunct terrorist group's example would make it unlikely that someone would utilize crude, improvised dirty bombs as their primary form of governmental influence.

The FSB chief rubbed his chin. The Celestial Hammer may have been a failure, but it was only because they didn't have a properly dedicated orbital weapons platform. Certainly they had the potential to cause millions of deaths, but their system of attack was a jury-rigged design that utilized easily available, low-profile technology, or insiders allowing them access to China's space program. Soryenkov hated to think what would have happened with a more dedicated system, like the proposed kinetic bombardment satellites controlled by various nations with space programs. The thought of a twenty-foot-long, one-foot-in-diameter chunk of high-density metal being "thrown" at a city at a velocity of 36,000 feet per second...

There wouldn't be any radioactive fallout, but the impact would be comparable to a ground-penetrating nuclear device. That was merely the calculations for a "crowbar" of tungsten of those dimensions. Basically, from low orbit, a projectile would carry thirty-two megajoules per kilogram of mass, a figure that was between six and seven times the equivalent power of a kilogram of TNT.

He looked out the window at the Moscow skyline. The U.S. military had a "smart" missile, essentially an artillery tube with steering stabilizer fins, a two-ton hunk of metal that could be dropped by a ground-attack fighter with enough force to penetrate one hundred feet of concrete. On a whim, he picked up his calculator and came to a figure of sixty thousand megajoules of energy. From what he remembered of World War II conventional weaponry, a ten-thousand-pound bomb only put out twelve thousand megajoules of energy. One of the proposed "Rods from God" had five times the punch of a weapon that destroyed entire city blocks in the air war between the RAF and the *Luftwaffe*.

"That technology is years off," he whispered, as if

to dispel the sudden dread that overwhelmed him. Out the window, he saw a puff of smoke. Soryenkov wondered if it had been a car bomb, but it was too far away and had kicked up too much debris. Something else blurred through the air and struck the ground. While the shock wave of the distant impact finally rumbled through the floor, the windowpanes cracked as the building flexed.

"I said that technology is—" There was a third, fourth and fifth impact, all occurring more or less at the same instant. Soryenkov's window shattered an instant later, but by then, he'd already thrown his arms across his face to keep the broken glass from carving him apart.

There were no more spears cast down from heaven, no more buildings vaporized into dust by two-ton hunks of steel striking them at terminal velocity. But when Soryenkov next looked through the broken window of his office, he saw a city rocked to its core. Columns of dust rose lazily skyward as alarms wailed across the city.

Damnation had rained down on Moscow in the form of a weapon that wasn't supposed to exist.

CHAPTER ONE

London, forty-five minutes after the Moscow incident

"Oy, lads, fancy a couple Britneys?" the bartender asked
Gary Manning and David McCarter as they focused on
the LCD-screen television hanging over the bar. The TV
news was dominated by the aftermath of the disaster
in Russia. The bartender's question pulled Manning's
attention away from the pad of paper where he'd been
scribbling angles he'd guessed at from video footage
and the oblique shapes of the impact craters.

McCarter looked at the bartender. Though he'd lost
most of his accent, McCarter still could hear a touch of
Polish in his speech.

Manning's look was quizzical in response to the pub
man's comment. He turned to his friend for an explana-
tion. "Britneys?"

"Rhyming slang," McCarter explained. "Britney
Sp—"

"Her name rhymes with beers," Manning cut him off.
"How'd she get across the pond to influence London
barkeeps?"

"Sitting naked in music videos does a lot to im-
prove international popularity," McCarter answered.
He looked at the bartender. "Two more pints, mate."

"The Babel concept," Manning muttered. "Languages

are far from immutable, more like living creatures. Viruses actually."

"Language is a virus?" McCarter asked.

"More appropriately, an information virus," Manning told him. "Viruses are a part of this planet. The first transfer of information was in the form of a virus, one simple organism transmitting DNA code to another in the creation of life. All data is viral in nature, be it a new word in a language or a catchy set of lyrics in a song. Every bit of information is a single permutation of that first virus."

McCarter looked at the pad on which the Canadian demolitions expert had been calculating trajectories. "What about those angles? Did someone put a satellite in orbit right over Moscow?"

Manning tapped the end of his pen against his chin. McCarter could see a brilliant light working behind the Canadian's eyes. "We don't have footage of their whole approach. All I can tell is that they came in off of a supraorbital arc. Whether it was akin to the supergun or a satellite-mounted kinetic weapons system I couldn't tell without proper examination of their approach vectors. Even then we'd be dealing with over-the-horizon launches."

"You know, maybe the Farm picked up something," McCarter offered.

Manning shook his head. "Unlikely. A release of kinetic darts would have a minimal thermal profile. There's no indication of any rocket thrusters so they would be untrackable except when they hit the atmosphere. Then the friction of their passage through the air would provide for infrared tracking, but we're looking at trailing a projectile at thousands of feet per second…"

"Terminal velocity. We experienced that kind of speed ourselves," McCarter replied.

"A little too closely," Manning returned. He smiled. "I bet you had the time of your life playing bumper cars with space shuttles."

McCarter held up his thumb and forefinger to indicate a small amount. "A bit, mate."

Manning chuckled, and McCarter looked away from him, his eye catching something going on in the corner. He'd come to the pub to watch the two booths full of young men wearing football jerseys. He counted twelve of them, all shaved-headed, with faces that looked as if they'd taken multiple punches over the years. These were soccer hooligans if they were anything, a breed of troublemaker with whom McCarter was quite familiar. A couple of them were looking at their cell phones, the brightly glowing LCD screens reflecting in their eyes lending them a haunting, soulless appearance.

"Gary, you know all about technology. What's it called when groups assemble due to instant messages?" McCarter asked.

"Flash mobs," Manning answered immediately. "Given a proper network of like-minded people, flash mobs are hard, almost impossible to anticipate and difficult to track. Why?"

McCarter nodded toward the hooligans who were assembled at the two booths. Manning narrowed his eyes, studying the group as the two men with the cell phones pocketed them and gestured to the other jersey-clad men. The group threw down their money on the table for the waitress to scoop up as she took their order for the current round. In a London pub, you paid before you got your alcohol. She returned with a tray of lager bottles, which the hoodlums grabbed off her tray. Where they had been garrulous moments before, now they had fallen into silence.

"As always, good instincts," Manning noted. "There's no game on tonight, and these guys are in a hurry for something."

"We've got a little bit of time before we're called in. Let's see where they're headed," McCarter suggested.

Manning nodded. He left a tip for the bartender and the two men exited the pub, staying back but still within sight of the small mob of ruffians. Both Manning and McCarter were members of Phoenix Force, the foreign-operations strike team of Stony Man Farm. McCarter had summoned Manning to London to assist him in checking out rumors that someone had been organizing the roughhousing young men of the hooligan scene. There had already been plenty of arrests of more enterprising hooligan gangs doing muscle work for organized crime and street-corner drug dealing. This had been part of a disturbing trend from London to Vladivostok. The clique mentality of the thuggish sports fans had given the roughnecks an impetus to organize, and they had found plenty of opportunity to make money from mayhem and destruction.

McCarter frowned. "Viruses tend to spread in patterns, right?"

Manning nodded. "Especially social constructs."

McCarter's frown deepened. "This isn't the normal kind of sport fan. These are ruffians who have taken their social ostracism and turned it into gang mentality. In the U.S., street gangs are nothing like the Crips and Bloods who developed in the 1970s into gun-wielding thugs. But right here, we're seeing the same kind of evolutionary changes occurring among the hooligans."

"In order to fund their lifestyle, they commit robberies or they sell drugs," Manning agreed. "And they could increase their level of violence—"

"As if they aren't savage enough in hand-to-hand," McCarter interrupted.

"Then you don't want to imagine them with shotguns or rifles," Manning said.

McCarter nodded. He kept his eye on the group. He'd kept watch over them all morning. The soccer thugs had been on a pub crawl all night long, and it was close to nine now. So far, he had Stony Man's cybernetics teams studying Twitter notification streams and other text message hubs to look for signs of organized communication networks. The young men were now on the move soon after a near apocalyptic event in Moscow. McCarter couldn't believe that this was a coincidence.

He pulled his phone and sent a secure text to the Farm, hoping to catch someone's attention.

"Hooligans in motion. Copy?"

There was no response, and the Briton wrinkled his nose. Of course the Farm wasn't going to take the electronic organization of London street gangs as a priority over a high-powered strike on a major international capital. He looked over at Manning, who gripped the strap of his backpack. Both McCarter and his Canadian partner were well-armed with handguns and knives, but the satchel contained more potent equipment.

McCarter was someone who had a predisposition to action and had developed a level of lethal ruthlessness when dealing with opponents who had no qualms about murder. However, the thought of opening fire on unarmed foes was something that the Special Air Service veteran found abhorrent. Manning's backpack had a pair of shotguns, but the twelve-gauge weapons were filled with nonlethal shells. The initial loads inside the pistol-gripped pumps were tear-gas-spewing ferret rounds, but there were bandoliers filled with mixed gas and spongy baton rounds. While the ammunition wasn't intended to be deadly, they could kill if Manning or McCarter chose their shots carefully.

McCarter felt that if he was going to drop an assailant permanently, he'd use either his beloved 9 mm Browning Hi-Power or his new backup pistol, a Springfield Armory Enhanced Micro Pistol. The EMP was also a 9 mm pistol, and it also shared the same mechanism that allowed him to carry the Browning locked and cocked; the EMP was simply a resized version of the Hi-Power's cousin, the John Moses Browning–designed 1911 pistol. The flat EMP fit easily into an ankle holster. Manning had his choice of sidearms, as well. The big Canadian had opted for a .357 Magnum Colt Python with a 9 mm Walther P5 for backup. For quiet but bloody work, the two carried chisel-bladed knives in sheaths around their necks.

"No response from the Farm?" Manning asked.

McCarter confirmed Manning's query. "On the bright side, they might have had the kind of data you couldn't access over a TV news screen."

"And far superior physics simulation programming

to allow for air current effects upon objects in motion," Manning replied.

"Would that make it easier to determine what the weapon was?" McCarter asked.

"Slightly," Manning answered. "They'd also know if a radioactive element was utilized in the kinetic darts."

"Radioactive metal? You think we'd have to deal with that again?" McCarter asked.

Manning shrugged his brawny shoulders. "I always assume the worst, but even with the rod assault being made of conventional materials, it carries enough kinetic energy to obliterate entire city blocks and infrastructure. You noted the flames."

"Gas mains and electrical lines disrupted," McCarter agreed. "They haven't confirmed the dead, but if just one of those rods hit a crowded tube, er, subway…"

Manning grimaced at that thought. "It wouldn't have to hit dead-on. If my calculations of the mass of the orbital impact objects are correct, we're looking at a landing within a quarter mile of a subway tunnel. According to the map I was working from, we're looking at between four and seven tunnels collapsed, as well as at least three transit platforms. The death toll underground can reach over two thousand, independent of above-surface structural collapse."

McCarter's mood matched the expression on Manning's face. Since the Canadian was a demolitions expert, the Briton had little cause to doubt his friend's calculations. McCarter returned his attention to the hooligans, whose numbers had tripled as they met up with more groups of their comrades. He felt a moment of uncertainty, judging the superior numbers he and Manning would face if their quarry decided to turn en masse and confront them. The Phoenix Force veterans were survivors of multiple riots, having fought off dozens of crazed opponents alongside their other three Phoenix Force partners, but in those situations, they had terrain and training advantages. The hooligans were something different from what they would be used to—men who used their strength of numbers as a lethal weapon against foes unlucky to get into their path.

McCarter spotted hammers and sharpened shanks of steel in some of the hooligans' hands, and the football fans were uniformly buzzed on beer, drunk enough to surrender their individuality to the madness of the mob but not so inebriated that they couldn't concentrate on targets of rage and opportunity. With weapons in hand, these men were a threat to anyone they encountered, and even though the group had tripled in size, they still hadn't reached their final destination. Manning slipped his backpack off his shoulder, allowing McCarter to reach in surreptitiously and withdraw the stubby shotgun and transfer it under his windbreaker. Suddenly the ex-SAS commando was wishing that he had his preferred Cobray submachine gun, a well-tuned little chatterbox that could spit out its deadly 9 mm kisses at 800 hits per minute.

"It's not going to be much if they turn on us," Manning noted.

McCarter managed a smirk. "As long as they don't have guns, we can at least use the shotguns as clubs."

Manning nodded at the suggestion. "Sometimes your optimism can be contagious."

McCarter snorted. "But this isn't one of those times."

"You read my mind," Manning replied with a chuckle.

McCarter's cell phone beeped, letting the Briton know that he'd received a text message from Stony Man Farm. He fished out the phone.

"Message received. Network shows thugs assembling at Piccadilly Circus," the text read. From the use of full words, but terse wording, McCarter could tell that it had been Carmen Delahunt who had sent the message. Akira Tokaido would have used abbreviated terms, while Huntington Wethers would have written out entire sentences, including prepositions.

McCarter quickly typed a reply. "Alert locals, incl Flying Squad."

The growing mass, headed to one of the most famous shopping districts in the free world, would turn into a rampaging stampede of bulls in a proverbial china shop. The sight of hammers and shivs in various hands showed a capacity for violence. He checked his watch. At 10:00 a.m. there would be hundreds if not thousands of shoppers on hand for the buzzed, hostile hooligans to menace. The mention of the Flying Squad, London Metropolitan Police's premier emergency response team, was one of McCarter's hopes for evening the odds, as well as limiting the chances of fatalities. The Met's Flying Squads were made up of rough-and-ready men, many of them veterans of the SAS like McCarter himself, or of the Royal Marines. But they were more than just gun-toting civil servants. The warriors in the "Sweeney" units, named for the Flying Squad's rhyme of Sweeney Todd, were also trained in emergency first aid, as well as riot suppression. If the Flying Squad wasn't on hand to immediately squelch the hooligans' violence, they could provide vital life-saving assistance to their victims.

"Notified," Delahunt's message returned.

McCarter ran his thumbs across his phone's mini-keyboard. "Moscow news?"

"Situation remains fluid," Delahunt told him.

"Fluid," Manning grumbled. "Moscow's football gangs are of a slightly more violent level of hostility than London's."

"Not by much," McCarter said. He typed a quick question to send to the Farm. "Riots in Moscow?"

"Confirmed," Delahunt answered. "Moscow police overwhelmed."

McCarter and Manning looked to the sky. If London was going to be the site of flash mob violence, there was the possibility that the city on the Thames would receive a hammering from the same weapon that had scarred the Russian capital. The Briton typed in another question. "We expecting rain?"

"Wish we could tell," Delahunt answered.

McCarter grit his teeth. "So while we're looking at these berks, someone could be targeting my city?"

"Berks?" Manning asked.

"Berkshire Hunts," McCarter explained. It was more rhyming slang, and Manning shook his head as he figured out the curse that his term stood in for.

"It's unlikely that our opposition could stage a second orbital weapon launch, nor probable that they would assault this city without a declaration of intent," Manning said. "According to the news, Moscow broadcast sources received a threat a few hours before the attack."

"And Carmen would have told us if there was something for London," McCarter said. He texted again. "No warnings?"

"None. Yet," was the response.

McCarter's brow wrinkled in concern. "Get C, R and T.J. on deck."

"Already done."

McCarter pocketed his phone. They were already on Haymarket Road, and in the distance, even in the morning daylight, he could see the bright, glowing signs of the Piccadilly Circus. McCarter could tell that they were on Haymarket due to the presence of four rearing horses off to one side. They were carved in black marble, and were beautifully polished. This statue, nestled in a semicurved corner over a small fountain, was one of McCarter's favorite pieces of art in London, a visage of natural beauty and power. Its fame would always be in the shadow of Eros at the center of Piccadilly Circus, the massive cherub that was poised on one foot, aiming its bow at some distant lover's heart, surrounded by the blazing neon of Piccadilly's shops. McCarter squinted and he could barely make out the tall form in the distance over the heads of the massing hooligans.

The throng they trailed had swelled even further in size. Four more groups had hooked up to form a mob of potential rioters that seemed like an army. Throughout the crowd, he and Manning took note of dozens of glass bottles held up like torches of liberty. A more ominous sight along the edges of the crowd were the black handles of knives poking out of waistbands here and there. A couple of men carried gym bags, signaling that they were devotees of the Manchester Blacks. McCarter was too aware that those satchels could easily conceal firearms, as he and Phoenix Force had managed to disguise their arsenal that way in the past.

"I see four men with those bags on this end of the throng," Manning stated.

"Who knows how many are mixed in with that lot," McCarter grumbled. "I'll need a distraction."

Manning nodded, knowing that McCarter would need to ambush one of the bag carriers to see what he had hidden in a nylon sack. The Briton slipped closer to a hooligan he'd picked since he was the rearmost of the group. This particular soccer thug looked sober and too well groomed to be in with this lot, despite the fact that he wore team colors.

It was a simple prisoner snatch, something he had done in both service to Britain and to the Sensitive Operations Group. Off to the side, a sudden crackle of a dozen firecrackers popping drew all eyes. That was Manning's distraction, utilizing a small portion of explosives that the demolitions genius always kept on his person. McCarter slipped his forearm around the bagman's throat and brought up his free fist, driving the bottom edge of it hard against his target's ear. The hooligan was paralyzed with agony as his eardrum was ruptured by the boxing of his ear, and luckily the man's nerves were frozen, maintaining the death grip on the nylon web straps of his bag. McCarter swiftly backed into a small nook between shopfronts, sliding down the narrow entryway.

The prisoner struggled to speak, but McCarter cut him off with a sharp blow that landed just above his navel, driving the wind from his lungs. He was unable to cry out for assistance in the dark and narrow walkway down which McCarter and his captive had disappeared. The thug reached up with one hand, fingers hooked like claws, but the Briton grabbed his wrist and burst his knuckles on the brick wall. McCarter was more concerned with what his opponent's other hand was doing, and he yanked on the hooligan's collar, pulling him off balance.

The man's hand rose, a snub-nosed revolver locked in it, but it was pointed toward the alley, not at the Phoenix Force commander. With a hard chop, McCarter jarred the thug's neck with enough force that he dropped the weapon, his knees buckling.

"Not nice. Don't you know they have laws against that shit here?" McCarter asked, yanking the hooligan's wrists down to the small of his back. He slipped a plastic cable tie out of his pocket and bound his prisoner's hands behind his back.

"Fuck off, Nancy," the goon snarled.

McCarter whacked him again, this time in the temple, sending him into unconsciousness. With the bagman out cold, he was able to look inside the nylon gym bag. He saw dozens of canisters that he recognized as grenades, their pin-laden tops ominously looking back at him. A shadow fell across the entryway opening and McCarter turned to see who it was. Manning was there, keeping watch.

McCarter pulled out one canister and saw that it was chemical smoke. There were three different kinds of hand-thrown bombs inside, none of them purely explosive, but there were plenty of tear gas and stun grenades on hand to sow terror in Piccadilly Circus.

"Four that we saw, maybe three more groups," McCarter mused.

"Whatever the amount, there are plenty of grenades to start a wild riot," Manning replied.

McCarter grimaced. He could hear sirens in the distance. The Metropolitan police were on their way, alerted to action by Stony Man Farm. He didn't know if that would be enough, however. He hoisted the confiscated bag, holding it out to Manning. "Forget about the shotgun rounds. We'll need this."

"How will we track where these came from?" Manning asked.

"Bugger that," McCarter grumbled. "You've got hundreds of hooligans ready to go crazy amid thousands of innocents."

Manning held out his backpack and McCarter gave him half a dozen flash-bangs. "We could just start the violence early if we throw these around."

"Or we could throw them off their timing—and pull their attention our way," McCarter answered.

Manning nodded. It was a standard bit of strategy on the part of the action-oriented Phoenix Force leader. If there was the potential for mayhem, McCarter chose to make himself a target to pull trouble away from those he'd sworn to protect. "I'll give us some room."

McCarter saw the brawny Canadian draw his Colt Python. The powerful revolver would make plenty of noise, being heard more clearly than any mere 9 mm pistol with its Magnum level loads. There was one thing that the Phoenix pair could count on—the reactions of everyday people to gunfire. They wouldn't be certain how the crowd of hooligans would react, but luckily the shoppers had thinned out at the sight of a mob of rowdy drunks.

"Let fly," McCarter said, and Manning aimed at a facade of a building, triggering three rapid, bellowing shots at the brick. The Magnum's hollowpoints were easily stopped by the stone and mortar, preventing dangerous ricochets or rounds cutting through a wall to harm a second-floor resident.

People scattered, running away from the heart of Piccadilly Circus while the throng clogging Haymarket whirled at the sudden burst of new violence. The Python was far more authoritative than the firecrackers Manning had dropped. The rioters glared at the two men who stood defiantly in the middle of the road.

Manning and McCarter were both the same height, six foot one, but Manning was broad-shouldered and barrel-chested while McCarter was leaner.

"Who do you berks think you are?" one of the bagmen grunted. He had noticed McCarter's bag full of tricks.

"The Peace Corps," McCarter replied.

"Why don't we promote you berks from corps to corpses?" the spokesman said. He turned to his mates. "Fuck 'em up!"

The wall of thugs surged, taking one step forward, but McCarter and Manning had been cooking their flash-bangs from the moment the loudmouthed bagman snarled his response to McCarter. The Phoenix pros hurled their flash-bangs in underhanded tosses, both canister grenades rolling between the crowd's feet.

Detonating, the distraction devices unleashed twin stunning pulses through the crowd of drunken thugs. The unified surge that they had attempted transformed into a snarl of limbs as dozens folded over with painful deafness. Those who were farther back in the riot crowd tripped over those who had been halted by the blasts. McCarter and Manning had produced a dam of humanity against the flood tide of rage that would have overwhelmed them, but the grenades were only the beginning of what they needed.

The bagman had pulled a pistol from his waistband. McCarter, a British Olympic pistol champion, saw him start his quick draw and hauled out his Browning Hi-Power, triggering a quick shot faster than the gunman. The hooligan jerked violently as the bridge of his nose exploded with a precision-placed shot straight to the brain.

Not being a dedicated handgunner like his British friend, Manning whipped out his shotgun and fired the .12-gauge ferret rounds into the knees of three rioting hooligans. The tear gas shells weren't designed to be fired directly at someone, but with the numbers they were facing, Manning erred on the side of injury rather than shooting someone in the chest.

Legs knocked out from under them, the thugs tumbled, providing a break that their allies, unhindered by flash-grenade deafness, had trouble passing. The tumble of stunned bodies created by the explosions snarled their path. It was a brief reprieve, and both Manning and

McCarter were facing down a dozen angry hooligans whom they weren't willing to gun down in cold blood.

Conversely, the surging rioters were out for Phoenix Force blood and outnumbered the merciful warriors six to one.

CHAPTER TWO

Normally, Gary Manning did not rely on melee weapons when it came to close-quarters combat. He preferred to utilize his great strength and skill to deal with opponents, but now he was faced with a less than optimal situation. The London roughneck charging at him had a brain-smashing weapon locked in his fist.

Manning quickly reversed the pistol-grip pump in his big hands and brought the weapon up to bat aside the whistling steel of a ball-peen hammer targeting his skull. Metal struck metal with a loud clang and a spark, and the Canadian knew that although his weapon would not be reliable anymore, it had saved him from a traumatic head injury. He knotted his left hand into a ham-size fist and brought it up hard under the chin of the hammer-wielding rioter. The uppercut literally lifted Manning's target off his feet and hurled him against another soccer hooligan behind him.

Manning didn't have time to celebrate his victory. Instead he whirled and jammed his shoulder against the chest of a third rioter, getting inside of the arc of the young man's scything knife. The shoulder block turned the blade-wielding hooligan into a plow, which allowed the powerful Canadian to run over four of the surging rioters. He reached up and snared the improvised battering ram by his football jersey and whipped

him around as a living club, bowling over more of the
rowdy maniacs.

Manning glanced quickly to one side and saw that
McCarter had trapped one of his foes in an armlock and
was utilizing the hooligan as a fulcrum and a shield.
The big Canadian returned his attention to the combat
at hand in time to hear his captive howl from the stab of
a sharpened strip of metal into his shoulder. Manning
hurled his charge aside, away from where he'd encounter
more rioter weapons, and snapped down a judo chop on
the forearm that held the bloody shank. Bones cracked
under the assault, and the ruffian stumbled backward.

The dam of stunned figures wasn't holding angry
rioters back as well as it had before, but Manning was
aware of the impermanence of a stun grenade's effects
on crowds. With a surge, the big Canadian whipped one
muscular arm out and clotheslined it across the throat of
a charging hooligan. The London gang member's feet
kicked out from under him and he toppled backward
into his compatriots. Manning knew that his only hope
was to exploit the number of bodies pitted against him.
He was not facing a unified group, moving in perfect
synchronicity, despite the singular mind the mob possessed. As such, he was able to trip up one attacker
with one of his fellow rioters, limbs entangling each
other as one hand was clueless about what the other
was doing.

Even so, Manning realized that he could only maintain this frenetic pace for so long. He kept his body
in tip-top condition, maintaining a level of endurance
that could carry him across deserts or up the highest
mountainsides. Combat, however, sapped that kind of

energy far faster than simple cross-country traveling. Manning was directing his muscles with precision and speed, as well as exploiting their phenomenal strength. Such fine manipulation required more intensive use of endurance, and he knew that he didn't have the kind of power to hold out against the entirety of this roiling throng.

If Manning's seemingly bottomless reserves were beginning to run dry, he wondered how his partner was faring as the hooligan horde surged forward.

FISTS AND FEET FLEW, trying to track the SAS-trained brawler, but they struck McCarter's prisoner, not the man himself. In the meantime, McCarter lashed out with his long, powerful legs, kicking rioters in the knees or groin. The low blows weren't pretty and were far from fair, but they were the swiftest and least harmful means of knocking down ruffians without causing undue death.

The maneuvers reminded McCarter of his favorite American slapstick comedians, who often repeated a gag where they ensnarled themselves against an enemy and utilized the momentum of that foe to spin them around, whirling out of harm's way while their opponents ended up battling each other. The weight of the man McCarter had hooked himself to was providing sufficient energy for McCarter to spear snap-kicks into abdomens and get enough height to break more than a few jaws. The SAS veteran was tempted to lose himself in the brawl, but his sense of responsibility kept him from full surrender. He pulled his punches and kicks, knowing that he didn't require that much force to hold his enemies at bay.

Somewhere in the course of the initial melee, the rest of the crowd that had been halted by the stun grenades had recovered their senses. They started to move in, surrounding both Manning and McCarter, a wall of bodies separating the Phoenix pros. McCarter released his fulcrum, putting plenty of muscle into a hip toss so that when he struck his compatriots, a dozen bodies tumbled together.

Dozens of hands clawed at McCarter as he back-pedaled. There were too many of them, and he didn't have the sheer muscle required to hurl rioters against each other. Fortunately, McCarter had a bag of heavy grenades, and he swung them hard. Their mass added to the strength of his swing, and the hard metal canisters for the smoke and tear gas dispensers proved to be unyielding as they struck hands, wrists, arms and shoulders.

Several of the hooligans stopped short, clutching shattered limbs. The rioting thugs didn't have much time to comfort their injured body parts as others behind them shoved them to the ground to be trampled underfoot by the surging tide of madness. McCarter whipped the bag of grenades around again and again, feeling the impact of his improvised mace against their bodies, scattering them in a wide arc. Each slashing stroke of the flailing nylon bag was testing the strength of the synthetic fabric, however. His weapon wasn't going to last forever, and the football hooligans had spread out, encircling the Phoenix Force commander.

McCarter grimaced, realizing that he was going to

have to try something drastic. He hauled the bag back to his chest, reached into its zipper and came away with three or four pins. The roughhousing throng paused as they saw the cotter rings fall away from his fingers, and McCarter lobbed the satchel into the waiting arms of one of the rioters. Before the grenades could detonate, McCarter equalized the pressure in his ears with a loud roar that further worked at slowing the madness-inflicted mob.

Sympathetic detonations accompanied the lone stun grenade's explosion, extreme pressure knocking loose safety mechanisms to extend the shattering blast, even as powerful jets of smoke and tear gas erupted from the bag of doom. Hooligans wailed as chemical smoke and concentrated capsicum solution blasted dozens of faces. McCarter was used to working in the clouds created by the smoker canisters, and he had also built up an immunity to the sinus-inflaming effects of the pepper extract. Even so, McCarter's eyes and nose were running freely. He had been almost at ground zero of the detonations, but the number of rioters had worked in his favor. The press of their bodies absorbed the concussion of the flash-bangs, as well as diluting the tear gas and smoke he would have taken full force otherwise. McCarter fired off quick rabbit punches, tagging sides and abdominal muscles, knocking air from the hooligans' lungs, forcing them to breathe in deep gulps of atmosphere that was no longer good for them. The cottony cloud that enveloped McCarter and his crowd of opponents provided a shield that limited the advance of dozens who could no longer find him.

McCarter pumped a knee into the gut of one ruffian

who tried to fight on despite his blindness. That foe collapsed to the ground, gasping for breath. Another man took a karate chop to the shoulder, the pain of a broken clavicle taking the fight out of him. The Briton had bought himself time with the use of the grenades, but smoke and tear gas dissipated, and the stunning force released by the high-pressure flash-bangs would fade, allowing enemies to recover their senses.

Suddenly, McCarter stumbled, pushed back by two of the rioters. He would have fallen on his ass had it not been for the presence of a pair of curved plasticine shields. McCarter glanced back, and hands reached in the gap between the two riot cops, tugging the ex-SAS man behind a wall of lawmen who pushed forward with rubberized clubs and their clear plastic but nigh invulnerable shields. The police were wearing gas masks to protect them from the choking clouds that had been unleashed by the Phoenix Force pros, so they went in with all of their senses working. The phalanx of officers also had the benefit of trained coordination. Each man covered himself and the man to his right, and they moved in step.

While the mob had a wild might, it was unfocused and undisciplined. They crashed helplessly against the wall of authority that pushed forward. In the meantime, McCarter found himself helped up by two cops who followed behind the living barrier that descended upon the riot. McCarter was relieved to see the Flying Squad's efficiency in herding the hooligans.

"You all right?" one of the bobbies asked.

"I've been better, but not by much," McCarter replied with a wink.

"Dispatch told us to keep an eye out for you and your partner," the other metropolitan policeman said. "They told us that the two of you would be holding the line as if you were a two-man riot squad."

"Where's my chum?" McCarter asked. He scanned around and breathed a sigh of relief as he saw the unmistakable bulk of Gary Manning among the policemen following the riot-squad phalanx.

"I hope that's him," the first cop said. "When the shield men passed him, he'd wound two of the rioters up in those hulking arms of his."

"Yeah, that's him," McCarter confirmed. "How is the suppression going?"

"Well, thanks to the two of you hammering this end of Haymarket Road, we were able to divert the fire hose trucks that would have been here to other approaches," the second lawman explained. "A good rinsing is taking the piss out of these drunken louts."

"Looks like you've got them all well and kettled up," McCarter said.

"You sound like you know a little of what the Met likes to do," the first police constable noted.

McCarter shrugged. "I've been around the Met and worked alongside the Sweeney a few times in a professional capacity."

The other PC sized the Phoenix Force leader up. It had been a while since McCarter had worn the short, close-shorn haircut of a professional military man, his hair naturally feathered and flowing down over his ears. Still, even through the layers of his windbreaker and shirt, it was easy for the lawman to notice that McCarter was fit and muscular in the way that a professional soldier would be, lean with very little bulk to get in his way. "Professional but unofficial?"

McCarter nodded curtly, indicating that further discussion along those lines was no longer open.

"Who are you and the barrel-chested bloke?" the first constable asked.

McCarter sighed. "Friends. Concerned friends. That's all I can say."

"Well, you're a right geezer in my book," the second constable said. "Anyone who can take on that many hooligans with only a few bruises…"

McCarter wondered what the lawman was talking about, but then he noticed that he was starting to feel stings along his face and arms. He'd been so wrapped up in battling the riot, he hadn't noticed where glancing impacts had connected with him. Had he been less quick and skillful, he would have suffered broken bones and muscle tears from the melee.

"You still with us, friend?" the first bobby asked.

"Yeah," McCarter replied. "Just taking inventory on all my bits and pieces."

The two officers studiously ignored the sight of McCarter's holstered pistol and the shotgun that hung through the tatters of his windbreaker, but their nonchalance only lasted so long.

"Would you want us to take those for you?" the first lawman asked.

"I'm keeping my Browning," McCarter said. "But you can take the riot gun."

The two officers looked at each other, then thought about the orders, the description they'd been given. They also looked at the stunned and battered dozens left in the wake of the riot police, men who had been knocked down mostly by the efforts of the man with the Browning and his partner. If McCarter was a threat to the peace they'd sworn to protect, he could easily have gunned down countless more of the soccer hooligans as opposed to leaving them alive but hurting. They could trust the Phoenix Force commander with his sidearm.

"Thank you for your assistance," the second of the officers said. He took McCarter's hand and shook it.

The "concerned friend" waved Manning over, and the pair disappeared down Haymarket Road. They had to contact Stony Man Farm.

McCarter and Manning lurched through the door of their hotel room, running on fumes from the energy they'd exerted in dealing with the Piccadilly riot. Manning secured the door while McCarter turned on the television, flicking it to the news. As it hadn't taken them more than a few minutes to get back from Haymarket Road, the news media was still in the dark about what was going on, putting up rumors as true information.

McCarter could see the news cameras focused on one arm of the riot for a moment. He could see himself and Manning amid chemical smoke and tear gas battling against a throng. Luckily, the quality of the camera images was too grainy and jumpy to be of any use in identifying them, and by then, Stony Man Farm would have grabbed extant copies of the video footage from where the files had been stored across the internet and doctored them to make any attempts at clarifying their features totally impossible.

Price and Brognola, back at the Farm, would be

gnashing their teeth that McCarter and Manning may have exposed their identities on international television.

Manning picked up the phone as McCarter continued to scan the channels, looking for more information on the riots. If he was going to risk the privacy of the Sensitive Operations Group, he might as well know the extent of the damage.

"Barb wants to talk to you, David," Manning said, holding out his cell to McCarter.

"Tell her it's not my fault," McCarter replied, checking the television.

"It's not that," Manning corrected him. "Besides, the Farm's running its own scans of local news."

McCarter looked over his shoulder, then held out his hand to accept the cell phone. "What did I do now?"

"Aside from risk exposing Phoenix Force's existence?" Barbara Price asked. Stony Man Farm's mission controller sounded only mockingly reproachful, which eased McCarter's nerves somewhat. The Briton was a man of action, but he dreaded paperwork and he also hated the subterfuge necessary to keep him on the front lines, battling against the forces of evil. He was a doer, not a politician who needed to massage the egos of law enforcement agencies or foreign governments.

"Any time Phoenix Force and a riot are in the same city, you know we'll bump into each other, even if we're outnumbered," McCarter answered.

"Luckily this time you bumped hard enough to stop the riot's spread in one direction," Price told him. "We have to keep you on station in London for a little while, but Cal and the others won't be coming to assist you.

We need to spread out in order to deal effectively with the nature of this threat. You might also have to go elsewhere in Europe."

"The other states in the G8 have been threatened, most likely," McCarter responded.

"Exactly, which is why we can't keep Phoenix Force as one contiguous unit. If it's any consolation, Lyons and his men are splitting up, as well," Price confirmed.

"Things are getting bloody serious if that's the case," McCarter muttered. "More riots?"

"We think that the riots and the orbital bombardment attacks are tied in," Price said. "The Russian soccer gangs went wild in full force. We're fairly certain that they've also been backed by the neo-Nazi movement in Moscow."

"Neo-Nazis," Manning muttered, listening in as the phone was set on speaker mode. "Now that there's been an influx of other people from the Middle East and other countries, the Russians are putting aside the bad memories of the battle of St. Petersburg and embracing racial purity."

"It doesn't hurt that the Russian economy is in the shitter," McCarter added. "White, young and jobless people tend to congregate and cast hairy eyeballs at the nonwhites who are taking jobs that the whites would normally turn their noses up at. It happened a lot in London with Jamaican, Indian and Pakistani immigrants. Bigots like picking at the edges of groups of disenchanted youth."

"It just so happens that the Moscow neo-Nazi sympathizers are well-organized, and they have a lot to pick from on the streets," Price said.

"Cal's going to be bloody useless in that venue. Rafael, too," McCarter pointed out.

"Cal's not going to Moscow. We've activated an old friend or two to deal with Japan and China," Price explained. "Hope you don't mind if he's hanging out with Mei."

"No. You said *or two*...are we thinking of my favorite ninja?" McCarter asked.

"John's going to be in action," Price said. "Cal's heading to Tokyo on a jet fighter right now."

"And what about Lyons and the boys?" McCarter asked.

"Right now it's all need-to-know. I'm just informing you of your teammates—"

"To keep my head straight, so I don't worry over their problems," McCarter finished. "Thanks, Barb."

"Any potential information on where the kinetic darts came from?" Manning asked.

Price paused for a moment. "The only thing we can tell is that there was a scrambling signal that interrupted observation satellite feeds for forty-five minutes."

"All of them?" Manning asked.

"We're not certain for other governments, but looking at our own reconnaissance satellites, we've got most of an hour missing due to active jamming," Price said. "From the tropic of Capricorn to the tropic of Cancer, it's one big blind spot."

"Equatorial satellites, meaning we've narrowed down the possible places where the enemy could have launched from," Manning said.

"That's still millions of square miles," Price countered. "Who knows if it's a land-based launch or someone utilizing a decommissioned submarine's missile silos."

"Or worse, converted a regular freighter to utilize such silos," Manning added. "Some tanker ships have the room and the strength to fire Atlas rockets if they wanted."

"No clue where the jamming signal could have originated?" McCarter asked.

"We've got our people on it. Whatever it was, it transferred from system to system easily," Price said.

"An opposing force of hackers," Manning surmised.

"We're looking at that. The nature of the interference was such that we couldn't tell if it was signal interruption or a viral computer program affecting satellite uplinks," Price said. "Either way, the jamming hasn't affected telecommunications."

"No. Even though they could utilize local cell towers to keep in touch with their people, this Fist of Heaven group seems to want us to know the kind of horror happening in Moscow," Manning said. "A sword of Damocles for the other seven member nations of the G8."

"David, I just got a hit on the picture you took of the bag man you wrangled in that alley," Price said.

"Something's better than nothing," McCarter replied. "What is it?"

"We've got his name, and he's on Scotland Yard's watchlist," Price explained.

"Given that he's on a watchlist, he's probably in with a neo-Nazi group like Combat 18," McCarter said. "Organizations like them see the soccer hooligan growth as a breeding ground for new recruits."

"His name was Kent Hyle, and he's part of the Jakkhammer Legacy," Price provided.

"Jakkhammer Legacy," McCarter replied, nodding sagely, his tone transmitting his understanding over the phone.

"What the hell is the Jakkhammer, and why are neo-Nazis holding it in high honor?" Price asked.

"Jakkhammer, in the '70s, was a righteously brilliant punk band. When I was in a band, too young for signing up, I was a great fan of theirs," McCarter replied. "Then around 1980, they became a part of the Rock against Communism movement, which just started a slippery slope."

"Nothing wrong about being against communism," Price noted.

McCarter shrugged. "I've seen communism's failures, but the RAC was simply blowing smoke up arses. The RAC was formed to be a counter to the Anti-Nazi League's Rock against Racism drive, because Jakkhammer was a pro-white power band."

"All the little white boys were feeling edged out of their lowest rung on the social ladder by the addition of Indians and Jamaicans to the London population," Manning added.

"Oh," Price replied. "And much like American politics today, communism or socialism is a handy slur that can't be used as the basis of slander by far-right extremists."

"Bingo," McCarter replied. "I wouldn't be surprised

if certain U.S. news network pundits weren't punk fans back in the late '70s."

"Regardless, Jakkhammer Legacy has a reputation with the British police," Price said.

"I know that," McCarter said. "When the whole team was in London a while back on holiday, we ended up having to teach a few of their number a lesson about accosting blacks and Latinos."

"Good times," Manning said, showing a rare grin at the commission of physical violence against anyone. "Punching a Nazi makes anyone's day a little better."

Price chortled. "You're going to have an excellent evening with the information we'll give you two, then."

McCarter flexed his fists, tendons popping, a cruel grin on his lips. "Give us an address, and we'll ask a few hard questions."

Manning opened the pair's "special" suitcase and pulled out two pairs of brown leather gloves. The gloves were designed for law enforcement and military, with reinforcement and padding to protect the small bones of the human hand when utilized for punches against people's heads and faces. He tossed a pair to McCarter. They would, of course, go with firearms to meet with members of the Jakkhammer Legacy, but going in guns blazing was a hard way to get information. On the other hand, it would take considerable damage to the lips and nose to leave an opponent unable to talk after being thrashed.

McCarter received the files from Stony Man Farm as he prepared to head out, the leather of his fighting gloves creaking as he fit them snugly over his hands.

He couldn't help feeling a slight bit of guilt over taking such glee in laying abuse on a violence-and-racism-prone group of disenfranchised young men, nor could he dismiss the irony that he was going to become to the hooligans what the hooligans were to honest, law-abiding people.

McCarter glanced at Manning. "Let's go teach some lessons tonight, Gary."

"Be Afraid 101?" Manning asked.

McCarter nodded. "Class is now in session."

CHAPTER THREE

Los Angeles

Carl Lyons was a man who had been born to hunt monsters. It had been apparent when he worked the rough streets of Los Angeles, patrolling neighborhoods in dispute zones between rival gangs with a determination that had earned him the title of Ironman. Hal Brognola had seen it after Lyons's chance encounter with Mack Bolan, the Executioner, and had guided the young cop to put his unwavering courage and sharp mind to work in Brognola's organized crime task force, going undercover against the most murderous of gangs. Finally, Lyons had found a home in the Stony Man Farm–based Sensitive Operations Group, alongside Rosario Blancanales and Hermann Schwarz as the leader of Able Team.

With his new position, Lyons had tackled gangsters, terrorists and psychopathic madmen from Alaska to Sri Lanka. All that experience gave Lyons insight into the minds of human predators. He knew that there was one certain place to find his prey and that was where it would find the tastiest meals.

Right now, it was in Los Angeles, where the President was returning from a trip to the G8 conference. The President would stay there for a few days, and there were rumors in the wind that something was going to happen. Those rumors tickled Lyons's honed instincts, informing him that he would be needed in the City of Angels.

Unfortunately, the intel fragments that had been picked up indicated that whatever was going to happen might occur on either coast, or both. That meant leaving his partners in Able Team behind while he went solo to L.A. His fears were confirmed when Moscow became the target of a volley of orbitally launched spears, then Britain came under assault by electronically directed rioters.

Brognola had just finished relaying the London situation over Lyons's earpiece.

"Two G8 nations in less than two hours," Lyons mused. "It looks like a lot of things are coming together right now. I don't like this one bit."

Brognola grunted in agreement. "We were lucky to have David and Gary on hand for London. But with the teams spread so piecemeal across the globe…"

"We'll cope," Lyons responded as he looked around the LAX terminals. There were dozens of Secret Service and other agency personnel assembled, their nerves on edge as they waited for Air Force One to touch down. Up in the night skies, United States Air Force jets were flying air patrols and their radar and infrared sensors searched for sign of any menace that would come close to harming the leader of the free world.

Lyons noted that he blended in with the L.A. police who had been pulled in to supplement federal agents in putting a protective ring around the President. It was standard operating procedure to draw from local law enforcement, and in a way, it had made things easier for Lyons to slip unnoticed among them. He had spent enough time as both a cop and a Fed to pass for the other when encountering either side. It was a two-edged sword, unfortunately. The very hodgepodge of personnel that had allowed him an anonymous presence, fully armed, in an airport on heightened security would make any other ex-cop or former federal agent blend in, and not every retired law enforcement agent was out of work because he wanted to leave the job amicably.

Lyons had encountered too many bent cops and corrupt Feds to make him feel complacent about the ease with which he operated within the supposedly airtight security cordon around the terminal. Lyons had come into the airport with an assortment of firepower that would give him a chance to grab something more substantial in the case of a full-blown gunfight. He had his favorite revolver, a Colt Python, on him as always. This particular .357 Magnum was a snub-nosed version with its frame cut and adapted to wear Pachmayr Compacs, tucked into an extralarge side pocket in his slacks. Speed loaders packed with 125-grain semi-jacketed hollowpoints weighed down the pockets of his sports blazer, ready to slam six rounds at a time into an empty cylinder. A .357 Magnum hammerless, five-shot Centennial revolver rode in an ankle holster under each of his pant legs for backup, even though the revolvers were only going to be supplementary to his main sidearm.

The three wheelguns were in reserve for the .357 Auto chambered Smith & Wesson Military and Police he wore in a shoulder holster. The high-powered autopistol was filled to the brim with sixteen windshield-smashing shots to start, and he carried forty-five more rounds in three magazines he wore in a pouch that balanced the MP-357.

"Carl, Hunt's picked up an anomaly on the radar over the airport," Brognola said. "The VOR radio had a burst of static for a moment, then the original image appeared."

Brognola referred to Huntington Wethers, one of the most meticulous and attentive human beings that Lyons had ever encountered. Wethers had an acute eye for detail, which meant that anything he considered an anomaly was a serious deviation from the norm. Lyons consulted his PDA, which had a map of LAX loaded onto it. "The VOR station had a hiccup, and Wethers is concerned about it? Time to take a look at the transmitter."

"Your identification will only get you so far if there's something truly kinky going on," Brognola said. "A gunfight on the tarmac will bring an army down on your head."

"I'll be careful," Lyons promised.

Lyons slipped out an exit door close to the VOR station and jogged out onto the tarmac. The speedloaders in his pockets kept the wind across the flat concrete from blowing his lapels up to reveal the arsenal under his shoulders. He was dressed in a dark blue mock-turtleneck sweatshirt, light enough for the Los Angeles weather, and his jacket was a plaid blend of navy blue, Lincoln green and burgundy stripes, tinted just right so that Lyons could disappear into the shadows if he had to. It was a concept his friend and armorer, John "Cowboy" Kissinger, had developed—true urban camouflage. If someone saw Lyons decked out in black from neck to feet skulking around at night, they would be suspicious of him. However, with a little bit of light, he looked just like a normally dressed man, not a black-clad commando on the stalk. If he needed to totally disappear, he had a pocketed do-rag that he could stretch over his blond hair, removing the glint of its golden sheen from his profile.

He didn't know what he would be looking for, and with grim concern, he realized that he wasn't equipped for a stealth probe, unless he counted the Protech automatic knife he had clipped onto his belt. With a touch of a button, its five-inch blade would flash out, and as a cop on the violent streets of Los Angeles, he had no illusions that five inches of sharpened steel was any less deadly a weapon than a contact blast from a shotgun. A knife, even an inch-long stub, could destroy much more tissue than the largest bullet in the world. He'd have to get up close and personal to kill silently with the sleek switchblade, but with lives and national security at stake, he would make the sacrifice if necessary.

As Lyons neared the VOR transmitter, he slid behind the shadow of a parked luggage cart. A man paced back and forth, his bright cell phone screen causing his face to light up. The glowing reflections in his eyes were the only warning the Able Team commander had of his presence.

He pulled out his own PDA, made certain its LCD wasn't too bright, then pulled up the cell phone cloning application that Hermann Schwarz had loaded into the powerful pocket device. He didn't know the exact programming science behind the process, but Schwarz had explained simply that cellular phones were just encrypted radios that connected to a regular telephone network. This was why so many transmitter towers were needed around towns, as the cells were effectively only short-range. Schwarz explained that his program located the transmissions of nearby phones, then decrypted the mathematical keys that kept others from listening in.

A row of digits appeared on the screen and Lyons recognized the area-code prefix on the phone was for a cell number. He copied the text, put it in his instant messenger program and fired off the number to the Farm to trace it. In the meantime, he'd wait and observe, keeping his senses peeled for friends and foes in the darkness. If the Secret Service or a police officer saw him skulking in the shadows, he knew that his identification wouldn't explain why he was acting like a ninja when the President was due any minute. If the menace targeting the President had posted guards to scout their operation, then a bloody fight would be inevitable.

For all of Carl Lyons's reputation as a berserker warrior, a man capable of phenomenal violence in the face of the enemy, he was still a policeman and had become the tactical leader of Able Team. Observation and planning were Lyons's two secret weapons that allowed him to appear as an unstoppable engine of destruction in addition to his great strength, endurance and fighting prowess. He studied his opponents, sized them up and found their weaknesses. By applying his strengths to his foes' flaws, he could blow through them as if they were made of tissue.

Lyons looked at the PDA screen and saw that Stony Man Farm had come up with the original phone number that his quarry was using. It was a cell phone owned by a fifty-eight-year-old woman in San Bernardino County. Right now, he was operating on a clone of a cloned phone. The cybernetic geniuses back in Virginia were running the recent list of calls that had been made on the line, but the other end of the line was well encrypted. There were regular numbers, and then there were lines of gibberish that couldn't be deciphered.

Whoever they were up against, they had good, secure communications. Naturally, Lyons sighed mentally; anyone who would dare go after the leaders of eight nations, let alone the U.S. President, would have to be highly organized and capable. When something showed up on Able Team's radar, it generally had to be a national-scale conspiracy seeking to achieve its goals by murder and mayhem.

Just wait and see who's calling in, Lyons thought. He fished along his belt for a small sheath that contained a compact Bushnell night-vision monocular. The device had a 4x magnification, which would allow him to get a better look at the man with the phone.

The man was clad in a denim jacket, and through the green tint of the night vision, Lyons could see what appeared to be sigrunes on his neck. Normally, Lyons wouldn't know about arcane, occult designs, but the sigrunes were on a list of identifying tattoos for the southern California Reich Highwaymen, a widespread gang of thugs enlisted by the prison-based White Pride Defenders as muscle for their outside operations. The makeup that covered the lightning-bolt *S*'s on the man's neck was very different from his normal skin color under the light magnification, and the dark ink underneath showed through. In regular vision, even under good light, Lyons knew that the man would have covered himself so as not to be noticed.

Lyons grit his teeth, then checked his PDA, sending a text message off.

"Any signs of neo-Nazi activity in London or Moscow?" Lyons asked.

"Jakkhammer Legacy in London," came the reply almost instantly. "Suspect RNCG organizing rioters in Moscow."

Lyons furrowed his brow in concern. Sightings of three different local neo-Nazi groups in relation to threats to G8 nations was a disturbing trend. He quickly took a snapshot with the PDA and entered the text CRLR. He got the rapid message and its attachment off as quickly as possible as he heard his quarry's phone ring.

Lyons listened in.

"Your phone is compromised. Ditch it," came the terse order. "Pull back for Plan B."

The Reich rider looked up from the cell, then dropped it to the tarmac, his boot heel crushing the device. Lyons cursed, but even this bit of activity had given him information about his enemy. They were able to monitor their phones, and somehow had picked up on the fact that their line had been cloned. Sophisticated technology plus a white supremacist biker gang with national prison ties added up to the kind of opposition that Lyons couldn't help but welcome.

Whatever the biker's contingency plan, Lyons hoped that they only had one mode of communication that they felt was secure. As it was, the Reich rider turned and jogged to the VOR transmitter building. The boxy red-and-white base of the building with its conelike tower was an unassuming little place, but it could hide at least three more men inside. Lyons was going to have to ask about Plan B before he got to the others.

Lyons exploded from his hiding space with the speed that had made him a star football player in high school and college. Powerful legs propelled him along like a human rocket, and he caught up to the anxious neo-Nazi biker before he could make out the thump of feet or the trainlike pants of breath escaping the ex-cop's nose and mouth. The denim-clad gang member turned just in time for Lyons's brawny arm to catch him right across the throat. Momentum and velocity slammed the Reich rider to the ground hard, his head bouncing on the tarmac.

Breath released in a subdued "oof," thanks to the force that Lyons had applied to his throat, and his face was clenched up in a painful wince. The undercover biker must have hit the back of his head hard on the ground, which was fine with the Able Team commander. A little pain was a handle with which he could convince his prisoner to talk. He didn't have much time before whoever the motorcycle thug had come here with came looking for him.

"Plan B?" Lyons growled, drawing his Protech automatic knife. A simple press of the button and the five-inch serrated blade flickered into being right before his prisoner's eyes. Shock registered on the man's face as he tried to squirm away from the razor-sharp cutting edge that ended in a wicked needle tip.

The biker had trouble getting enough breath to speak

louder than a harsh whisper thanks to Lyons's weight and the placement of his forearm. There was also an enraged madness flickering behind Lyons's eyes, informing the downed criminal that if he cried out for help, the burly warrior would slice his face off and leave him to die slowly.

"I'm not asking again," Lyons said, resting the edge of the knife against the biker's left eyebrow. One flick of the wrist, and the biker knew he would be blinded and mutilated. It was a basic, inborn fear. The blind rarely lasted well in the days before the modern world. The biker himself not only had the gruesome mental images of his eyes punctured running through his mind, but also the realization that he would be ostracized by his circle of acquaintances. Riding with the gang would be out of the question, as well, as he would have failed his brothers. There was also no guarantee that Lyons wouldn't take out the other orb, too, leaving him blind. He would lose the life he'd known for the past decade or so.

"We're supposed to meet up with another group. They tell us the location when we call them," the man said.

"You guys are too tight not to have a password on hand," Lyons mentioned. "A code word to let them know everything is all right."

"I don't have that," the thug confessed. "Bones does."

"Which one is Bones?" Lyons asked.

"He has a baby skull on a necklace," the biker told him.

"How many others?" Lyons asked.

"Two," the prisoner confessed. "Don't mess my eyes up, man."

Lyons nodded, but that didn't preclude reversing the blade, then punching the pommel of the knife against his temple. The steel-reinforced fiberglass handle was less fragile than the small bones of the human hand, which broke easily when punching a man in the skull. Out cold, the biker wouldn't be much of a threat now.

Lyons rose from the ground and scanned the VOR station. One thing in his favor was that few such transmitter buildings had windows installed. Unfortunately, such structures had very limited numbers of entrances. In this case, there were two, parallel to each other. Lyons could try to go through the front door, but that would leave him a target for armed men inside. Three-to-one odds wasn't new for the Able Team commander, and indeed, he'd handled far worse.

Lyons preferred to fight smart, as well as hard. He scooped up the unconscious biker and put him in the luggage cart's driver's seat. The cart itself was hardly a step up from a riding mower, except with an engine that let it pull thousands of pounds of luggage a day. Lyons strapped the biker in, started the engine, then steered toward the VOR station's door. His final act was to push his former prisoner's foot against the accelerator.

He was setting bait, getting the bikers inside the building as bunched up as possible. A slow-moving cart bumping against the side of the station would draw curiosity, while anything faster striking the structure would send everyone packing.

With the cart set up, Lyons jogged along in its shadow, easily keeping up as he moved in a crouch behind the low-speed hauler. It struck one of the doors and crunched to a halt, its wheels grinding against the ground and causing the door to rattle. Lyons slipped out of sight behind the hauler and the unconscious biker.

Sure enough, the door opened a crack. Then a little farther. Lyons stayed hidden in the shadows, his do-rag tugged down to hide the glint of his blond hair in the ambient light.

"Toady? Toady, what the fuck? You drunk again?" a voice challenged.

"What's up?" another asked.

"Damn fool passed out riding a goddamned luggage trolley around," the man at the door said. Lyons saw a bone-white globe around the man's neck. He stepped out into the open, and the other two men joined him.

Lyons had set his bait well, as Bones stuffed his big shiny stainless revolver into his waistband. The three of them walked closer to Toady in his perch, and one of the bikers leaned over the dashboard, looking for the ignition to stop the cart's unrelenting "assault" on the locked door.

"Of all the—" Bones began.

Lyons didn't let him complete his curse toward his fallen comrade. With a lunge, the big ex-cop burst into view, his forearm crashing against Bones's jaw with the force of a sledgehammer. Lyons wanted the skull-wearing freak out cold and out of the fight to prevent the possibility that the other two could keep Bones from speaking. The biker toppled backward like a felled tree, but Lyons didn't hear him fall, as he was too busy concentrating on other problems. One of the bikers was stooped over to catch Bones, but the last of them reached for a black 1911 he had tucked into his belt.

The handgun made him a target for Lyons, who lashed out with *mae geri,* the Shotokan front kick. Lyons had been a *karateka* for several years, since just before he'd joined Able Team, and his familiarity with the blunt, direct Shotokan style had proved to be more than an edge in countless fights at home and abroad. The blow struck the biker in the stomach, just below his navel, driving the wind from his lungs and folding him over reflexively. Thus positioned, Lyons automatically transitioned to a *ushiro empi* chop, bringing his elbow down savagely on the enemy's back.

The gunner struck the ground face-first, mouth and nose gushing blood as they rocketed against the concrete. Lyons flipped the man onto his back and plucked the 1911 from his waistband. He dumped the magazine and worked the slide to eject the one in the pipe. He followed with a press of the thumb and a flick of the slide stop out of the frame. Now the weapon was useless, in two pieces and tossed away in two directions.

"Think you're hot shit?" said the biker who'd lunged to Bones's aid.

Lyons regarded the opponent who was reaching for his own iron. With a *suiki uki* block, Lyons scooped the man's hand away from the handle of his sidearm, and he followed it up with his one-knuckle fist, his favorite punch in the art. With his knuckle projecting like a spearhead, he struck the biker in the breastbone with enough force to halt his breathing. Lyons stiffened his hand for a *shuto* strike and plunged the hardened blade of flesh and bone into his foe's sternum. Fetid breath escaped from the man's lungs, but Lyons withdrew and stabbed into the man's clavicle, right at the juncture of nerves and blood vessels running along the side of the neck.

The biker was unconscious within moments.

Lyons turned and saw Bones struggle to get to his hands and knees. Lyons swept the biker's hand out from under him. A quick frisk revealed that his shiny .44 Magnum was accompanied by a claw hammer, a favorite biker weapon. He threw both of them aside and hauled the stunned criminal to his feet.

"Come on, Bones," Lyons said. "We're going to talk about Plan B, and about that skull around your neck."

CHAPTER FOUR

The Blue Ridge Mountains, Virginia

Hermann Schwarz entered the cybernetic paradise that was known as the Stony Man Farm War Room. He paused, looking at the wall of digital LCD monitors that offered a tapestry of views from around the globe. Workstations sprawled out, each indicative of their owner, all of whom were at work right now. There was an optional side station that Schwarz and Manning had appropriated for themselves whenever they were working at the Farm. The Canadian utilized the station simply for research on his varied fields, from ballistics to structural physics. Schwarz, on the other hand, fiddled and experimented with computer codework, constantly updating and improving the efficiency of the programs that he ran on his personal cell phone and the combat Personal Data Assistants that he'd assigned to his comrades in the action squads Able Team and Phoenix Force.

Right now, his Able Team partner and friend Carl Lyons was in Los Angeles, already in town on a rare moment of much-earned leave. With the veiled threat against Russia and the rest of the G8, Lyons had gone back on duty immediately. Schwarz was watching his combat PDA, knowing that it was possible that he'd be called to action to deal with problems along the coast.

In the meantime, Schwarz was working with the rest of the cybernetic team at the Farm in an effort to backtrack the kinetic shafts that had struck Moscow. They surely weren't the only ones trying to figure out the trajectory of the deadly missiles, but at least they could act on that information almost as soon as they received it, as opposed to a more conventional agency, which needed at least four hours of logistics and even more time for intricate planning.

It wasn't that Able Team and Phoenix Force could ever be accused of going off without a plan. However, the two Stony Man Farm teams had enough experience and skill, as well as the ability to think unconventionally, that they could be called upon at a moment's notice. They trained for as many contingencies as possible, honing and refreshing their skills in the time between their missions. Their intelligence, training and the technology they were able to fall back upon had all combined into a cohesive catch-all for whatever they could face.

That had been proved by the events in London less than an hour ago, when two members of Phoenix Force had been the deciding factor in what could have been a tragedy, containing mass violence and allowing innocent civilians to escape from seething, violent soccer hooligans. Schwarz made certain to listen in on Lyons's conversation with Brognola, though the big Able Team leader had gone silent as the VOR station at LAX was mentioned.

Aaron "the Bear" Kurtzman turned his attention

toward Schwarz. "You come up with anything yet, Gadgets?"

Schwarz looked at Bear, the Stony Man cybernetics expert, and shook his head. He was still running mathematical calculations in his mind, but the Able Team electronics genius was the kind of a person who could mentally multitask with remarkable ease. When his teachers complained that he, as a youth, seemed to be antsy and distracted in class, he realized that it was because the lessons they gave him only occupied a small fraction of his brain power. He needed other distractions. Schwarz would hum to satisfy the part of his mental focus that needed music, while he idly designed circuits or performed complex equations as mere doodles. He literally had designed some of his gadgets in his sleep, the burning intellect trapped in his skull looking for something to do even as he dreamed.

In one way, it was a godsend for the brilliant technician. The burning need to create, to tinker, to modify and program allowed him to live in the moment, to focus on nothing and thus able to experience everything. There were times when he seemed to have an almost paranormal danger sense, but while the genius believed in the possibility of ESP, he knew the truth was a matter of being able to reconcile his conscious and subconscious minds. The human subconscious was vastly aware of the world around it, but very few people had tuned their upper mental faculties to pay attention to those background cues. Schwarz's subconscious awareness was a directly accessible part of his mind, allowing him to process the sound of a scrape as either a breeze blowing a twig or a boot sole scuffing concrete.

"The nearest I could make out was that we're looking at an eastward launch," Schwarz replied. "The people who fired those darts were using Earth's rotation to add to the relative velocity of those missiles. And who knows how many times they orbited the planet before they struck."

"Given an equatorial launch, we could assume two or three cycles around the earth to angle in on Moscow," Kurtzman replied.

"Maybe more, since those darts came in almost directly from the east," Schwarz mused. Something caught his eye in his peripheral vision, and he turned his head, focusing on it.

"What is it?" Kurtzman asked.

"Something on the world map," Schwarz said, getting up and walking toward the plasma screens. He headed toward the monitor panel that contained northern, equatorial Africa. It was a small flicker in Cameroon.

The monitor screen kept watch for anomalies that would add up to flags for potential problems that would end up in Stony Man's lap. The computer would look for trends in increased criminal or terrorist activity, either smuggling or intensified violence. Then it would take regular census numbers of American or allied agents in those areas. Operatives who had not reported in for three consecutive days raised the flag.

"What do we have in Cameroon?" Schwarz asked.

"Nothing for CIA or NSA as far as we can tell," Barbara Price spoke up from her liaison station. She frowned. "I'm checking Department of Defense."

"You think this might be relevant?" Kurtzman asked.

Schwarz pointed at the proximity of the African coastal nation to the equator. "What were we just talking about, launchwise?"

Kurtzman grimaced. "Barb, what is the DoD looking at?"

"Two operatives were sent to the Congo to look into reports of kidnapping among the local population," Price answered. She looked up. "Modern-day slavery, and in that region, slaves equal diamond mines."

"Not necessarily in this case," Schwarz said, "But then, there had to be something done to fund a potential launch pad."

"Construction teams for a launcher," Price murmured. "The Congo is akin to a million square miles…"

"One point four million square miles to be exact," Schwarz corrected. "That's just for the river basin, which is one of the top three largest unspoiled rainforests in the world."

"Even with satellites, it's going to take a lot of time to look through all that jungle," Price noted, taking a deep breath. "And it's not as if we have a lot of eyes in the sky looking down at the Congo."

"Things are more interesting with piracy off the Horn of Africa or around the Mediterranean," Kurtzman added. "Reallocating orbital surveillance for something that's only a hunch is going to take a lot of effort and might raise too many flags."

Schwarz turned, regarding Kurtzman. "I know it's just a hunch, but everyone else is looking to the sky and pointing fingers at China and the U.S."

"The only two countries with the resources to launch orbital bombardment satellites," Price noted. "Though we're concerned with something in the U.S. Lyons informed us that the Reich Highwaymen were skulking around LAX."

"Reich Highwaymen in the U.S., Jakkhammer Legacy in England," Schwarz mused. "Anything on our Nazi watch?"

"There've been funds flying around the backtrails, but nothing that points in any solid direction," Carmen Delahunt spoke up. "All we know is—" she looked at her screen, her green eyes flashing as she did some quick math "—the amount of money in the stream is increased."

"And no old artifacts or gold has turned up," Schwarz stated.

"That's true, but violence has increased in Europe among diamond smugglers," Delahunt replied, anticipating Schwarz's next supposition.

The Able Team genius frowned. Being right while he grasped at rumors and hints to form a plan of action was no victory. While he'd put together circumstantial evidence for where Stony Man should direct its attention for the origins of their unknown enemy, the conspiracy seemed to have links to violent, neofascist, racial supremacist groups from Moscow to Los Angeles. Putting boots on the ground in Africa would do nothing to stem the tide of mayhem that humans could cause, as opposed to the destruction wrought by throwing giant crowbars at cities from orbit.

Able Team had encountered the adherents of racial intolerance in the U.S. and engaged them in brutal combat. They were bloodthirsty and ruthless in their ideology, and recently the white supremacist scum had gone from supplementing their income with drug dealing and weapons smuggling to becoming full-time players, exercising their greed at easy money, power and prestige.

The Reich Highwaymen were symptomatic of this trend, being among the most successful smugglers across the border between California and Mexico. There were also five warrants for RHM members wanted for questioning in regard to twenty murders.

That's just what the police knew. Unreported killings, in Schwarz's experience, would be exponentially more.

"See if the Highwaymen have any friends here on the east coast," Schwarz suggested. "It's not as if the FBI and the CIA aren't following more obvious, less arcane leads, right?"

"It could just be that you've got a bias against those gangs," Price noted. "We could be spinning our wheels for an old grudge against a particular type of biker."

"What was that about Jakkhammer Legacy?" Schwarz asked. "British neo-Nazis who are the strong-arm behind the British Imperial Revival Society? Looking for the day when all the brown peoples in the world know their place, and it's usually toiling for a white limey?"

"You're fast on the research," Kurtzman noted.

"I heard Barb talking about it with David," Schwarz said.

"A worldwide fascist conspiracy, and they're working out of darkest Africa," Price said.

"Using black slaves to mine diamonds and build launch pads," Schwarz added. "Can you think of something a white supremacist wouldn't like more than having Africans work themselves to death for their purposes?"

Price shook her head reluctantly. "Racist bastards… For once I completely agree with Carl about dealing with them."

"Shoot first, ask questions, then finish shooting," Schwarz explained for the computer experts in the War Room.

A phone warbled. Price picked it up. "Gadgets, it's Pol."

"Pol" was short for "Politician," the nickname for the diplomatic and smooth-talking Rosario Blancanales, the third and final member of Able Team. When Lyons had activated and stayed on station in Los Angeles, the ex-LAPD cop had suggested that someone go on alert in Washington, D.C., preferably working from street level to avoid duplicating the efforts of federal agencies who were looking at terrorist groups and foreign governments. Lyons had been a beat cop, and while he had the advantage of electronic, satellite and internet-scoured information, he had never given up on the reliability of rumors and chatter on the mean streets. Blancanales, an affable, nearly chameleonlike person who could disarm an enemy with his words *and* his hands, had volunteered, leaving Schwarz free to utilize his particular skills.

Somewhere Blancanales had come through, prying loose some nugget of information that would give Stony Man Farm an edge.

Schwarz punched the speaker phone button, so that Blancanales could be heard by the rest of the War Room staff. "What's the news, Pol?"

"I stumbled my way to a town just a mile past Chevy Chase," Blancanales answered. "Don't tell Carl, but his primitive, stone-age cop ways still work."

Schwarz grinned. "A town?"

"Barely a town, actually. Basically, it's the runoff from an interstate. It's got some fast-food restaurants, two major gas station franchises and a bunch of small rest stops catering to the nomadic sort," Blancanales explained.

"Bikers and truckers," Schwarz translated for Price. She rolled her eyes, exasperated by the assumption that she hadn't learned the verbal shorthand utilized by the field teams.

"I work at a desk for a few hours a day. I'm not a hermit stuck on an island," Price responded.

"Anyway, there's a congregation meeting. It looks as if they're getting set for a holy revival," Blancanales said. "Be nice if you got here."

"Is Jack or Charlie around?" Schwarz asked, referring to Jack Grimaldi or Charlie Mott, Stony Man's two resident pilots.

"I've had Charlie keep a helicopter on standby," Price said. "Get to the pad, and he'll take you up as soon as you get there."

"I'll be there in a few minutes, Pol," Schwarz said. "Tell Barb your exact location so Charlie can take me there as the crow flies. Need party favors?"

"I'm pretty well strapped. Just bring plenty of ammo," Blancanales replied.

Herman Schwarz raced out of the War Room.

It was time to ask some questions, Able Team style.

The Congo

JOHN CARMICHAEL TRIPPED but recovered his balance by hugging a tree trunk. The trouble with doing that in a rainforest was that creatures started crawling along his arm, making a beeline for his shoulder and neck. It took five hard, quick slaps to make certain everything had been either knocked off or crushed, and the smashed insects that clung to his dark arm left behind a gooey mess that attracted hungry flies. He mopped the stuff off his arm, not wanting to catch a bite from a tsetse fly or some infection from a disease-ridden set of insect mandibles.

"Congratulations, you made it another hundred yards before something else tried to kill you," he panted. He glanced back, trying to take consolation in the fact that the only things that had been after him, at least those that he could see, weren't men packing assault rifles.

"Only problem with that," he told himself, "is you can't shoot bugs."

Carmichael felt that he could relax his pace now. Too much exertion in the heat and humidity of the jungle would drain and dehydrate a man, despite the amount of moisture in the air.

He checked his satellite phone again, as if somehow the bullet hole through it would have disappeared. Naked electronics, a shattered silicon board, peeked out, and Carmichael sneered. Arcado had been carrying the device when he'd been hit. The memory of his partner came unbidden, and he clenched his teeth.

"Don't think about it," he told himself, putting one foot in front of the other. Each step was closer to civilization, another step toward warning the world of what was going on. He checked his watch; it was only hours since the rocket went up.

That didn't mean much, Carmichael calculated. At orbital velocities, whatever had been launched could have gone around the world a dozen times in just sixty minutes. He could just be too late to raise the alarm that death would be raining down from above.

If that was the case, Carmichael would have to bring in someone to avenge those killed, including his best friend. Raw anger gnawed at him along with the willingness to channel that rage.

Carmichael glanced over his shoulder again, looking back toward the jungle-camouflaged base. He frowned as he realized that the enemy wouldn't give up. There was someone on his trail, willing to enter the sprawling rainforest basin to keep their secret. They couldn't afford to let Carmichael reach civilization alive. Once he spoke, they would die.

Carmichael had only given himself a lead on the enemy; he hadn't given them the slip. He didn't know what kind of cushion he had. Slowing down would be the only rest he could get. Stopping for any length of time would give his hunters a chance to catch up. He wiped his brow and sighed. There were only two spare magazines for his Kalashnikov, giving him ninety rounds for the rifle, and the four magazines for the 1911 he used for a sidearm. He also had five shots for the tiny .357 Magnum Centennial he wore in the small of his back, but if it got down to handguns, especially the two-inch-barreled snubby, he was doomed. The enemy would have a full combat kit and outnumber him at least four to one, putting him at a disadvantage when it came to a fight.

Arcado's advice, from back when Carmichael was a rookie operative for the DoD, came to mind. "Guns make you fight stupid. Sure, firepower could possibly save your ass when it comes to bad-breath distance, but if you want to fight smart, you stay away from fights. And if you can't avoid a fight, then don't fight stupid. But I don't have to tell you that. When you're in the shit, you'll be scared. And when you're scared, you'll fight smart."

It wasn't until Carmichael had read Sun Tzu's *The Art of War* that he realized that Arcado was paraphrasing the brilliant Chinese general. Carmichael paused and assessed his situation.

What were his strengths? He knew how to get through a jungle and survive off the land, thanks to his Robin Sage Green Beret training. As only one man, he was a low-profile target, making him more mobile and able to hide in smaller places. He knew he was being hunted, and he knew how vital it was for the enemy to capture him, so he could gauge how much force they had and how well-skilled his pursuers would be. He knew in which direction he'd been heading as he smashed his trail through the rainforest while moving at full-tilt.

What were his enemy's strengths? They outnumbered him. They outgunned him. They had a home-field advantage. They had communications and could call on extra resources if necessary. They were trackers, and they had been good enough to be within sweating distance for at least the first hour of their pursuit. They were smart enough to ease up and let Carmichael burn himself out running like hell, so they had been resting for the past two hours while he exerted energy and used up vital reserves.

Carmichael was already painfully aware of his weaknesses; no apparent water source to replenish his lost fluids, low on ammo, far from his allies. Carmichael looked for *their* weaknesses, even as he trod through the jungle, taking care to move slowly and easily, not breaking branches or tearing leaves with his passage. He made certain to step on exposed roots and fallen, heavy branches to minimize his footprints, though most of them were readily swallowed by the thick undergrowth that somehow thrived on faint rays of sunlight that had penetrated the forest canopy.

"There are more of them, so moving quietly will be more difficult for them," Carmichael reminded himself. As he made that assessment, he added another strength that they possessed over him. Because they had numbers, they could fake him out, distracting him with a larger number, thus herding him toward a scout who would be moving singly and with stealth.

"They have confidence," Carmichael said. "They have the perception of certain superiority. I know I'm in the hole."

He went back to Arcado's words. "When you're scared, you'll fight smart."

Carmichael continued his march. He was scared, but his training and determination kept him from blind panic. The shots of fear kept him wary, attuned, in a state where his body was able to pump all manner of energy into fight or flight, but his mental processes were clear and focused.

"Survive for David," Carmichael told himself as he continued into the dark rainforest, demons nipping at his heels.

CHAPTER FIVE

Maryland

Rosario Blancanales lowered his binoculars as Hermann Schwarz pulled up behind his van. He was parked far enough from the biker bar that even the four men who were watching the near side of the perimeter wouldn't notice the arrival. Just the same, Schwarz had kept his headlights off. It was a couple of hours before dawn, and Schwarz's vehicle was a low-profile, nonreflective dark blue. He joined Blancanales in the van.

"Did I miss anything?" Schwarz asked. He looked Blancanales over, and noticed that he was dressed in dark blue overalls with a county waste-management patch. "Oh, the old Dumpster trick?"

"Slapped a sign on the side of the van, rolled up behind the bar, got called a spic by the troglodytes working security," Blancanales said.

"Didn't they wonder why you weren't driving a garbage truck?" Schwarz asked.

"Dumpster inspection. Clipboard and a few stickers and said that their can wouldn't need to be replaced because of the rust on the bottom if I got a few bucks," Blancanales explained.

"That's one way to get your ass stomped by those

slope-headed knuckle draggers," Schwarz growled. "Yet I note the lack of bruises."

"Sure way to find out that these pricks are doing some serious dirt if they don't want to draw attention by smacking a county worker around," Blancanales answered.

"So it could be a gun or drug deal," Schwarz noted, musing. "But if that were the case, they'd have brought some vans and automobiles."

"This is a rabble-rousing meeting," Blancanales said. "Just standing out back I heard them revving the crowd with hate metal."

Schwarz frowned. "Sure?"

"I could hear the lyrics," Blancanales said. "And I can't make a mistake about Nick Cobb and Night Heat."

Schwarz nodded. Able Team, as a component of their general domestic awareness, made certain to keep an eye on two particular brands of music. One was *narcocorridas,* the songs glorifying the life of Mexican and Central American drug dealers. It was a genre of music that had expanded into Texas, Arizona, Nevada and California. The other genre of music they kept familiar with was the aforementioned "hate metal" or "white power rock," which was far more widespread than the chosen medium of the Latino drug dealers. Rosario Blancanales, the son of Puerto Ricans who had immigrated to the U.S. to give their children a good life, had taken a special interest in Nick Cobb and his band, Night Heat, a group of so-called Minutemen who sang the anthems of the white supremacists, the same racists who corrupted the immigration-reform movement. Cobb and his group jabbed a raw nerve on the first-generation-American Blancanales, so he became intimately familiar with the bigoted venom they spewed as a form of political protest.

"We could shake things up," Schwarz said. "A few flash-bangs, maybe one of my headbanger specials..."

"It'd be fun to knock these assholes around, but right now we're just gathering intelligence," Blancanales replied. "Patience, Gadgets."

Schwarz took a deep, cleansing breath and put aside his anger for another moment. He noticed that Blancanales had aimed a rifle microphone at the bar and was listening in on one earbud. The oscilloscope that measured the level of noise inside the biker's den suddenly flared, then dropped off.

Blancanales turned on the speaker. "Business is picking up."

Schwarz settled in to listen to the hatemonger's speech to his white supremacist, motorcycle-riding flock. As always, when it came to battling the forces of terror, combat was only a small percentage of what had to be done. The Able Team warriors had to investigate and observe to locate and identify. Once they had their target, then it would be time to destroy the enemy.

Bonn, Germany

RAFAEL ENCIZO PULLED BACK the slide on his Heckler & Koch USP Compact, looking into the breech to make certain that the chamber was clear. The slide stop was locked into a notch on the top half of the pistol, keeping it locked back so that he could check down the barrel and the feed ramp for damage or imperfections. He looked over to T.J. Hawkins, who did his own maintenance on his personal Glock 19. Encizo had always been a fan of Heckler & Koch's weaponry, even before it became a popular brand and the must-have weapon of armchair commandos, as well as real-world operators. The small USP 9 mm Compact was a good fit for him in civilian dress, easily concealable and still holding 14 shots, and he balanced it out with another German handgun, his .32-caliber Walther PPK.

The Cuban Phoenix Force veteran didn't miss the irony that he was in Bonn to search for potential neo-Nazis who were the henchmen of choice for the group threatening the G8 nations. Germany and its chancellor were already unpopular with the hard-core racists who had been enraged by the relaxation of immigration standards. Riddling Bonn's neo-Nazis with Teutonic weaponry just seemed right.

Encizo and Hawkins had been in Germany already, catching some R & R not far from their allies in England. The only member of Phoenix Force who had been missing was Calvin James, who was off in San Francisco. Encizo and Hawkins were on a working holiday, posing as U.S. Marshals engaging in cross training with the GSG-9.

The laptop beeped, prompting Encizo to load and sheath his H&K before answering the video call. It was the Farm, and they didn't transmit without good reason. Barbara Price's face appeared on the laptop screen.

"Barb?" Encizo asked. "What's wrong?"

"We're on the fence about committing you to a neo-

Nazi hunt in Germany," Price told him. "You might be more useful elsewhere."

Hawkins raised his head at the mention of that. "We're going hunting for the launch pad?"

"If we can narrow down the location, yes," Price replied.

"So we're looking at equatorial Africa?" Encizo asked.

"Figured that out so soon?" Price countered.

"We've done enough with covert and overt launch facilities to know that the closer to the equator, the easier it is to use the Earth's rotation to establish a proper orbit," Encizo answered.

"Like, duh, Barb," Hawkins added.

Price smirked. "We've got a few hints that are pointing us to a possible location."

"One of the Congo states?" Encizo suggested to Hawkins.

"The Congo River Basin is a big, untouched area," the Southerner replied. "You could hide battalions in that rainforest."

"Our little ex-Ranger is growing so fast," Encizo said with an ironic, wistful smile.

"Like T.J. said, the Congo River Basin is one of the largest rainforests in the world, and even if we did have satellites looking down into that jungle, they could have all manner of camouflage," Price explained. "We need to narrow things down."

"So we should do our initial investigations here," Encizo said. "I hate sitting on my thumbs waiting to be told to do something."

"Waiting is a big part of covert operations, Rafe," Price reminded him.

"Waiting while observing is doing something, at least mentally," Encizo answered. "T.J. and I could shake a few things loose so that we could hand it off to the BND before we leave."

Price sighed.

"Barb, it's me and T.J., not David or Carl," Encizo added. "We know how to stay low profile."

"You tell me that, but I've seen what you can do on your own," Price said. "You said you were going to shake things loose, and that means conflict."

"Look at it this way, ma'am," Hawkins said. "If we didn't ruffle the feathers of locals, you wouldn't have much to do other than arrange airplane tickets."

Encizo stifled a snort as he saw the look on Price's face on the laptop monitor. Her clear blue eyes promised Hawkins an ass kicking should he ever return to the Stony Man War Room. "Keep writing checks your butt can't cover, T.J. Keep it up."

Encizo cleared his throat, putting some distance between himself and Hawkins's last comment. "Besides, we're going to be knocking neo-Nazi heads together to get this information. They're not the kind to bother German civil liberties lawyers about harassment, especially since we're not local authorities and we won't exactly be leaving our calling cards."

"All right. Hit the streets and see what you can find out," Price said. "It'll take a while for us to arrange a drop for you two into Sierra Leone."

"We've got a pilot to take us the rest of the way?" Hawkins asked.

"That's part of the holdup," Price explained. "We need a bush pilot with a plane and jump gear for you two. Add in that it's going to have to be a secure pilot, or at least a good cover…"

"And so we have some time before we go," Encizo concluded. "Good. Any word on David and Gary or Calvin?"

"David and Gary are in the same boat as you two," Price said. "Calvin's still en route to Japan, and we're not even certain we can get him to Africa."

"We're just working against the ground forces, the dog packs utilized to stir up trouble," Hawkins said. "What can any one or two men do against the equivalent of five tons of TNT striking a city at 150 miles per hour?"

"That's why we have the cybercrew working overtime," Price answered. "Maybe we can find where the orbital attacks are originating and intercept or jam them."

"The last time we did this, we were lucky enough to steer our efforts to where we could catch a ride to the appropriate location," Encizo said. "It's not as if we've earned free tickets on the space shuttle, and even so, it'd take a week to prepare one for launch and a second for backup."

"Have you checked with some of the friends we've made with the Chinese space program?" Hawkins asked.

"That's a good idea. There's been a lot of talk about adding the People's Republic to the G8 core as it is rapidly becoming one of the largest capitalist economies in the world," Encizo agreed. "Beijing has a lot to gain by helping out against someone who's threatened the member nations."

"Not that much," Price replied. "They're already in the G8 Plus 8, and China can handle its own economic and international issues. The warning issued doesn't sound like them, either. They can sit out and remain neutral without incurring actual bad press or ill will."

"I didn't think we'd actually be going through official channels," Hawkins replied. "This could just be a large-scale distraction for something else."

"Like a threatened move on Taiwan or Japan," Price added. "We've thought about that. Considering that the southern coast hasn't shown any launch data, and troops haven't been assembled in position to make a move on either island, it's slim, but we're not taking our eyes off them."

"The only potential chance for intel either comes from a trip into deepest, darkest Africa, or punching it out of the heads of neo-Nazi groups," Hawkins said. "And since the common street soldier isn't exactly the brightest light on the tree, anyone who would have the kind of information we could actually use has a cushion we'd have to cut through."

"That's something Phoenix Force does well," Encizo reminded his partner. "Plus, we've got a head start in terms of where to look for people to talk."

"It pays to have you guys develop individual intelligence assets," Price conceded.

"I prefer to think of them as friends," Encizo countered.

"Losing friends hurts more than losing assets," Price reminded him. She killed the connection, leaving

Encizo and Hawkins to continue preparing for their intel hunt.

Encizo remembered one of Phoenix Force's closest friends, the German BND investigator and former commando Karl Hahn. The man had even become a reserve member of the team when Encizo had fallen in combat against another neo-Nazi conspiracy. A trusted ally, Phoenix Force had risked their lives to rescue Hahn from kidnappers, a move that had drawn worry from Stony Man Farm itself, as the covert team could have compromised the secrecy of the Sensitive Operations Group. Hahn had since fallen, assisting Phoenix Force in combating a threat that could have incited a global war. Encizo's frown deepened as he realized that the maniacs who had killed Hahn were also fanatics who sought to resurrect the Third Reich. He rubbed his forehead, feeling the scar left there by a neo-Nazi's bullet.

"You all right, pard?" Hawkins asked.

"Just remembering all the 'fun' I've had with bigoted fascists," Encizo told him. "Dead friends and old wounds, mostly."

"Can you remain objective, or should I just do this by myself?" Hawkins asked.

"I'm a professional," Encizo said.

Hawkins smiled and gave his friend a light punch on the shoulder. "Just remember, this doesn't mean you're not allowed to enjoy yourself. Just do it within our ethics."

Encizo nodded, his signature easy grin returning to his handsome, swarthy features. "Who do you think taught you half of those ethics?"

Hawkins allowed himself a chuckle. "Getting the info

we want is going to be hard. Torture is slow, sloppy and inefficient, and Cal's not here to dose anyone with truth serum."

Encizo made sure his gear was all in place, from the knife on a leather thong around his neck to his two handguns. "I'll show you a few tricks we used before Calvin joined the team. Come on."

Hawkins followed Encizo out into the Bonn streets, the two Phoenix Force members grimly determined to get what they could out of their Nazi opponents.

Stony Man Farm

Akira Tokaido double-checked the figures that both Hermann Schwarz and Gary Manning had provided in regard to the trajectories taken by the twenty-foot-long hunks of iron hurled at the city of Moscow. Schwarz's figures were slightly off from Manning's, but Akira realized that Manning had taken wind deflection into account.

The young Japanese-American computer expert sent this to Schwarz as he was on stakeout, and received an almost instantaneous text response.

"Leave it to a sniper to figure atmospheric activity into an equation while I didn't," Schwarz had written.

"Anything new there?" Tokaido texted back.

"Tired old bigot rhetoric," Schwarz answered. "Anything there?"

"Plans to send Dave and the gang down south," Tokaido replied cryptically. "Based on your observations."

"But nothing until you can see a launch pad?" Schwarz asked.

"Which could take weeks," Tokaido answered. "If we did find it, what's the plan then?"

"Hopefully we'll be able to raid their communication links and find their mission control center," Schwarz typed. "If mission control is not at the launch pad."

"Most likely not," Tokaido responded. "If they've been mining diamonds…"

"That's another thing we'll have to take care of," Schwarz interrupted.

"The mine," Tokaido clarified.

"Could be used to fund other terrorist activity," Schwarz explained.

Tokaido thought for a moment, then looked over to Hunt Wethers. "Hunt, can you access Carmen's money track for the neo-Nazis?"

"I presume that you're looking for recent large real-estate transactions," Wethers commented.

Tokaido nodded. "Just throw everything you find to my workstation. I'll sort it out once I figure out what they'd need for a mission control station."

"Don't forget support staff and fortifications," Wethers added.

Tokaido grinned. "I love it when a team comes to-gether."

Grand Castle of the Fist of Heaven
Tennessee

AUGUSTUS HAMMERSMITH liked standing in the computer annex of the manse, especially thanks to the ionic air cleaners, which attracted motes of dust or debris that would otherwise have left an imperfection on his uniform. He was proud of the suit, which was charcoal-black with red piping, and he made certain there was not a fleck of white marring its perfection. He kept his hair short, styled as what the modern media called the Roman look because it resembled the style seen in sculptures of Caesar. In this cut, his hair was pale enough that it looked as if he had a golden polish applied to a bald head.

Hammersmith had chosen the Roman symbol for Mars as the group's badge, a black circle with an arrow pointed to the northeast in the center of a red disk. Unlike the neo-Nazis he'd employed in southern California and elsewhere, he went to Hitler's inspiration—the original thousand-year reich created by Rome. While he and the organization were devout Christians, they picked the unmistakable symbol of war—Mars—as their emblem and name: the United Legion of Messianic America. The Roman legions were unbeatable, and Rome had spread across the globe, and had ground the lesser, servitor races under their sandaled feet, their progress halted by even more ferocious and dedicated white men. The only thing keeping Hammersmith from choosing to name the group for the mighty barbarians who had eventually weakened the Roman empire was the lack of success at ultimately defeating Rome.

Around him, in the darkness of the room, the blue-and-white monitor screens cast their glow, illuminating the faces of computer operators to make them appear ghostly. Up on the wall, a map of the world showed the position of their satellite, as well as blips of light for dozens of cities across North America, Europe and Asia.

"Sir, I'm picking up some monitoring of real-estate transactions we've gone through in the past five years," Darius Dispenza, his chief technician, said. Dispenza, like the rest of Hammersmith's personal staff, had clear blue eyes, though his hair was reddish brown, not blond. It didn't matter to Hammersmith, as it made him clearly a peckerwood—a pure white in the slang of prison folk. Dispenza had European Latin blood, and had become a soldier of the White Pride Defenders while he was serving time in prison for identity theft and computer fraud back at the turn of the millennium.

Hammersmith looked down at the man, then at his computer screen. Confidence swelled in the commander's heart, as he knew that the United Legion of Messianic America was safe in that regard. It had owned the manse for decades. The addition of this nerve center had occurred in the late '90s, and the updates to its technology and earth-to-orbit communications equipment had grown naturally. The ULMA had been there for the ground floor of the white power movement's invasion of the internet, and right now, its equipment had been kept cutting edge. It rivaled any government agency, and in many cases, superseded its access to electronics, thanks to the wealth accumulated from members' dues and other sources of income.

"Let them," Hammersmith said.

His voice had a grim, booming authority, as if he were a lion recast in the image of a man. "What about our loss of signal in Los Angeles?"

"It was a temporary disruption, but our intermediaries are in contact with the airport team," Dispenza told Hammersmith.

"Are you certain that this is uncoerced communication?" Hammersmith asked.

"The Reich Highwaymen aren't sophisticated enough to have codes set up for a compromised operation," the computer man said. "They're very paranoid about their security, but their arrogance keeps them from conceding a plan based upon possible failure."

"Alert the Plan B squad to expect unwelcome visitors," Hammersmith ordered. He looked at the satellite track. According to the wall monitor, their kinetic launcher was only two minutes from the optimal position to fire on London. He didn't need to give orders either for the satellite or for the flash mobs that were poised to wreak more havoc.

"Cameras?" Hammersmith asked.

"Slaved to your station, sir," Wallace told him. Wallace was another computer criminal who had cleaved to the side of the WPD for protection in exchange for services. On the inside, it had been seeing to the carnal needs of the white supremacist prison gang. Outside, Hammersmith had put him to work raising funds through computer scams. Hammersmith didn't trust the man as much because he had profited in internet child pornography. Still, the Fist of Heaven mastermind appreciated the subservient tone of voice from the sexual deviant.

Hammersmith smiled, walking to his monitor.

The Scorpion, their satellite named for the Roman legion's ancient arbalest, was poised to sting another city. This Scorpion, like its forebear, didn't need venom.

It simply needed mass and velocity. The legionnaires' giant crossbow artillery had easily torn through British castles and forts with their massive, iron-headed bolts. The ULMA's Scorpion did it with old recycled steel pipes filled with concrete and steered by GPS-guided tail fins.

The ULMA computer crew had hacked into traffic cameras around London, which superimposed targeting loci for their missiles. The first Scorpion launched could only carry ten of its bolts into orbit, so five targets had been chosen: New Scotland Yard, MI-6, MI-5, Interpol's British Headquarters and the Ministry of Defense. They were big, showy targets, and though Hammersmith doubted that anything would actually be snarled in the English investigation, the destruction and death toll would be spectacular.

The Fist of Heaven project was ready to rain hell upon a city overwrought with mayhem.

The countdown numbers blinked down toward zero....

IN THE VACUUM OF SPACE, a simple release of CO_2 gas was all that was necessary to rotate the Scorpion satellite precisely. The orbiting machine was built on the basis of simplicity and low cost. Electronics and microprocessors made its maneuvering seamless. The launcher wasn't much of a mechanism. It was another puff of carbon dioxide after a small motor released the kinetic dart. That soft push, in no atmosphere and negligent relative mass, was more than enough to hurl the twenty-foot-long bolt into Earth's gravity well.

All of the fuel for the launch vehicle was necessary

to put the Scorpion into orbit. The satellite wasn't meant
to stay up for long, and few conventional satellites had
fuel supplies or engines. Momentum and altitude were
all that was necessary to keep the vehicles up. There was
an old joke that flying was simply throwing yourself at
the ground and missing. Orbit was just that, falling from
such a great altitude that the satellite simply missed the
Earth completely. Such a method helped satellites stay
aloft for decades, only requiring batteries to maintain
their functions such as relaying signals or operating
cameras.

The Scorpion's bolts, however, were given a trajectory to where they wouldn't miss the ground. Now, hundreds of pounds of steel accelerated at thirty-two meters
per second. Had there been no atmosphere between the
missile and the ground, its velocity would grow exponentially until final impact. The only thing preventing
obscene levels of speed was Earth's atmosphere, limiting it to falling over six miles in a second, the terminal
velocity of a streamlined object in uncontrolled acceleration through the atmosphere.

It didn't matter that the top speed was so low. Even
at that speed, the impact would punch through concrete
as if it were a soap bubble.

It literally would strike a building like a fist from
Heaven.

In Tennessee, a madman's smile grew as he watched
buildings erupt into clouds of powdered stone.

CHAPTER SIX

London

The Jakkhammer Legacy lieutenant, Rupert Evanston, screamed his lungs out, despite the fact that Gary Manning of Phoenix Force had a firm grip on his ankle. Evanston was dangling upside down from the fourth floor of the building where the Legacy owned the Morningstar Crossing pub. The pub itself was a front company for the Jakkhammer Legacy, and had been studied by MI-5 and the Metropolitan Police. While Scotland Yard and MI-5 only had it under surveillance, with no real evidence to move in on the British neo-Nazis, Manning and McCarter were not limited by the need for warrants to enter the building.

Manning and McCarter had managed to skirt the surveillance team and slip into the upper three floors. Through trickery and stealth, they had cleared out four Jakkhammer security men picked more for their muscle than their brains. Chokeholds and cable ties made certain that they would remain still while Manning and McCarter put fear into Evanston.

Holding up the 165-pound owner of the pub with one hand was easy for Manning, a power lifter who could bench press nearly four times that amount. Evanston didn't know the kind of strength that Manning possessed, and fear gripped him completely. McCarter could already smell the release of the neo-Nazi's bladder.

"Shut your gob, you nancy!" McCarter snarled.

Manning faked a shoulder spasm and Evanston dipped two inches. That kind of drop felt like a mile to Evanston, eliciting another howl of horror. McCarter looked down at the street, realizing that the surveillance teams watching the Jakkhammers would now be aware that something was wrong. Sure, they were facing away from the street, over the back of the Morningstar Crossing, but the cries of terror would echo loud and wide.

Not having the time to engage in a proper interrogation, and loath to use conventional torture methods, they decided to resort to blind fear and the urge for self-preservation to loosen Evanston's tongue. It had been a gamble, but McCarter knew that men like Evanston weren't disciplined enough to resist scare tactics. Breaking a man psychologically with a minimum of physical harm would be relatively easy to do, and quick, as well.

The roof shook around them suddenly, and all three men froze. Throughout the streets and alleys beneath them, they heard the rustle produced by hundreds of windows cracking as buildings shifted.

"Aw, no," McCarter muttered as the sonic boom of the first kinetic dart rumbled through the air.

Manning hauled Evanston back onto the roof so the shuddering rooftop didn't cause him to fall. "You're lucky we're not as rotten as you lot."

Evanston curled up on the tarpaper, cringing as the city shook violently again. "The hell is going on?"

McCarter grabbed up the neo-Nazi by the throat and

turned his head to look at a rising cloud of debris from the first impact. "The bastards paying you to throw riots are now blowing your city to hell, and they don't care that they're targeting white people."

Evanston tried to swallow, but McCarter's grasp around his throat prevented that. He tried to shake loose, and Manning's admonishing glare convinced McCarter to ease the strangling grasp. "Half of this bloody city are race traitors, you bleeding-heart Commie."

"Commie?" McCarter would have laughed if destruction weren't raining down on his hometown. Instead, he head-butted Evanston, breaking the Jakkhammer leader's nose and tearing his lips against his teeth. "Bloody berk."

Manning had his PDA out to contact the Farm. He turned away from Evanston, speaking in a low voice that kept the Jakkhammer leader from hearing him. Not that Evanston was paying attention; he was too busy groaning over his broken nose and teeth. Still, even with the heavens crashing down around them, Manning didn't relax his radio discipline. "Barb, they're hitting London."

To punctuate that phrase, the thunder of a kinetic dart's sonic boom reverberated, the air echoing the vibrations that the weapon had emitted through the ground.

"We just lost contact with the MI-5 and MI-6 computers as you called," Price said. "No news reports… where are you?"

Manning turned on his PDA's video camera and swept the skyline of the city. Four clouds of pulverized stone hung in the air over the ugly craters that belched them up. He narrated for Price's sake. "Only four hits this time."

A spear of lightning flashed and sliced right through the giant Ferris wheel standing next to the Thames. The tall white structure's center vaporized on impact, spokes tumbling out of the air to meet the sudden geyser of water that bloomed from the Thames.

"Five hits," Manning corrected. He tried to keep his voice clinical and emotionless, but he hadn't noticed if the Ferris wheel had been turning. If there had been people in the cars, they would certainly be dead. He also didn't want to think about the people in the buildings hit by the orbital spears. He'd been in the offices of MI-5 and MI-6 and knew that while there were agents working in them, the majority of staff were noninvolved civilians—clerks and janitors. The agents and investigators had at least signed on to risk their lives. The paper shufflers and mop pushers hadn't extended that willingness to die for their country. They were bystanders just trying to earn a paycheck.

That didn't take into account the people in the debris radius around the collapsing buildings. Falling rubble would crush dozens, hundreds of people. The death toll in Moscow had been over 3,500, with ten times that injured. The subway cave-ins had been the most deadly, and London's tube system was far more extensive than in Moscow, and much busier.

Busier would mean more corpses being dug out of the ground.

Manning realized that he hadn't heard Price speak for a few moments as his brain raced through the potential destruction wrought by the assault on London.

"Barb?" Manning asked.

"We're getting more data on this," Price answered, her voice stoic.

"Bad," Manning said.

"Terrible," Price corrected.

McCarter glanced up from Evanston as he lay, his face smashed, on the roof. "What did they do to my bloody city?"

He struggled to pull his PDA out to get in on the call, but Manning handed over his own. Manning could tell that McCarter had been unnerved at the sight of his home being hammered from orbit. Sure, McCarter had grown up during the days when the Irish Republican Army detonated bombs across London, and had joined the SAS just to take the battle to the terrorists, but he'd never seen thick columns standing like grave markers for hundreds, if not thousands, of his fellow Londoners. "What did they do?"

"The emergency services are prepared for this. They saw what had happened earlier to Moscow," Price said. "Subway traffic had been redirected away from major—"

"What did they bloody do?" McCarter growled.

"We're looking at the Ministry of Defense, MI-6, MI-5 and New Scotland Yard all hit," Price confessed. "No estimates of casualties, but it's likely that they have been working under bomb-threat protocols since the Moscow incident."

McCarter looked back to glare at Evanston. Manning could see a brief tic in the corner of the Briton's eye, and he remembered the SAS veteran who had been transferred to Phoenix Force all those years ago. That McCarter had been a man with a short fuse and a large payload of anger. He'd calmed enough to be considered the leader of the team with the retirement of Yakov Katzenelen-bogen, but that temper had only been put on a leash, a stored form of energy reserved for combat. Still, that fiery rage was something just below the surface, and the sight of a thug who had called hundreds of murder victims "race traitors" was just too deep a stab to ignore. He started toward the fallen Jakkhammer leader, but Manning stepped between the two men.

"I can't let you, David," Manning told him. "He's unarmed and injured."

McCarter looked over Manning's shoulder at the neo-Nazi struggling to his hands and feet. "The little prick is going to regret—"

"Do you think he's the kind of person who has re-grets?" Manning asked, putting a strong hand against his friend's chest. "No. But you would."

"Because you're too soft to do what real men would," Evanston chided.

"I'll get what needs to be gotten out of his skull," McCarter growled.

Manning shook his head. "Not manually."

"You pussies going to play good cop, bad cop all day?" Evanston asked, his voice thick as if he had a bad cold. "If so, can you run down to the corner to get me—"

Manning grabbed a fist full of Evanston's collar, hauling him up as if he were a bag of laundry. "Good cop and bad cop? You think that this man isn't willing to skin you alive because you might know who trashed his city?"

"Hand the turd over," McCarter said. "He'll see this isn't an act."

Evanston laughed, sputtering blood all over the two Phoenix Force commandos. "Kiss my arse."

Manning sighed heavily, then wrapped his fingers around the Jakkhammer lieutenant's throat just under his jaw. With a push, Evanston was suddenly hanging two feet off the ground, his legs kicking as all of his weight seemed to press on his windpipe. "You know, if you're that crazy, I'm just going to let David play with you."

Evanston slapped helplessly against the Stony Man warrior's forearm. It was like trying to karate chop a tree branch. Manning's limb didn't even display a flinch from Evanston's mightiest blows, which weren't all that strong thanks to the air cut off from his lungs.

Disgustedly, he dropped Evanston into a gagging, gasping heap, right at McCarter's feet.

"Do what you want, David. I'll have a change of clothes ready for you when you get back to the car," Manning said dejectedly.

McCarter hooked his fingers into Evanston's nostrils and used them as a handle to get the man to his feet, tears pouring down his cheeks as his own weight stretched the skin of his nose painfully. The angry Phoenix Force commander cupped his hand and cuffed the neo-Nazi's ear. White fire burned through Evanston's brain as his eardrum ruptured. The Jakkhammer officer stumbled backward, blood pouring between his fingers as he held it to his ear. He couldn't focus for what felt like an hour, legs wobbly and rubbery.

"Ask a question!" Evanston sputtered through his torn lips.

McCarter yanked Evanston close, snarling in his good ear. "Just making sure you remember that you're half-deaf because I'm laying the blame square on you, and unless you tell me who threw you and your mutts the bones to start the Piccadilly Circus riot, half-deaf is going to be the least of your problems."

Evanston's bravado disappeared as he was nose to nose with McCarter. Looking into the British commando's eyes, Evanston came to the conclusion that any form of defiance would make him wish McCarter had murdered him in cold blood.

Hours later, handcuffed and in the custody of the London Metropolitan Police, Evanston realized the seeds he had sown throughout his life. The fury of David McCarter was echoed in the grim faces of the lawmen in the station, men who had lost coworkers and friends at New Scotland Yard. Anger seethed below the surface, and the agents who had picked up Evanston had the additional frustration of having Phoenix Force attack the headquarters and escape without a trace, all under their noses.

But the anger that stuck with Evanston the longest was McCarter's. The eyes were the windows to the soul, and the glass Evanston had peered through showed the depths of hell.

Tokyo, Japan

CALVIN JAMES WOULD HAVE been alone in the Japanese city if it hadn't been for the presence of his friend and martial-arts master John Trent. Trent was born to an American diplomat and his Japanese-born wife. As the son of a Southeast Asian diplomat, Trent had learned Japanese and Chinese to levels of fluency that would have made Trent an invaluable resource to James, who had learned much of his Japanese and Cantonese from his friend. However, what made Trent truly a treasure to Phoenix Force was the legacy he'd inherited from his mother's family. Trent's Japanese ancestors were part of a lineage of ninjas, the legendary spies and scouts of the shogunate.

James met Trent at the door of his hotel room, carrying a black duffel bag. Trent was six feet tall, with black hair and skin a rich tan. He was dressed in a cheap black shirt, and James could recognize the black clip-on tie the martial artist wore. The clip-on was a part of Trent's martial-arts preparedness. A conventional tie with a Windsor knot would have given an opponent a handle with which to strangle or break the ninja's neck. If an enemy grabbed the clip-on, he'd only have a handful of cloth, and be thrown off balance.

Trent entered and then put the duffel bag on the bed in James's hotel room, unzipping the top. "It's been too long, Calvin."

"It took a while to convince Barb that you wouldn't compromise our missions," James explained. "There were a dozen instances when we would have loved to look you up…"

"But now you're by yourself in Tokyo while London and Moscow are under attack," Trent said.

James frowned. "The teams are spread pretty thin."

Trent smirked and held out his hand. "I'm not taking this personally."

James shook with his former teacher. "I am."

Trent guided James to the duffel. "Hal sent me a care package so that we could do something together."

"Ninjas' night on the town," James said with a weak smile. He reached into the bag and pulled out a Heckler & Koch USP 9 mm pistol. He looked under the hammer on the pistol, and saw no control lever on either side of the grip.

"That's mine," Trent said, holding out his hand. "I've been following firearms design since we last teamed up. I asked for an H&K with a law-enforcement-module trigger."

James nodded in approval. "Makes the USP work like a revolver—no need for a control lever, but the hammer is resting on a safety shelf to keep it from firing if it's dropped. Simple and fast, and very easy for someone who doesn't regularly use handguns."

Trent pointed to the other pistol. "Yours is a Variant One trigger system, so you can carry it locked and cocked, just like your Colt Commander."

James smiled and pulled the pistol from the duffel bag. A press check allowed him to see that there was a round in the chamber. He thumbed back the hammer, then flicked the control lever to on-safe. With a fluid motion, the Phoenix Force medic would be able to draw and fire with a crisp four-and-a-half-pound trigger pull, while still delaying the USP from being used against him should someone pry it from his holster by surprise. He saw bundles of spare magazines and two boxes of ammunition. Two Steyr TMP submachine guns and magazines were in a separate compartment on the other side of a nylon and cardboard divider. Like the LEM-triggered H&K, the TMP machine pistols' only off switch was the trigger. It was easy to use for new-comers, especially with the mounted shoulder stock, holographic red dot sight and under-barrel T-grip. The holo-sight would make targeting easier, and the stock and extra grip would help control the weapon's recoil.

"Good choices," James noted. "So what's been going on locally? Any racial incidents?"

"So far, no youth riots, nor incidents of foreigner harassment above the norm," Trent said. He produced a notebook full of scribbles. "I hope you can read my writing... I've kept my ear to the ground, and my pitiful few Yakuza contacts don't have anything for me point-ing toward trouble."

James looked at the notes and scanned them. "You have a strange idea of what nothing means."

"Unusual happenings that don't fit into the situation the Farm provided for me," Trent said. "I didn't have a lot of time to look up and corroborate half of that."

James took out his PDA and turned on its camera, scanning the pages Trent had provided him. The high-megapixel digital imager inside the personal data assistant was of sufficient power to be able to photograph and copy documents down to the smallest print. Reading Trent's handwriting through the images it recorded would be easy. Once he'd completed the sheaf of notebook pages, he transmitted them to Stony Man Farm.

"We can have our people do the confirmation on what you've picked up," James said.

Trent nodded. "That works. Anything pop out specifically for you?"

"This ship that your Yakuza contacts don't have a manifest for," James answered. He looked up. "We both know that the Yakuza gets a good look at everything that comes through Tokyo. If they're in the dark and security has kept them out, then that means…"

"It means we're going to be looking at a boat," Trent replied. He smirked.

"Did you do a preliminary check on the *ship* already?" James asked, emphasizing the proper term for the craft.

"It did take about eight hours for you to get here," Trent said. "And this was in the half that I ran the confirmations on. Security is tight."

"Too tight for you to penetrate?" James pressed.

Trent shrugged. "It looked like it. All I did was dress up in a sailor's coat and go down acting as if I were looking for a new berth."

James sighed. "Ninja magic sure loses its luster when you encounter the real thing."

Trent shrugged. "Running around in black hoods and pajamas with a sword over your shoulder is a way to get noticed. Ninjas were information gatherers, which meant dressing and looking like you belonged where you went. The martial arts, the swordplay, that was because ninjas posed as *bushi*."

"I know. *Bushi* were nonsamurai soldiers. Ninjas also had disguise and training regimens to appear as traders, farmers, traveling entertainers…" James added. "So-called ninja martial arts mastery was just to give them a cover to infiltrate opposing armies to get troop movements as loyal officers or low-echelon infantry. So what about the ship?"

James flipped back to the notebook page and spotted where Trent had marked off different positions for sentries on the quick sketch of the ship. Attention to detail and strong recall was something every ninja honed. Taking notes in the field was a good way to be spotted as a spy, then shot and executed. "Good map. We should be able to arrange an assault plan based on this."

"If it's a lead worth following," Trent countered.

"This sparked your interest enough to map the freighter," James said. "And it was brought in below the Yakuza radar. If it's not related to the current worldwide threat, then it's something just as dangerous."

"That fills me with confidence," Trent answered.

"Come on, we'll do a little more recon," James said. He typed into his PDA's minikeyboard, texting the Farm that he was going to follow up the lead on the ship.

Trent nodded. The ninja felt good to be working with Phoenix Force again.

Los Angeles

THE BIKER NAMED Bones was born William Morgan. An unassuming young man, he had grown tired of being afraid of the blacks and Hispanics who populated his old neighborhood. While serving a stint for nearly killing a black kid with a lead pipe, he'd been approached and wooed by the White Pride Defenders of California. They'd taken him under their wings, but only put the lightning rune tattoos on his neck when he'd spilled blood in jail.

Bones had lived up to the motto "blood in, blood out." The ceremony had given him the confidence he'd wanted, and the teachings of the WPD had provided him with the "courage" to do what had to be done. Graduating back to the streets, he saddled up with the Reich Highwaymen, an offshoot of the WPD, and spent his time doing side projects in stemming what he considered the tide of impure blood poisoning his country's ethics and goodness. Bones lamented that his work hadn't been enough to keep one of the mud-blooded out of the White House, but in his opinion Washington, D.C., had been a lost cause for decades.

His neck was raw where the thong that held one of his best projects had been torn off by the brawny blond man behind the wheel of the RHM's SUV. The baby skull rested in a cup holder between their seats, and cold blue eyes flicked to him every so often.

"You move, I will make you sit still," he'd growled. That was two broken fingers ago.

Bones was supposed to be strong, remade into a powerful warrior by the WPD and the RHM. And yet he'd been manhandled by someone who seemed to care more for the brown sewage flooding the streets of America than a fellow white warrior. And they were going to the Plan B site, thanks to his squealing. Guilt over his betrayal of his brotherhood and the cause churned in his gut. He'd shown weakness, and there were few things that he could have done to make amends.

"You're just one man," Bones spoke up. "And you're fighting true knights of the new order…"

"Shut your suck hole," Lyons snarled. "'True knights'? Knights were warriors, not sniveling cowards who murder people who can't fight back. Or was the owner of this skull six feet tall and two hundred pounds?"

"Nits grow up into lice," Bones countered.

Carl Lyons was so quick that Bones didn't see the punch. When his vision cleared from a blurry haze and the ache inside of his skull faded enough for him to form coherent thoughts, Bones saw the cracks in the passenger-side window where his skull had struck. Blood poured down the side of his head and soaked the collar of his T-shirt.

His wrists were handcuffed together, and a gag had been stuffed into his mouth.

"You're going to have to sit still while I visit your fellow 'warriors,'" Lyons told him. "I'll send your regards."

You're dead, race traitor, Bones thought.

As if reading his mind, the brawny, blond ex-cop smiled. "You want them to take me out. I hope they try their hardest. It'll make me feel less guilty about chewing them into stew meat."

The Able Team commander slipped out of the van, stalking off toward the Plan B headquarters.

CHAPTER SEVEN

Stony Man Farm

Encizo was on camera, and so was Hawkins for a moment until he saw Barbara Price, who was still irritated from his prior comment. A bruise on his chin hadn't won any sympathy from her, and it showed in her eyes.

"Still angry, or just teaching T.J. a lesson?" Encizo asked.

"What did you learn?" she asked curtly. Price was in no mood for small talk, especially since Hawkins had called her merely a glorified ticket agent.

Encizo wiped his mouth, then tapped a key on his laptop. "I'm sending you serial numbers we found on grenades and firearms we encountered at a local neo-Nazi HQ."

Price looked at the list of numbers entered into the laptop via USB wire, and when they registered in the system, the initial serial number runs were recognized by the Stony Man mainframe, at least according to the brand and manufacture of the explosives and the rifles. She frowned, disturbed by the fact that the information was so readily available on the firepower, which had "fallen off of a truck in Brazil."

"We know where they came from, but they're out

of the mess that is the Brazilian arms market," Price replied.

"So this trail isn't going to help us much," Encizo replied.

Price shrugged. "It's still more than what we had. Who knows, we might be able to figure something out by the arms dealers who pushed these through to Germany."

"In the meantime, we're on the road to Africa?" Encizo asked.

Price nodded. She said the next sentence with a sneer that didn't even need the conference camera to convey it. "I arranged for your flight."

Hawkins leaned back into view. "I'm sorry, Barb."

Price pointed for him to step out of the camera's sight. "You'll be landing at the same airfield as David and Gary, but Calvin's going to be running late."

"Why?" Encizo asked.

Price shook her head. "He picked up a lead. That's all you need to know."

"No need to worry about OPSEC," Encizo replied, referring to operational security. He was a trained professional, so all he really needed to know was that Calvin James was all right. "I didn't ask for specifics, just if Cal was healthy or hurting."

"He's all right, and he's hanging with your old buddy," Price answered.

Encizo knew that Price wouldn't say anything more than first names over the connection, and even here, she was guarded. It didn't matter, Encizo knew she referred to John Trent, a man who had fought beside Phoenix Force on several occasions, even being tapped by Mack Bolan himself for a couple of operations when the Stony Man crews needed some extra muscle and language skills in Japan. The Cuban felt better that James had good backup. "Thanks, Barb. David and Gary know?"

"Yes," Price said. She sighed. "David's fit to be tied, though."

"We heard," Encizo answered, indicating that he was aware of the chaos that had struck London. "How bad is it so far?"

"Forty-three hundred confirmed dead so far," Price said. "Another six thousand missing. They don't have enough beds for the injured, so we could lose more lives."

Encizo grimaced. "All we have is to hit Africa and see where their mission control is."

Price nodded. "We've done some calculations, and we're certain that the orbital assault platforms are going to be small, so their payloads will be small."

"Two cities with over eight thousand dead is small?" Encizo asked.

"We didn't say effective, but the launchers couldn't be too much larger than a standard multiple impact rocket vehicle," Price said. It was a reference to the warhead setup of the old ICBMs, the InterContinental Ballistic Missiles, which carried a payload of three to five nuclear bombs in one capsule. When the MIRV was launched, it would travel to its destination, then release all of its warheads at once, giving the ICBM a better chance of hitting a city-size object, even if antimissile systems intercepted one or two of the nukes. "In fact, we would be looking at a smaller device, given that we had trouble tracking its launch."

"A smaller rocket booster means a lower profile, but less weapons in the air," Encizo agreed. Price could see Encizo's concern for McCarter troubling his swarthy features. "David's going to get medieval on anyone we encounter."

"He's still got some control left," Price explained. "Otherwise he might have done more than popped an eardrum and broke a bigot's nose."

Encizo nodded, again glad that his brothers in arms were in a good place. McCarter had been a wild card in the early days of Phoenix Force, but the Briton had kept himself to a standard of ethics that had earned him leadership of the team. Encizo shuddered at the thought of a younger McCarter unleashed on someone even peripherally associated with such a bloody attack on London.

No situation that he thought of ended with anything less than a power hose and a wet-dry vacuum for biohazard cleanup. "Sorry we pushed so hard for so little."

Price shook her head. "You got us something. Carmen's been following ODESSA funds, and she's picked up a link to the arms dealer who those serial numbers were traced to. It's tenuous at best…"

"But it's not a confirmation that these are the same bastards behind London or Moscow," Encizo countered.

"Manning held on to a gym bag long enough to take down serial numbers from the London incident. These were from the same lot," Price replied. "London and Moscow aren't going to be the last, and it looks like

Los Angeles and Washington, D.C., are both going to be drawing some heat."

"Send Carl and the boys my best wishes," Encizo offered. "They usually don't split up like that."

"Just make sure you make it to Africa safely. Even that pompous hick who thinks I'm just a travel agent," Price said.

Encizo nodded. "Don't worry. I'll make sure T.J. comes home for his ass-kicking."

Price almost felt the laugh she released as the two Phoenix Force commandos signed off.

"Godspeed," she whispered.

Maryland

HERMANN SCHWARZ HELD his earphone tighter as he scurried in a crouch behind Rosario Blancanales. The two Able Team commandos were infiltrating a suspected Fist of Heaven compound and had just gotten over a privacy wall topped with broken glass mixed in with mortar. Such measures would have taken a conventional intruder by surprise and left him bleeding and at risk of infection. However, the two Able Team veterans had invaded countless compounds and secure fortifications. A quick perusal of the scene had given them the foresight to lay a thick Kevlar and Nomex blanket over the top of the wall, making it easy for them to penetrate the perimeter. They'd folded and stashed the blanket away, knowing that they hadn't left any evidence behind on the material, which had been opened from a sterile packet.

"Anything?" Blancanales asked, his voice low and hurried.

Schwarz shook his head. He was listening in on the communications of the compound, and the two Stony Man warriors decided to move once the order was given to completely lock the place down. They had moved quickly, and had only barely avoided being caught in the glare of flashlights as they darted into the bushes, disappearing into the shadows past the searching cones of light.

"Hold it," Schwarz urged.

Blancanales held up, remaining silent as the electronics genius looked at the screen of his combat PDA. A flicker in his peripheral vision caught Blancanales's attention, and he noticed that the lights were dimming through the windows of the manse. It had even surprised sentries who were standing outside of the building.

Schwarz's face turned into a frowning mask, illuminated by the soft red tint of the screen. As the teams often operated in stealth, the Able Team inventor had put a red filter on the LED screen. Since the red wavelength of light was relatively low frequency, the soft glow of the LED would be harder to see at a distance. It was a carryover from the lens caps on military flashlights used during the Vietnam War, and just one of a dozen little tried-and-true ideas that had been unified and updated to maximize the pocket-size personal computer for operational use.

"Power surge in the basement, as well as an initial signal test," Schwarz said.

Blancanales frowned. "That's a lot of juice just to send out text messages."

"Not if they want to ensure their communications can punch through a radio field jammer," Schwarz replied. "The best-equipped bomb squads bring one to make certain that the explosives aren't triggered by a cell phone."

Blancanales nodded. "They'd be foolish not to have a contingency for such countermeasures."

Schwarz checked a few boxes on his PDA's touch-screen display. The stylus had brought up two different maps, one for the local power grid, and one that had mapped out local wireless internet signals. His forehead wrinkled with concern.

"The power grid picked up a glitch, but not as large as it would seem for the brownout we observed," Schwarz said. "That means they have their own generators."

"So what's with the quizzical look?" Blancanales asked.

"There's a cell tower on the premises, and it's putting off a lot of noise," Schwarz answered. "The transmission is so strong, I can't get a good fix on it."

Blancanales pulled a small night-vision monocular from his assault vest and swept the grounds. They were far enough from the fortified central house that they could see a good portion of the compound, and his gaze came to a halt on a small building with a thick cylinder jutting through its roof. He picked up signs of newly buried utility pipes on the ground, and there was a significant guard force around the structure. He pointed it out to Schwarz with a hand gesture, and the electronics genius nodded in confirmation of Blancanales's observations.

"We don't have much time," Schwarz said. "I fired

off a message to the Farm to coordinate the D.C. Police and the Secret Service in protecting Washington."

Blancanales swung aside a tube mounted on his SIG 551 carbine's forearm. What looked like a large-mouthed pistol, complete with its own grip, was a Heckler & Koch M-320 grenade launcher. Chambered for the standard 40x46 mm low-pressure grenades, it had a maximum effective range of 400 meters, and was designed specifically to fit the shorter length of compact assault rifles like the SIG-Sauer carbine that Blancanales used. He slipped an M-406 high-explosive shell into the breech, then flipped up the sights along the side of the stubby cannon's barrel. The steel-wrapped grenade had two purposes: anti-personnel and light-armored or emplaced targets. Against people, it would lash out a sheet of fragmented, notched steel over a five-meter radius. Against the barrel-like tower, it could possibly do the trick with a direct hit.

"Gadgets, watch to see if the signal is interrupted, but be ready to fight," Blancanales whispered. "Once I fire, we're going to attract a lot of attention."

Schwarz nodded. With the combat PDA in his left hand, and the pistol grip of his own 551 in his other, he indicated that he was ready. He looked at Blancanales. "That's why they needed so much power...the Farm says that they've got D.C. EMS communications scrambled."

Blancanales grimaced. Washington, D.C., had been put in the dark by the transmitter he was aiming at, leaving the city wide open to coordinated flash mobs of angry white supremacist marauders. He triggered the H&K launcher, and felt the stock of his SIG bang against his shoulder under recoil. The M-406 spun out of the barrel, centrifugal force arming its impact fuse after fifteen meters of spiraling travel. It would sail another 120 meters before it came down on the roof of the comm building. As the fuse reacted to its sudden deceleration due to its contact with a solid surface, its high-explosive payload was sparked. A wave of overpressure pushed along scythes of razor-sharp steel fragments. What the shrapnel didn't chew up on the aluminum transmitter antenna, the shock wave hammered into a twisted pulp of useless metal.

The security guards surrounding the building had been shielded from harm by the roof, and they dropped into ready positions, searching for the source of the weapon that had cut loose on them.

"Gadgets?" Blancanales asked.

"One more round," Schwarz answered. "Still have the wireless network active, but the scrambler's down."

Blancanales popped open the side of his M-320, the shell ejecting under its own power. He fed another shell in as Schwarz cut loose with his SIG 551, its suppressed barrel cutting down on the flaming cloud of gasses released from a rifle discharge, making them harder to see in the dark. The Fist of Heaven sentries knew they were under attack, but didn't know from which direction. Schwarz intended to keep that advantage for as long as possible as he hammered short bursts into the gunmen around the shack.

The second 40 mm grenade was off with a throaty *bloop,* and Blancanales transitioned his hold on the compact 551 carbine to fire it conventionally, laying down suppressive fire while Schwarz reloaded and checked his PDA monitor. The grenade hit and the comm building shook again, its windows blowing out under the high-pressure concussion.

"WiFi's down," Schwarz announced.

"Explosives two, technology zero," Blancanales replied, noting the score.

"I'm more worried about regular old-fashioned bullets right now," Schwarz answered. "They saw the flash of your grenade launcher."

"Split and close in," Blancanales ordered. "We'll surround 'em."

Schwarz nodded. As always, Able Team may have been outnumbered, but they would fight with a ferocity that few could match.

As the enemy gunmen opened fire, however, Schwarz was aware that he and his partner were merely men. A bullet in the right place would end their storied careers as easily as any other man's. Bullets tore into the bushes to the side of the electronics genius. He would have caught all of them had he not sidestepped and changed his position for a new vantage point. Staying still in the middle of a firefight was only good for a few moments, perhaps as long as a minute if you had sufficient cover and good shooters on your side batting cleanup. With a small, personal army on one side and two veteran commandos on the other, Schwarz and Blancanales had to rely on mobility and stealth.

Another boom filled the air, this one accompanied by a brief buzz, as if a thousand angry hornets had taken flight. Schwarz knew that sound all too well from several jungle battles against insurgents—it was the unmistakable signature of a fléchette grenade. A salvo of forty-five needle-sharp darts had been fired, obviously from Blancanales's underbarrel launcher, and the miniature javelins sliced through the night and impacted on a trio of riflemen who were moving on Schwarz's position. The three men were perforated, any fléchettes not striking bone slicing clean through even the toughest organ meat before carving on to the next body in its path. The effect was devastating, their bodies tumbling in a tangled mass of mutilated mayhem.

Blancanales had drawn the defenders' attention back toward himself, but the wily old wolf of Able Team would have instinctively maneuvered immediately after firing, or would have cut loose from behind a solid barrier like a tree trunk. That didn't mean Schwarz was going to let his friend be shot at without response. He shouldered the SIG 551 and triggered it on full-auto, quick taps of his finger releasing precision bursts that ripped three and four rounds of 5.56 mm NATO lead into a single target. In the night, he couldn't quite be certain of the effectiveness of his carbine, except for one man whose head peeled open like a watermelon struck by a sledgehammer. The explosion of gore incited panic in the decapitated man's partners as he still continued to walk, spastic signals from his spine sending messages to his legs before he toppled messily to the ground.

Two sentries dragged another man back toward the manse as a third knelt beside an unmoving body. Schwarz was about to hammer him with another burst when the guard who stood the line jerked violently under assault from the side. Blancanales was approaching at a right angle to Schwarz, the two men forming a perfect cross fire, able to lay down lead in wide arcs without fear of striking the other man. One of the two guards dragging their wounded ally buckled, then collapsed as Blancanales's rounds stitched him from hip to armpit. The second "rescuer" dropped his wounded charge and accelerated toward the main house, firing his weapon one-handed.

Schwarz slammed the fleeing Fist of Heaven warrior between the shoulder blades, dropping him like a rock. He paused for a moment, ejecting the spent magazine and feeding another one into the rifle's hungry well. Things had gone quiet, but the Able Team veteran had seen too many battles flare up after he'd assumed they were finished to let down his guard. He tapped his LASH headset to bring up Blancanales on the radio. "Hostiles?"

"Quiet as far as I can see," Blancanales replied. "Not going to confirm it's clear, though."

"I'll cover you," Schwarz said. "Get to the house."

Rosario Blancanales broke into a run, keeping his eyes open for signs of the enemy, confident in his friend's marksmanship. Only a few steps after he started, he spotted the ground to one side erupt in divots of dirt and grass, a figure rising, then falling amid the churning autofire. Schwarz was on target, nailing a gunman who had reacted to Blancanales's movement. The wily Puerto Rican warrior continued his race across the open field between himself and the manse, knowing that his life relied upon his speed as much as Schwarz's accuracy with an assault rifle. Finally, after a race that seemed to last forever, he skidded to a halt beside a doorway.

Blancanales was thankful that he was in great physical condition; otherwise he would have been too winded, gasping for breath, to be in any condition to fight after such a sprint. He opened his H&K M-320 launcher and ejected his spent casing, fishing for a door-breeching 40 mm round. The "door knocker" was akin to his buckshot and fléchette rounds in that they were self-contained shotguns, high-pressure charges that launched a variety of missiles, except with six times the energy of a conventional .12-gauge pump gun. The breecher was a two-part frangible slug that could serve multiple purposes, either smashing a fist-size hole through the heaviest of doors, tearing through a human being as if he were composed of tissue paper, or smashing the engine block of an automobile like a cheap teacup. Once he was loaded for bear, he pumped his fist in the air, then looked out for Schwarz as the younger man charged in a hundred-yard dash to meet up with Blancanales.

The elder Able Team veteran's eye spotted movement in the shadows, and he lowered the SIG 551, milking the trigger the moment his front sight was locked on the patch of darkness that had alerted his combat instincts. A flurry of 5.56 mm NATO rounds sliced across the three-hundred-foot gap to the enemy. As they struck, the gunman twisted in pain, his death throes tightening his fingers to fire a burst of autofire into the night sky. The muzzle-flash of the Fist of Heaven gunner's weapon illuminated two other killers stalking in the night.

Blancanales swung on them, his SIG sputtering through its suppressor. He tried to keep up with the enemy's muzzle-flashes, but they were in fire-and-maneuver mode, reaching cover and laying down suppressive fire to aid each other. Schwarz stopped thirty feet out and dropped prone to the ground in a skid. For a moment Blancanales was worried that his partner had been hit, but it was simply a case of the Able Team commando making himself a smaller target.

One muzzle-flash stayed still, despite the amount of fire that Blancanales laid into it. That meant heavy cover.

"This is why I'm glad I bring extra ammunition," Blancanales whispered as he reached for the M-320's trigger. The oversize shotshell belched. It was a straight shot, as opposed to the low-pressure, low-velocity standard 40 mm grenades. The case for the breecher, like the rest of the shotgun-style grenade launcher ammunition, was reinforced enough so the pressures of its launching charge wouldn't overpower the chamber of the H&K blooper. Moving much faster, and developing a spin thanks to its design, the frangible double slug sailed like a regular bullet, Blancanales only allowing an extra foot to account for the missile's weight versus gravity.

The slug broke apart when it struck the tree, but since it was so massive, so did the section of trunk the enemy rifleman had been hiding behind. Aside from a face full of splinters, the Fist of Heaven sentry took a quarter of a 40 mm projectile through his breastbone while a second fragment tore off his arm. That enemy rifle fell silent just as Schwarz's withering fire took down the second guard.

"That the new MOUT slug?" Schwarz asked.

Blancanales nodded as he reloaded his grenade launcher. "Not that new. Step back. This will get messy."

Turning, Blancanales put the second breecher round

to work on what it had been intended for. The oak coating on the manse doors was a facade for a heavy steel core, complete with a powerful lock. The frangible slug struck the bolt that kept the doors closed. It disintegrated on impact, but then, so did the locking mechanism, and the heavy doors bounced open.

Schwarz had kneeled behind a stone planter and aimed at the entrance, knowing that there would be response inside. The crack of the breecher round against the heavy doors had been startling, and Schwarz saw a brief glimpse of surprised faces before he pulled the trigger on his carbine, ripping out 5.56 mm NATO rounds at 800 rounds per minute.

Blancanales tucked himself behind one of the damaged steel-cored doors for cover, listening to wood splinter and steel ring as enemy fire hammered toward him in response. He poked his rifle around the corner and fired to keep heads down before he backed off and slipped an M-406 HDP round into his launcher. "Give me some cover."

Schwarz nodded, knowing that this round needed fifteen meters to arm itself. That meant that Blancanales had to move to a standoff position. He kept on the heat as his partner scurried into the darkness at an angle to the doorway he'd opened. The stone planter he was using for cover had chunks torn out of it by enemy rifles, but nothing had penetrated through one side, let alone the packed dirt and second curved wall of stone. His position wasn't going to last long, however.

"When can we expect that big kaboom?" Schwarz asked over his radio.

"At ease," Blancanales replied just before the familiar

thwoop of the 40 mm launcher. Moments later a big brass egg sailed through the doorway and down the hallway held by the Fist of Heaven soldiers.

Even behind the big concrete planter, Schwarz felt the pressure wave of the explosion. It was light and soft out here, twenty feet away from ground zero, but inside the hallway, the enemy riflemen were done. If a five-foot radius of flying steel slashing through flesh didn't, the force of a dozen atmospheres squeezing on the air-filled cavities in the human head would have been enough to end their fighting days. He peered around the corner and saw one man laid out on an Oriental rug, dark red pools where his eyes had once been.

The fight for the manse wasn't over yet, however. The bark of a heavy handgun roared from inside, and Schwarz winced as a two-inch-wide crater was smashed out of the planter he'd taken cover behind. "Once more, with feeling!"

Blancanales took the cue. He'd already reloaded, and this time he aimed deeper into the main house. The manse shook with the second explosion, and Schwarz recoiled away from a splatter of pulped flesh skipping along the ground in front of him. More body parts landed around Schwarz's position, and he knew that it had to be because the hallway was confined enough to turn it into an improvised shotgun barrel of dismembered limbs and organs.

He sneered, looking at the shredded remains of the man who tried to hold them off on his own.

"Think that's it?" Blancanales asked.

Schwarz shrugged. "We wouldn't let down our guard inside anyway."

Blancanales nodded. "Who first?"

"Age before beauty," Schwarz replied.

Blancanales looked around. "So then you're not going in at all?"

Schwarz stifled a chuckle. He'd needed the laugh in the wake of the grisly conclusion of the firefight, and Blancanales had sensed it.

The two Stony Man warriors entered the main house slowly, ready for any more opposition.

CHAPTER EIGHT

Tokyo Harbor

Hanging in the windy night air wasn't Calvin James's favorite place to be, especially suspended ninety feet above the unforgiving steel deck of a cargo carrier. His legs were wrapped around the dynamic rope that John Trent had anchored to the crane boom that was parked over one of the ship's closed holds. While James would have preferred entering the ship from the water, he had neither the equipment nor the opportunity to exploit that route. There would have been some potential in crawling up a mooring hawser to the bow or stern, but with the regular patrols on both ends, it was unlikely.

Security was tight. So Calvin James was dangling like a spider descending on his web from a crisscrossing steel trestle behind him. His armor-padded climbing gloves and the synthetic nature of the rope kept him from receiving burns as he lowered himself. His carabiners had the dynamic line interwoven between them so that if he lost his grip, they would snarl and keep James from hurtling to the bone-smashing metal hatch beneath him. The elasticity of the dynamic rope would also stretch it between five and ten feet, providing vital deceleration that would spare the Phoenix Force commando from a broken neck.

Alone in the shadows, away from the lights of the bridge and behind every member of the security team who was looking out over the rails, James was an invisible ghost in the darkness. He tried to suppress the grim irony of the term *ninja magic*. Like most feats of prestidigitation, it was all a matter of perception and knowing how to take advantage of it. The men on the cargo ship were certain that any attack would come from without, which meant guarding the anchor windlass and the hawser pipes, as well as keeping an eye on the gangplank. No one looked up.

James and Trent had taken a long and circuitous route to sneak into the giant freight crane that the ship was parked under. Their route had been chosen to keep them out of sight of the enemy gunmen on board. James looked up and saw Trent rappelling down from the other side of the crane boom. Just a little ninja magic to get them onto the ship, and then they had to stay quiet and stealthy. Despite the firepower both carried, and the suppressors mounted on their TMP machine pistols, even a suppressed gunshot wouldn't be certain to end a fight before noise was made.

Trent had a small assortment of martial-arts weapons, as was his style. Between his shoulder blades, tucked out of the way, the ninja had a plain, black, flat sword. It wasn't a traditional *ninja-to,* as it didn't have a square handguard, and it wasn't curved like a *wakazashi* short sword. Rather, it was a modern take on the sword design, something tough and durable but disposable if necessary. Around his waist was coiled, in quick-draw fashion, a meteor hammer. Though the weapon was of Chinese ancestry, the meteor hammer was a six-pound circular ingot of steel attached to twenty feet of tough, static rope. In the hands of an expert, it could be used as an improvised grapnel or shatter skulls across a room. Finally, Trent had a pair of *sai,* two blunt, three-pronged, dagger-shaped truncheons. While they looked as if they would have razor-sharp spikes, they were actually blunt-tipped. Unfortunately for foes of a *sai* master, the blunt points were dangerous, capable of rupturing internal organs or crushing bone with a single punch.

James's silent-assault gear was limited to a combat dagger and a knife concealed in a neck thong. The neck knife was a Hoffman Mini-Harpoon, a device that looked exactly as it sounded: a triangular flag of steel atop a hard-to-bend shaft that could go through a throat or a forehead easily. His other tool was a six-and-a-half-inch bladed Combat Bowie, a thick-spined blade that flowed like a wave to a sleek, lethal tip.

The blades and martial-arts weapons, however, were only items of last resort. There was no confirmation that the men on this ship were up to anything dangerous or illegal, and even if they were criminals, it could have been that they were drug smugglers, hence the firepower and the paranoia. James didn't think so, if only because the Yakuza had been kept in the dark. Even if these were rivals trying to horn in on the clans, there would have been rumors and knowledge of the market opening up.

The Yakuza were deeply entrenched, and they wouldn't overlook such an intrusion on their territory. It was bad enough that different crime families had to deal with their compatriots; an outsider would simply not be tolerated, and anyone with half a brain would steer away from the Yakuza's home market.

The two men alit gently on the hatch they had targeted, and in moments they had dropped down into the shadows of its raised lid. In the dark, the black ropes they had used wouldn't be seen and would provide an egress if things remained quiet and innocent. If not, it wouldn't matter that they had left two lengths of rope behind.

James scanned around to see if their arrival had drawn attention from the guards patrolling the rails. While the Phoenix Force commando searched for attention laterally, Trent poked a small hand mirror over the edge of the hatch and looked at the pilothouse to see if anyone on its balconies or on the bridge had noticed their presence. The lamps set up around the structure didn't spill their light too far out over the deck, and there were no search lights sweeping the area. That hole in their security couldn't be watched over too easily as the spray of floodlights would inform even the most casual observer that something was amiss. It was a small convenience, and it had gotten them this far.

Both men performed the hand signal that indicated their sweeps for detection were clear.

James pulled out his combat PDA and looked at the screen. Kurtzman had uploaded the schematics of this particular container to the microcomputer. From their descent, James was able to get a fairly good idea of where they were on the ship. James withdrew his Combat Bowie, its blade phosphate treated to be as black as night and to absorb not reflect light. He had been tempted to pull out the 9 mm USP, but a miss would ring out like a gong. He had to work smart.

Trent rested one hand on the back of his neck, keeping his elbow in tight, giving him lightning-quick access to his sword. Trent shrugged, indicating he wanted to know which way they were going.

James led the way, the flat of the blade tucked to his forearm as he crouch-walked toward a maintenance hatch. Trent followed so quietly, he could have been James's shadow. They had to pause two times before they got to the hatch and its ladder leading down into the bowels of the ship. A patrol of sentries on deck had passed close enough to force them to hide to avoid contact.

Even these delays helped James and Trent. The guard force was a mix of whites and swarthy men, the whites having sway over the swarthier members of the group. James understood snatches of Spanish passing between them, which was logical, as the freighter had Argentine registry according to the Farm. Argentina was one of the more cosmopolitan nations of the world, with an influx of Europeans to increase ethnic diversity in the country.

It had also been a place where Israeli agents had tracked down more than a few Nazi war criminals on the run from justice. Given the situation that neo-Nazis and other white power groups were involved in the London and Moscow conflagrations, James couldn't avoid thinking about that factor, and had seen too much time in the field to pass it off as coincidence.

This is a soft probe, James thought as he worked the hatch mechanism quietly. Luckily the sounds of the ship, even with its engines powered down, concealed what noise had risen above his efforts to work the wheel lock in silence. Once the lid was open, Trent was first down the ladder. James followed a heartbeat later, pulling the door carefully closed behind him. His shoulder burned from the effort of keeping the lid from clanging against its seal, but finally the hatch was closed, and he turned the lock, securing it again. In the darkness, Trent flicked on the power switch for a red-filtered flashlight and scanned upward.

"You all right?" he whispered, illuminating the ex-SEAL.

James nodded. "Took a little effort, but no one will sneak down that hole to surprise us."

Trent turned off the light. Blackness engulfed the two men again, and they moved slowly and carefully down the rungs of the ladder, both to minimize whatever noise they would have made and to make certain that they didn't slip in the darkness while searching for the next foot- or hand-hold. It seemed to take forever, and James's stressed shoulder began to complain some more as it maintained his weight.

They reached the bottom of the ladder, entering a corridor that appeared to run the length of the ship. Fortunately, no one had secured the bulkheads down here, so it was relatively clear sailing, at least as far as the dim red glow of James's torch indicated. He consulted the deck plans of the ship and noted that this deck allowed access to the cargo holds.

That lights weren't burning this deep was a fairly good sign for the Phoenix Force amphibious warrior and his ninja cohort. It meant that no one was on duty down here, or apparently there was no one. James pulled a night-vision monocular and scoped the hallway, checking for sources of nonvisible illumination that would be picked up by the light-sensitive electronic filters.

Sure enough, there was a "hot spot" down the hall, and he glanced at Trent, handing the monocular over to him. Trent frowned.

"If there were someone live manning that light, they would have seen your filtered flashlight," Trent noted in a soft voice.

James knew his facial expression would be invisible in the dark, but he couldn't help nodding in agreement. "It's definitely a stationary light source."

"When we get closer, we should keep an eye out for motion sensors," Trent added, pulling out his own night-vision monocular.

"That's one possibility, but there's another, too," James said. "Live guards on duty."

"Don't regular NVDs cause headaches if worn too long?" Trent asked.

James fought the urge to shake his head and correct the ninja. "That's an issue because they're worn on a so-called aspirin point on a helmet. The weight and leverage of the device hurts users in either position. Goggles, however, don't put that stress on a head, though the straps do tend to chafe if worn long enough."

"Which would mandate regular shift changes of the guard," Trent replied. "I still think we're more likely to encounter unmanned sensors."

"Prepare for everything, and you won't be taken by surprise," James answered. "C'mon."

Stalking carefully through the absolute blackness,

only the spill of infrared illumination pouring out of an open hatch giving them anything to see by, James and Trent moved in silence. They stopped three yards from the causeway, looking for electric eyes or tripwires.

The glow through the hatch had concealed the presence of four smaller "lights," the glowing sensors of an electric eye. James and Trent looked at each other in the glow through the door, realizing that the backlight that poured through the open hatch would have washed out the smaller, more focused beams of infrared radiation.

After listening for several moments, the two men decided that they were free to speak softly without undoing their stealth.

"A neat little trap," Trent mentioned.

"It won't be comfortable to slip under those trip beams," James said, "but we can do it."

Trent noted the hesitation in James's voice. "You don't want to try it?"

"This is an awful lot of effort to conceal a cargo, yet they left this route wide open," James said.

Trent's frown wasn't visible under the headscarf that concealed his face even in the most direct light, but his tone pointed out that he agreed. "We've been steered in here."

"Trouble is, do they know we're already present? Or are they just expecting us?" James asked.

"Either way, whatever would be in that hold is just a red herring," Trent mused.

"Bait for a trap, and we nearly jumped on it," James said. He scanned their back trail, but there was no indication of stalkers in the shadows creeping up on them.

However, James couldn't trust the lack of their visible presence, as they were backlit by the invisible light from the doorway.

"It's quiet," Trent told James. "No one's breathing, so we haven't been followed."

James sheathed his knife and drew the silenced H&K, aiming at a bulkhead near the ladder they'd descended. "We'll know in a moment."

Trent swallowed audibly, but even that was drowned out by the muffled bark of the suppressed pistol. Almost instantly, ten yards away, the Parabellum slug clanged on metal, ringing out loudly.

Curses sounded in the distance, and James grabbed Trent by the sleeve, pulling him behind the cover of a steel support beam as return fire chattered in the distance, slugs clanging off metal.

"The best way to cripple a trap is to spring it," James mused to Trent, sliding the TMP machine pistol into his hands. Even the enemy's weapons, despite their own suppressors, produced dully glowing flares as they discharged in the absolute darkness of the ship's bowels. James realized that this was going to be a relatively comfortable gunfight thanks to the cans on the guns of all involved, but he was tempted to unscrew the suppressor from his TMP. "Too bad we don't have any flash-bang grenades."

Beneath his ninja hood, Trent smiled and reached into one of the many pockets of his *gi* to pull out a pair of egg-size capsules. "No bang, but I brought some flash."

James clapped Trent's shoulder. "I'll give you some cover while you dazzle their razzle."

Trent chuckled. "Fo' shizzle."

The Phoenix Force pro leaned out, the TMP in one hand and his red-filtered flashlight in the other. As the TMP fired, its muted muzzle-flash would still be a bright glow in an enemy's night-vision goggles. The red flashlight would also be like a bright sun, masking Trent's movement behind him. It was a good tactic, and James felt lucky that he had steel between himself and the Fist of Heaven crewmen, as they concentrated their fire on him.

"Eyes!" Trent rasped, loud enough for only James to hear over the muffled burping of his machine pistol.

James pressed himself back against the bulkhead and clenched his eyes shut. Whatever Trent had been packing must have been powerful, because he could see a brief flare through his eyelids. He opened his eyes and smelled burned sulfur. He flicked on the high-powered LED lamp mounted beneath his TMP's barrel, showing a trio of armed Fist of Heaven sentries rubbing their eyes after being exposed to the candlepower of a twenty-first-century flash-egg update.

Cast in the stark fire of the TMP's illumination module, the blinded enemy gunmen were helpless as James cut loose with a trio of short precision bursts.

"Even with all of this gunfire suppressed, those three will have called in that we're down here," Trent said.

James gestured past the infrared trip beams. "Then let's head to the pilothouse. No harm in breaking the electric eyes now."

Trent nodded in agreement. "I just hope the ninja union doesn't pull my credentials for willingly tripping an alarm."

James chuckled, relieving some nervous tension. "Just tell them it was all my fault."

"You're a lifesaver," Trent responded.

The two men hurried up the corridor, aware that they were about to bring down the wrath of the Fist of Heaven.

Stony Man Farm

THE CALL FROM Calvin James's PDA made Barbara Price stand at her workstation, adjusting the earpiece/ microphone that she wore to keep her hands free.

"Barb, the ship is definitely related to this Fist of Heaven bullshit," James announced. "We've just sprung a trap left for anyone investigating them."

Price frowned as she looked down at her monitor. Tokaido had pulled up a satellite view of the ship that James was on. Men were shown in bright contrast to their surroundings thanks to their body heat on the IR camera peering down from orbit. "Was it specific for you, or just anyone sneaking on that freighter?"

"We haven't stopped to ask the opfor, not that anyone we've encountered is alive to discuss it with," James answered. "We counted about ten on deck."

"There's twice that now that you've stirred up the hornet's nest," Price informed him. "Can't tell who's down in the bulkhead with you."

"We're alone for now," James said. "But we're coming up on the pilothouse. I think we'll encounter some heavy opposition there."

"It's likely, but there's a sizable group entering a

hatch to one of the freighter's holds," Price told him. "Are you anywhere near there?"

"No, but that's the hold they wanted to dupe us into for an ambush," James said.

"Well, their heat signatures disappear once they go through the hatch," Price replied. "And if it was an ambush, then there were more forces in that hold."

"Upper level of the hold, most likely," James mused. "They'd have the high ground, better cover and a good angle to rain lead down. Now they have to come down after us, and they don't want to…"

Static hissed loudly in Price's ear, a burst so loud she had to tear her headset off. Still wincing from the stunning sound, she looked around the War Room. "Do we still have Calvin's signal?"

"Nope," Kurtzman announced. "The Fist must have a radio-frequency jammer on the ship, like the one Gadgets and Pol found in Maryland."

"See how big the radio blackout is," Price ordered. "If it's just on that boat, we only have to worry about Calvin and John."

"And if it isn't, then Tokyo is going to have a very hard night," Kurtzman concluded.

On the main board, a digital map of Tokyo and its transmitters appeared as differently glowing indicators for each type of radio emission—GPS, cell phone tower, radios and wireless internet connections. The whole city shimmered like a galaxy of stars, with one area in particular being a near solid mass of transmissions. The electronics wonderland and mecca called Akihabra was the most brilliant, a giant footprint of multicolored stardust left by some god in the southern part of Tokyo. Price swallowed at the scope of energy pouring off that epicenter of technology.

"That's what Tokyo looks like on a normal day." Kurtzman spoke up. "Throwing up a live feed now…"

Price watched as a spreading cloud of interference swept across the city. It struck and overwhelmed Akihabra, the multifaceted, gemlike footprint filled in by a muddy floodtide of jamming energy. The RF jammer on the Fist of Heaven's ship looked as if it were spreading a vile infection across what had once been a glimmering constellation, stars snuffing out as the signal strength grew.

Price grimaced, knowing that the Fist of Heaven organization was spreading an infection.

Without cell phones and internet, vast channels of communication collapsed. With that failure, a virus spread among the blinded and deafened users.

Kurtzman looked up from his computer. "They're not just jamming. Something took out multiple landline hubs across the city. Conventional telephone is as dead as cellular down there."

Already, the infrared camera on the surveillance satellite picked up flares of fires starting in different neighborhoods.

Fear was the ultimate information virus in the world, and it would spread across any city in minutes. Tokyo's residents had more discipline than most across the globe, but they were only human.

They would crack under the stress of felled lines of communication.

There were only two men who could hope to return a city to normal before riots began, and Price was unable to tell Calvin James and John Trent the stakes they were fighting for.

Helplessly, she watched the initial flickers of unrest spark across one of the largest metropolises on the planet. The Fist of Heaven had struck a knockout blow against the thirteen million citizens of Tokyo.

CHAPTER NINE

Southern California

It was almost sunrise in California. Carl Lyons calculated that Calvin James, his fellow Stony Man pro, would be operating in the middle of the night across the ocean in Japan. According to Barbara Price, there was the possibility that Plan B would be some form of communications blackout. His Able Team partners, Rosario Blancanales and Hermann Schwarz, had prevented a transmission jammer from knocking out communications infrastructure in Washington, D.C. Without radios or cell phones, the emergency services would have been left confused and incapable of dealing with citywide rioting incited by the white supremacist gang members that the Fist of Heaven had hired.

Lyons was fully aware of the type of people that the Fist of Heaven considered usable minions. The Reich Highwaymen and their White Pride Defender sponsors in Lompoc and other California prisons were there for very specific reasons. Most of them involved violence, or profiting from the pain of innocent people. That was why Lyons didn't feel too much guilt over leaving Bones, the biker who wore baby skulls as jewelry, with multiple facial fractures. These men were murderers and drug dealers, savages who fed on suffering. His mentor, fellow Stony Man warrior Mack Bolan, was someone who didn't approve of a little extra enthusiasm in dealing with people, and Lyons agreed, despising police brutality, the abuse of prisoners as a means of reveling in the power of a badge. Since leaving his badge behind, however, Lyons felt the freedom to act against the most heinous criminals he was absolutely certain were guilty. The Able Team commander kept enough control to leave Bones alive, but the renegade biker would remember his encounter with the grim, blond bruiser who'd taken him prisoner.

Lyons crouched and observed the Fist of Heaven's Plan B headquarters. It was situated in an industrial park that, thanks to the wreckage of the California economy, was a ghost town. The building he observed was a squat, five-story box of glass and steel on the far end of the office plaza from the only company that still stuck it out. Lights burned in the windows as cleaning crews did their duty and cubicle workers arrived early to prepare for a particularly long day of business. The only clue that Lyons was looking in the right spot was the sight of a torn tarp that was in the process of being repaired.

The Fist of Heaven took great pains to make their southern California hard site seem unmanned, going so far as to cover the windows of office suites they had appropriated. Lyons swept the building with his night-vision monocular, determining that three floors were under Fist of Heaven control, thanks to the blacked-out windows. He checked the roof and scanned for small outlying buildings that would have served as annexes to the base. He wasn't a technology expert like his partner Hermann Schwarz, but he was savvy enough to know that there wasn't an antenna on the site of the old, abandoned office building. Whatever their alternate plan was, Lyons knew it likely wasn't going to be a blackout. He frowned, then pulled his PDA to contact the Farm.

"Carl?" Price answered the phone.

"What were those bikers doing at the VOR station?" Lyons asked.

Price cleared her throat. "They had attached a laptop computer to the transmitter controls and had configured it to knock out Los Angeles airport."

"Just like they had planned for Washington, D.C., then," Lyons mused.

"How did you guess?" Price asked.

Lyons held up the PDA and used its built-in camera to get a snapshot of the Fist of Heaven fall-back site. "No obvious antenna for radio-frequency jamming on a large scale. On the other hand, a VOR station is just a great big transmitter. Simple deduction."

"You want us to do a sweep of the building for you?" Price asked.

"I'd appreciate it," Lyons said. His MP-357 pistol and its two revolver backups were live and ready for action, so he didn't need to run a check on them. His assault vest had a threaded suppressor for the Smith & Wesson autoloader in case he needed stealth. The silencer was balanced out by two magazines of 147-grain hollow-points sitting atop a .357 SIG charge. There was the possibility of a sonic boom accompanying a suppressed shot, but the can would muffle most of it, and the heavy .357 SIG projectiles would pack a considerable wallop when they struck their target.

Stealth would help Lyons close with the enemy, but he was going in to cause major disruption. That was why he had gotten his AA-12 shotgun from the back of his van. The big weapon resembled an M-16 flat-top on steroids, complete with an oversize box magazine to accommodate eight rounds of 12-gauge buckshot. It was the twenty-first-century update of what Able Team had affectionately called "the Lyons Crowd Killing Device," an Atchisson autoshotgun that had been tuned and modified by long departed Stony Man Farm armorer Andrzej Konzaki. Lyons took a measure of solace that the designers of the AA-12 had incorporated many of Konzaki's design improvements into the high-tech, polymer-shelled shotgun, right down to the ability to fire 12-gauge grenade shells. The original "Konzak" had been retired to a place of honor at the Farm, and now Lyons had his brutal shotgun back.

It was the exact opposite of a stealth weapon. Lyons attached a hip pouch to his battle harness to hold two 20-round drums, all the while musing that this could easily be a trap. He dumped the 7-round magazine and inserted it into a pocket on his load-bearing vest, and worked a third drum into place on the shotgun. The Fist of Heaven had proved that they had the power to attack cities with impunity, and had the lack of concern for human life to unleash those deadly assaults in the form of orbital bombardment or widespread rioting.

The time for beating around the bush with these maniacs is over, Lyons thought.

"Carl," Price said, getting his attention. "We have a satellite in position, but they must have insulation on that building. We can't get either infrared or radar images of who's in there, or where."

Lyons's lip curled. "That's okay. I've done enough high-tech investigation for now. This is where I earn my title of 'brutal caveman.'"

"Just be careful," Price admonished. "Who knows what could be stored in that building. You might puncture a barrel of radioactive waste with a stray shot."

Lyons looked around. For now, after a perimeter sweep of the building, there were no signs of heavy transport trucks parked around it. That didn't mean that they couldn't have made their delivery, then rolled off, job finished. Leaving vehicles around an abandoned building defeated the purpose of keeping the offices appearing empty. "I'll keep that in mind. Any more news from Gadgets and Pol?"

"They're looking for intel in the Maryland compound," Price said. "Bear and the gang are helping Gadgets crack hard drives, but so far, very little in the way of stored communication."

Lyons turned his head at the sound of a distant rumble. He didn't need the light-amplification properties of the monocular as the sky turned orange-yellow with the approach of the sun, and from the line of single headlights, he also didn't need the image magnification of the pocket nightscope. Once more, Lyons turned on his PDA's camera to transmit images.

"Not sure which gang it is from this distance, but the Fist of Heaven called in some extra muscle," Lyons said. "Looking at about twenty sleds."

Price sighed deeply. "Want to pull out and we can call in reinforcements?"

"No," Lyons answered. "It'll take too long, and the Fist of Heaven wants to do something spectacular to honor the President's presence in L.A. Send in a cleanup crew and someone to secure my killing box."

Lyons could hear Price emit a low groan of apprehension at his suggestion. "Give them hell, Ironman."

A smile split Lyons's face, one devoid of mirth, humor or good feelings. It was the peeled-bare rictus of a grim reaper, for death had sent one of his favorite sons to bring justice to those who dared to call themselves the Fist of Heaven. Lyons knew that the thought was nothing more than a boast, but there was one thing he had learned in his years of fighting impossible odds around the planet.

Attitude is everything.

Lyons flicked the safety on the AA-12 and stepped to a steel fire door that would have been secure against a quiet, conventional entry. A 12-gauge volley shredded the fire door's hinges, and one through the doorjamb lock turned the secured barrier into a toppling flap of metal that clanged nearly as loud as the shotgun when it hit the ground. From inside, Lyons could hear curses and shouts of surprise.

They were the gravelly voices of big men, not the yelps of any cleaning crew. Again, they were present in force, and they had no vehicles outside. Even if they had carpooled together, no van, SUV or sedan was in evidence to deliver them. Lyons darted through the doorway and into an area of shadow, AA-12 locked to his shoulder, the sights following his eyes' focus. Two figures rushed into view when a third hauled one of them back around the corner they'd erupted from.

With his vision acclimated to the darkness thanks to a night-long trek to the Fist of Heaven headquarters, Lyons could make out the unmistakable outline of a Kalashnikov rifle in the hands of the man who remained behind. Long hair twirled greasily out from under a do-rag.

Lyons held his fire, waiting to see if the enemy would provide more information or if his eyes could make out more details. He saw a diamond-shaped badge on the man's vest reading 1/100, the Reich Highwaymen's proud boast that they were in the same One Percenter league of outlaw bikers like the Mongols, the Breed and the legendary Hell's Angels.

"There's nothing there," the RHM sentry with the AK shouted.

"Damn it! Get to cover!" the voice around the corner snarled.

"Fuckin' paranoid pussy," the greasy-haired guard grunted. He started toward the fire door, though he kept the AK locked in his big fists, making the rifle seem like a child's toy. Lyons lowered the AA-12 and slipped behind a desk counter. As he crouched, he could see the outlaw through a hole cut in the desk for computer and phone cables. He could also smell the man, making Lyons glad for a particularly strong gag reflex.

"We've got some shot shells by the fire door," the big biker announced. "But just like the boys upstairs, I don't see anyone out here."

Lyons heard the jingle of spurs accompany the quiet footsteps of another man as he came down the carpeted hallway.

"Someone blows the door off our building, then cuts

out? I don't buy it," the newcomer said, stepping warily. "Look around."

"We'd have known if a team rushed inside," the big man countered. "And when people kick down a door with a shotgun, they're usually part of a team."

"We didn't call in reinforcements to deal with figments of imagination," a third voice said on the other side of the desk.

"Get back up front. Nobody's watching out there," the spur-wearing outlaw said.

"The teams on the second and third floors are," the third guy countered.

Spurs stepped closer to him. "What about blind spots, like right beneath their windows?"

"Whoa, tap the brakes there, Baby Huey," the third biker replied.

Lyons had enough to know that he was facing a good-size guard force. He fired the AA-12 through the plaster board, rifle slugs smashing through as if it were tissue paper. Spurs went down immediately as a .72-caliber bulldozer struck his right hip and exploded out the left. With his pelvis shattered, the Reich biker collapsed, the gun flying from his hands. The other two were in motion, but Lyons tracked the giant of the trio, the deer-hunting slug burping from the muzzle of his autoshotgun to strike the big man below his sternum. As Lyons was firing upward on an angle, the fat projectile blew a ventricle out of his heart on the way to snap his spine like a twig before exiting.

Panic seized the remaining sentry. He had gotten out of the foyer as his two comrades were destroyed by Lyons's shotgun. The guard had the presence of mind to trigger a salvo of bullets at the desk area, but he was firing from a quarter of the way down the hall. Rounds chopped through the reception desk at an angle, missing Lyons. The Able Team leader swung out from behind the desk, dropping another .72-caliber hammer on the remaining gunman. The biker's rib cage collapsed under the brutal blow, and he toppled backward lifelessly.

Lyons stepped to the fire door and looked out in the distance. The motorcycles were close now; he had maybe a minute before they swarmed the building. Had he been Gary Manning or Hermann Schwarz, Lyons would have been able to rig some form of improvised booby trap to hold them off. Instead, Lyons only had one course of action. He had to draw them into the building, where their movements would be limited by their numbers. He rushed toward a stairwell to get to the second floor to see how fortified the Reich Highwaymen were.

Stony Man Farm

BARBARA PRICE WATCHED the monitors, a blip representing Lyons fading to dark as the Global Positioning System tracker in his PDA was blocked by the insulation of the Fist of Heaven hideout. "We need a better way to keep an eye on our people."

"Whatever is in the building, it's almost as shielded as one of our secure computer chambers," Kurtzman said.

Price's brow wrinkled as she thought. "Like perhaps lead lining?"

Kurtzman frowned, then turned to his workstation.

He ran a quick check for Los Angeles County thefts of radioactive waste. A ton of it had disappeared two weeks earlier, and police were still on the lookout for it. "You're right."

Price winced. "Why can't I be wrong about the worst-case scenario for once?"

"It might not have been the bikers who took the waste," Kurtzman said.

"So someone else is sitting on fodder for a dirty bomb?" Price asked.

Kurtzman took a deep breath. "Akira, could you run a wind-pattern program to see how bad a cloud of radioactive particulate matter would spread through Los Angeles from there?"

Tokaido nodded over the tinny crash of heavy metal escaping his earbuds. He started typing to pull up weather information on the area when he paused.

"Weather patterns," Tokaido said.

Kurtzman tilted his head. "The launch site in the Congo?"

"If we narrow down favorable launch windows in the region, we can narrow down the part of the river basin we have to search through," Tokaido explained.

"Do it in a minute. We need to know what it's going to look like for L.A. if that building is a dirty bomb," Kurtzman said. "Also, run a check to see the results if it is an artillery firebase."

"I'm on it," Tokaido said, his fingers flying across the keyboard in a blur. "Carmen, could you…?"

"I heard you two. You run those figures for Aaron— I'll check the weather patterns for the past week," Delahunt said.

Wethers looked up from his keyboard. "Don't forget conditions in the jet stream."

"You'll have to get that yourself, Hunt. We can overlay them to see what we're looking at," Delahunt replied.

Wethers nodded. "Fair enough, Carmen."

The black former professor chewed on the stem of his pipe as he searched for data concerning recent jet stream patterns.

Price walked over to Tokaido to look at the screen over his shoulder. All that was there were two windows, one loaded with mathematical equations, the other displaying a map of Los Angeles County. The equations were pure code, woven by a masterful young programmer into what Kurtzman needed. It was like watching a musical genius composing on the fly.

She turned and regarded the screen showing Calvin James's operation in Tokyo harbor, and the communications blackout that smothered the city. Infrared cameras picked up violence in the streets now, but it was nothing compared to the rioting that had occurred in Moscow and had been averted in London. She gnawed on her lower lip, thankful that the disenfranchised youth of Japan had other focuses than racial jingoism. There wasn't a large community for the Fist of Heaven to mobilize and incite into riots.

On the other hand, clashes between French youths and their immigrant Muslim counterparts had started a new conflagration in Paris's suburbs to mirror the eruption of mayhem occurring in Berlin and Bonn. Italy had been relatively quiet, which gave Price some pause. If the Fist of Heaven couldn't stir up violence in Rome, then they were a likely target for orbital bombardment.

Price had also noted increased clashes in South Africa, something that added to her worries. South Africa, along with China, Brazil, India and Mexico, was part of the G8+5, an extended group that had assembled to discuss solutions to global warming. The Fist of Heaven's cryptic warning of the G8's failures might have spread to South Africa, but she couldn't be certain. Contributing factors were that there had always been violence between whites and blacks in South Africa, and coupled with news from overseas about racial tensions flooding the world, that country's infestation of white supremacists might have taken inspiration.

The Fist of Heaven had been quiet, except for their flash mob riot assemblage, ever since the first threat to Russia. It had been a good move on their part. Without a known agenda, the governments of the world could only rely on the vaguest of clues to deal with the opposition.

"Barb, it's done," Tokaido spoke up. She looked down to his monitor and saw that the office building had been placed just right for the Santa Ana winds to flood Los Angeles with radioactive dust.

Price frowned, then gave Tokaido a squeeze on the shoulder. "Thanks, Akira. Take a look for trouble brewing in Italy."

"It's not as if we can get the teams to do anything about it," Tokaido replied.

"No, but we can warn the authorities of the coming storms," Price answered.

The Santa Ana winds were blowing now, meaning that the whirlwind was about to be reaped if Lyons didn't succeed.

Southern California

THE STAIRWELL BETWEEN the second and third floors had become the choke point that Carl Lyons picked to make his stand. Bullets chopped upward from lower landings as Reich Highwaymen tried to get a good angle on the Able Team commander. As soon as they burst into view, however, the AA-12 bellowed out its deadly message. Four bodies were sprawled at the base of the steps, their torsos and faces shredded by the lethal swarms of buckshot unleashed by the autoshotgun. Three more shattered corpses lay on a lower landing.

Lyons had picked this position to hold the line because he knew that the pallet of waste material on the third floor had been their destination. The barrels of radioactive waste were lined with as much plastic explosive as Lyons had ever seen, making it the second biggest bomb he'd ever stood near. The largest had been a cement mixer filled with fertilizer and fuel that Schwarz had cobbled together to destroy the mountaintop headquarters of a Colombian drug lord. Lyons wasn't sure what the effects of the blast would be, but he knew enough basics on dirty bombs to realize that a good part of Los Angeles would be affected by airborne particles.

The radioactive cloud, coupled with the hot Santa Ana winds, would be lethal.

"Hey! You with that cannon! Hold yer fire!" a gravelly voice bellowed.

The Reich Highwaymen had either run out of ammunition or there was some manner of truce being called for. The leader of the group wanted to parley with Lyons, a wise strategy since he'd lost a lot of his brother bikers to the big ex-cop.

"We know you ain't no pig, nor a Fed. What's your beef with us?" the biker called.

"You plan to pop a dirty bomb near my city, that's what," Lyons snarled in response.

"Things have to get a little dirty in order for there to be a proper cleansing," the Highwaymen leader said, stepping slowly into the open, his hands raised to show that he was unarmed.

Lyons sneered at the cleansing comment. "You want cleansing, how about you take a bath, you filthy animal?"

"We're trying to come to an agreement here," the biker pleaded. He started toward the bottom step of the flight that Lyons stood over, when the AA-12 boomed. The Highwayman froze, covering his head, but Lyons had emptied his shot into the wall above the outlaw's head.

"You take another step, it's your last," Lyons warned. "I know you One Percenters like the back of my hand."

"Then you know, brother, that we don't take kindly to insults," the Reich rider said. "Especially from some clean-cut bitch like yourself."

Lyons smirked. "I just fucked this whole building, dimwit. You honestly think that you can deal with me when a force just as large as yours went down in the time it took you morons to park?"

The biker leader was starting to betray his impatience. Lyons knew that this was a distraction, especially when the man's eyes flickered to a spot over his shoulder. The Able Team commander whirled and ripped off a full-auto blast from the AA-12, catching two knife-wielding ambushers at chest level. Four 12-gauge shells pulped the two RHM killers in the blink of an eye, but that meant the autoshotgun was dry.

"He's out!" the leader bellowed, reaching for a massive revolver he'd tucked down the back of his waistband.

Lyons didn't bother to reach for a fresh magazine for the AA-12. Instead he let the weapon drop, its nylon sling allowing it to swing out of the Stony Man warrior's way as the MP-357 practically leaped into his hand. Weapon transition training was one thing that the Able Team leader took seriously, especially since his favored close-quarters longarm was a shotgun. The AA-12 was locked empty, and his fast-draw reaction was instantaneous, the front sight leveled at the Highwaymen leader's face.

The Smith & Wesson barked out its first round, 125 grains of jacketed hollowpoint rocketing across the distance between the two men. The .357 bullet punched through the biker's nose, and his long, filthy hair suddenly puffed out as the high-powered round dragged a four-inch section of skull out the back of his head. Another of the Reich Highwaymen had rushed to his leader's side, but before he could act, he caught a cloud of brains and blood in the face, blinding him.

Lyons would have ignored him for another threat, but the One Percenter still had a gun in his hand and was firing blindly. Two .357 rounds sliced through the blinded biker's upper chest and exited from the small of his back. Along the way, they must have struck a few important organs, because he folded like laundry.

"Holy shit! He's still shooting!" a third neo-Nazi outlaw shrieked as two of his partners pushed him ahead of them. "Wait! Wait! He'll kill me!"

Lyons saw that the frightened biker had thrown aside his weapon rather than tempt certain retribution. Opposed to killing an unarmed man, Lyons fired at the knee of one of the Highwaymen behind him. The .357 SIG cartridge had been developed to emulate the power of the .357 Magnum though it could still be loaded into a 9 mm autoloader. The 125-grain bullet that it fired had proved a fair match to its revolver relative, able to punch through the windshield of a semi truck, or in this case, turning the patella and lower femur of a renegade motorcyclist into a free-floating collection of splinters suspended in pulped muscle.

One RHM gunman was down, howling as he toppled off to the side of the human shield they'd grabbed. The pain of his knee's destruction had helped the biker forget that his weapon was only a foot away from him. Another neo-Nazi grunted and pushed his shield aside, thrusting a MAC-10 machine pistol at Lyons. The Able Team leader stepped to the side and crouched, all the while adjusting his aim to take this second outlaw. Lyons had worked with MACs before, and firing it one-handed was a good way to put lead in the sky, not on target, depending on which cartridge it fired at 1000 rounds per minute.

Before the angry gunman could readjust his aim to bring down Lyons, the biker took two hits to the heart from the MP-357. The dead man stood for a moment, then his machine pistol clattered on the stairs as lifeless fingers no longer had the strength to hold it. He finally toppled on the steps, blood slowly draining out of his two chest wounds.

The former human shield looked at the eight corpses scattered around him, then cast his bulging eyes upward to look at the grim wraith as he reloaded the Smith & Wesson.

"Where's the rest of your crew?" Lyons asked.

"They took off when you smoked Demon," the Reich Highwayman answered, trembling in terror.

Lyons looked down at the leader he'd shot through the head. "That's Demon?"

The frightened biker nodded.

The others must have left the bottom door of the stairwell open, because he could hear the snarl of big sleds powering up before peeling out and away from the Fist of Heaven headquarters.

"Do you know anything about the Fist of Heaven?" Lyons asked, calmly removing his empty shotgun magazine and giving it a new stick of 12-gauge shells.

"Who?" the biker asked.

Lyons nodded, as if answering his own question. "Figures. Blow before I get tired of looking at your ugly mug."

The terrified former biker would have left a smoke trail if he'd disappeared down the stairs any faster.

Lyons was sure that the man would disappear from the neo-Nazi outlaw culture after coming closer to death than he'd ever imagined.

Lyons needed to get outside and back in contact with Stony Man Farm to arrange for a Nuclear Emergency Support team to deal with the improvised dirty bomb. Then it would be time to find out who had put the Highwaymen up to this task.

And finally, after that, it would be time to call down some true thunder, fire-and-brimstone-laden retribution for the Fist of Heaven.

CHAPTER TEN

Tokyo Harbor

Calvin James and John Trent had been about to separate to cover more ground in the bowels of the Fist of Heaven's cargo ship when they did a quick radio check. They wanted to make certain that they could talk to each other despite their separation, to coordinate their efforts against whatever forces the Fist of Heaven could throw against them. James especially was nervous because of how abruptly he'd lost contact with the Farm. Given his position in the belly of the ship, it could have simply been that they'd wandered into sufficient infrastructure to provide a natural form of jamming, especially for a satellite phone. At close range, however, with the hands-free communicators they wore, even the nest of steel beams that formed the ship's skeleton wouldn't be enough to cut the LASH units off.

"Testing," James whispered softly.

"We're right next to each other," Trent said. "Nothing."

James took out his combat PDA and looked at its screen. "It might be all the metal around us, but this thing isn't picking up any outside signals."

"That can't be right. We're still as deep in the ship as we were when you called the Farm," Trent answered.

"Which is why I think we'd better get back to that hold we thought was such a certain trap," James answered. "Because if I'm right, this might be the effects of another weapon in the Fist's arsenal."

"There'll be guards between us and there. Should we do it quietly or guns blazing?" Trent asked.

"If we can't talk to each other, they can't. Loud or stealthy, it's not going to matter much," James mused as he tapped a few buttons on the PDA to bring up its wireless connection wizard. On a whim, he clicked "autoseek" and the pocket computer ran for a few moments before displaying a result.

"Unusable wireless signal."

"What does that mean?" Trent asked.

"Radios are out, and there's some form of wireless internet connection signal, but the PDA is unable to hook to a server because all it is picking up is white noise," James explained. "Radio field jammer. They're not compact, and they need a lot of power. They might be able to fit one into the pilothouse of this freighter, but there's one ideal place to set one up with electricity and everything."

"There was a hum of a generator in the hold we passed," Trent said.

"We got played," James admitted.

Trent snorted through his nose. "I won't tell if you won't."

"Come on," James said. The two men hurried back down the corridor to the hold.

Grand Castle of the Fist of Heaven,
Tennessee

AUGUSTUS HAMMERSMITH LOOKED at the two flags on his personal monitor screen, indicating that their Fist of Heaven projects on both coasts had stopped communicating with him. He frowned, his thumb rubbing the pale, nearly invisible stubble on his chin. Blue eyes flicked toward another contact indicator across the Pacific Ocean, Tokyo Harbor to be exact.

"Anything from Tokyo?" Hammersmith asked to his room full of technicians and communications officers.

"Their blackout has blanketed the city," Darius Dispenza spoke up. "Thanks to tight-beam transmission to one of our preliminary satellites, they're still in touch from the bridge."

Hammersmith nodded in approval. The launch base in the Congo rainforest basin had been put to a lot of work to prepare for their attack on the world's mightiest governments. For several months, they had managed to discreetly place communications satellites in orbit that were capable of snagging broadcasts from powerful transmitters on the ground. Parked in geosynchronous orbit over their target cities, the ULMA would never be out of touch with the Fist of Heaven operators, even when they had deafened and blinded most electronic transmissions. Thanks to the focused power of their tight-beam broadcasts, the radio jamming wouldn't interfere.

Dispenza had described it in layman's terms. It was akin to a solid icicle thrown into a puddle to stick into the muddy ground beneath. Ice was a hardened, crystalline concentrate of water, and thus wouldn't be disrupted by the water, at least not immediately. Similarly, their link to their field operatives came in the form of hardened, concentrated radio energy. Since their transmissions went in quick, short bursts, there would be no signal degradation. A bonus to this method of communication was that the messages would be hard to intercept by listening posts.

"We have at least one bit of good news," Hammersmith noted. "Unfortunately, there aren't enough true believers in Tokyo for us to make the impact we desire."

"You said that we would emulate the first empire, not the failure that proclaimed it was the third such," a raspy voice said from the doorway to the war room. Hammersmith turned in his chair, seeing the speaker, even though the voice was unmistakable.

It was Niklaus Radulf, a tall, raw-boned man who had seen better decades. He was shaved bald, and a black patch covered an eye that had two fused claw marks he had received from a one-armed commando's razor-sharp prosthesis. That had been one of the last of the operations he'd been involved with, realizing those who wanted to revive the Third Reich, or more accurately, the Third Empire, marched down the wrong road to history.

In his younger years, he had been the wolf of ODESSA as the organization rebranded itself. He was there in 1979 when the organization went from trying to protect former members of the Nazi SS to firing the opening shots of revenge and revival of their power base. After a brutal car bombing, ODESSA had become recognized as a dangerous worldwide terror group, though much more low profile than the various Soviet-backed

Red Army factions scattered across Europe. Radulf had seen ODESSA take several crushing blows over the years, both from Israeli intelligence and a mysterious international team of five deadly commandos.

The man who'd torn out one of his eyes had been a Jew; there was no mistaking the profile of a man's nose, nor his accent as he spoke to his four companions, though Radulf and his partners had learned too late that they had not been in a battle with the Mossad. He'd never heard the name Phoenix Force, but already he had seen similar pitfalls plaguing the Fist of Heaven.

"We are, Niklaus," Hammersmith said.

Only one of Radulf's eyebrows had the ability to express his discomfort, half a forehead wrinkling with worry. "Then why trust a Japanese royalist?"

Hammersmith sighed, hating to go over this conversation once more with his partner. It was a sacrifice he was willing to live with to exploit Radulf's connections to mobilize armies of rioters in England, France, Germany and Russia.

"Because Tadashi is the closest thing to a Christian that we can count on in the Orient," Hammersmith explained for the umpteenth time.

The corner of Radulf's mouth flickered with a checked sneer. Hammersmith did not like that Radulf was not a true believer in the United Legion's religious fervor, but again, sacrifices had to be made. Hammersmith knew that there would be a time of reckoning once they had crushed the Marxists who ruled the most powerful nations in the world.

Radulf would either convert or he would stand against the wall.

"Tadashi," Radulf repeated. He spit on the floor. Tadashi Takeo was the founder of Masa Minori, or Just Truth. Masa Minori was a religious organization that took elements of Christianity, Islam, Hinduism and Buddhism to create its own undeniable message. Outwardly, for a good many years, that message was one of world unity, despite religious differences. However, a few years ago, the truth had come out when a group of Tadashi's released poison gas in an office building, killing thirteen people and injuring a hundred others. Tadashi had warned that he would engage in a war of attrition until he was crowned the holy emperor of Japan and the voice of God on Earth.

Needless to say, the Japanese government didn't concede. Tadashi and Masa Minori slipped into the shadows, still with many followers, but also plagued by hunters in the form of angry authorities looking to make Tadashi pay for his thirteen murders.

"I will say, the slope's efforts are effective," Radulf said, noting the screen. "Radios out, and the signs of a dozen fires across Tokyo. Much better than your motorcycle hoodlums."

Hammersmith shrugged. "We have contingencies here."

Radulf bit his lower lip to hold back a comment, but his sole eye rested on two images on Hammersmith's monitor. They were the skylines of Washington, D.C., and Los Angeles, and neither showed any sign of damage. A video capture forwarded from Masa Minori's freighter in Tokyo Harbor showed the glows of Tadashi's attacks, and of course, the European cities bore their scars from space attack and from urban riots.

Hammersmith grimaced. Radulf hadn't needed to say a word. His gaze was accusation enough.

His minions in the U.S. were unsuccessful.

Hammersmith pounded the arm of his chair.

Radulf managed a smile. "It is no wonder you allowed a black man into the White House. Pathetic weaklings."

Hammersmith glared at the second-generation neo-Nazi. "Don't you have a flight to catch, old man? After all, you let a black man escape your men in Africa."

Radulf smiled, clapping Hammersmith on the shoulder. "You found your fight again, young friend. Good job."

Hammersmith thought about it for a moment. Radulf's criticisms of the ULMA high sorcerer had always been the old neo-Nazi's way of strengthening him like steel was tempered—in fire. When Hammersmith's ire rose at Radulf's prodding, his thoughts became clearer, his resolve purer. Hammersmith smiled at his mentor. "Be careful in Africa. We have no idea who is on to us."

Radulf took a deep, cleansing breath. "I do. And you are right. We must be very careful, for we fight an enemy unencumbered by political sanction and possessed of great warrior skill."

Radulf turned and left Hammersmith to his thoughts, waiting for the next burst transmission from Tokyo.

Tokyo Harbor

CALVIN JAMES KNELT BEHIND John Trent as the ninja used a small mirror to see around the corner into the hold. Trent's machine pistol hung on a strap around his neck, but his free hand was wrapped around the hilt of one of his throwing knives in case there was a sign of trouble.

Rather than have the pocket mirror hug the rim of the hatch, where it would catch any light source easily and betray his presence, Trent kept the small rectangle of reflection a foot back into the shadows of the corridor. Slowly, tortuously, he used the mirror to cut the hold into small sections. Among firearms trainers, this was known as "slicing the pie," moving slowly and steadily to see the enemy with a minimum of stimulus to be noticed by said opponent. So far, Trent had counted four gunmen on the access balcony of the hold. It was nothing more than steel grating for a floor, and a pipe providing a rail to stop sailors from accidentally plummeting onto storage containers.

The sentries on duty didn't have any cover, but they did have the advantage of a good firing angle and the ability to all fire at once against anyone entering from above or below. When Trent turned the mirror far enough to see the hatch that emptied onto the balcony, he noticed that there were two more riflemen visible through the hole.

Six up top, and the potential for a few more down among the storage containers, or even within one. Trent had spotted one container with its doors open, the glimmer of a lamp spilling out onto the floor of the hold. It might have been another trap, or it could simply be a fortress for the ship's defenders to pick off the intruders. Trent slowly withdrew his mirror and pulled out a small notepad to scribble down a quick tactical map for

James, which he read by the low glow of his filtered flashlight. Trent also drew a stick profile of the rifles that the Fist of Heaven guards carried.

James frowned, then nodded, killing his flashlight before someone caught sight of its feeble halo of light. His instincts were on high alert, especially after passing one particular hold that sounded as if it were offloading cargo. He didn't want to think what the cargo was, and he especially didn't savor the idea that the Fist of Heaven operatives were using the giant crane that he and Trent had descended from unseen.

"What is the plan?" Trent asked softly.

"We're going back to the other hold," James said. "They're making enough noise in there that we won't be noticed."

"And if it's locked?" Trent asked.

James patted a pouch on his belt. "I've got a key."

The two men headed back down the corridor, and Trent tried the door. Sure enough, it was locked, but the sound of banging was obvious on the other side. He looked at James, who placed four prepacked sheets of rubber at the corners of the locked bulkhead after taking a careful measurement of the door. James unrolled four spools of slender electrical wire from the sticky sheets, and wound them together around a screw and electrode on a portable detonator.

"They'll hear those, won't they?" Trent asked.

James put his hand to his ear. "Ninja magic. They're expecting noise in there, and those sheets are stuck to the door by coils of low-velocity detonation cord."

"Low velocity...so instead of a sharp crack, they

hear a dull bang," Trent replied. "Which fits into the environment…"

"Ninja magic," James repeated. He pressed the detonator, and four simultaneous thumps resounded, metal being hammered together, blending into the chorus of rattles and clangs filling the air. It became louder in the corridor, and when Trent returned to the hatch, he noticed that the explosive sheets hadn't blown the door off its hinges. What it had done was cut four holes big enough for a man to fit his arm through. From there, throwing the latches that kept the bulkhead locked would be ridiculously easy.

In moments, Trent and James entered the noisy hold, shielded by the shadow of a packing container. From their vantage point in the darkness, they saw a pair of miniature utility forklifts rolling toward the far side. James tugged Trent back behind cover.

"I didn't get a good look at what was on those pallets," Trent said. "What, are those oxygen tanks?"

James's mouth was a tight, bloodless line despite the darkness of his lips. "Those are chemical artillery shells. U.S. designation, specifically."

Trent swallowed. "Damn. What now?"

"We get our asses into gear and keep these bastards from taking those shells somewhere else," James answered. "There's nothing else we can do."

"How?" Trent asked.

"It'd be great if we could hit them from two angles," James said. "But they have a similar setup to the one we just avoided going into."

"Except there are bright lights and hard shadow," Trent countered. "Though it looks like they're close to finishing their work. We might need to get up on deck."

James remembered the nearest ladder, which led topside. "If they're doing any unloading, there will be a considerable guard force present."

"It's how we can have the two fronts," Trent mentioned.

James had worked alongside Trent before, but that had been in concert with the full five-man contingent of Phoenix Force members. Just the two of them would be a difficult situation, especially with their lack of communication equipment. "Too risky, and we'd be spread too thin."

There were curses in Spanish in the distance, and James poked his head around the corner to see that the Fist of Heaven gunners were using a lift that resembled a window washer's platform to raise the shells. Fortunately for the Phoenix Force commando, the weight of the pallets had been underestimated, because one end of the lift was higher than the other. James felt some relief. Skill had kept them away from the ship's crew after the initial skirmish, and now luck had intervened in slowing the chemical weapons' offloading.

"Plan?"

James looked at the snarled platform. "Head down to the other hold. See if anyone's distracted in there."

"And if they are?" Trent asked.

"Signal me with your light, and I'll be right over," James answered.

Trent stalked off and James kept his eye on things at his current position, casting a glance over every few seconds to check for a red light. In the meantime, the

Phoenix Force warrior checked his gear and the supply of prepackaged demolitions that had been designed by his teammate Gary Manning. He rubbed his brow, trying to come up with something that would even the odds without accidentally detonating the two dozen chemical weapons shells on the lift, and whatever was left in the hold. Both Manning and Rafael Encizo had cross trained the rest of Phoenix Force so that they could utilize explosive charges with some creativity to provide themselves an advantage.

You just have to think outside of your normal box, James thought. As soon as the word *box* moved through his mind, he glanced at the container in front of him. Made of metal, it wouldn't take much to turn the relatively thin walls into a sheet of shrapnel. He would need something stronger than the low-velocity panels that he'd used to cut through the hold's bulkhead, but the prepackaged charges had that. He also noticed that there were eight assembled eight balls—an eighth of a stick of military-grade plastic explosives with a blasting cap. They had been dreamed up by soldiers in Iraq and Afghanistan as a poor man's stun grenade. A smile formed on James's lips.

The container wouldn't need to make shrapnel. Just noise. And James wouldn't need explosives for that.

Trent's red-filtered flashlight blinked to life, and James moved over to share his plan.

FLAVIO GENOVEVA had been doubtful of his orders to bring part their stockpile of nerve gas to the Japanese Masa Minori, especially because of their previous actions with such a weapon. An attack on a single office building through its ventilation system should have been more successful. The cultists were incompetent fools, though he had to admit that their leader, Tadashi, had had a decade in which to learn from his mistakes. Genoveva had met the cult's master as he and his men had come to Argentina to train properly in how to deploy them with maximum efficiency.

Now, here on the freighter, Genoveva's doubts had disappeared. He was finally loosed to unleash the full power of the Argentine Justice Coalition against the enemies of the master race everywhere. It wasn't on home turf, but Genoveva knew that there would be time enough to return once the Fist of Heaven operation weakened those who diluted the blood of the true people of God everywhere.

So currently his impatience grew as the last load of shells choked up the lift platform. All this while his men hunted throughout the ship for the two invaders who had slipped past their security. Genoveva bit back his curse. There were simply not enough men to secure their radio-frequency jammer, transfer the cargo to Masa Minori and hunt for the intruders.

By all rights, his warrior elite should have had the two spies sewn up in the infrastructure of the pilothouse, or in the decks below, but they had been looking for several minutes without success. It was doubly hard to track them down since radio communication was impossible with their jammer active, so coordination would be difficult. Gaps in their sweeps might let them loose, one of the reasons why Genoveva had a half dozen of his best men on the catwalk halfway up the hold's walls, in a position to deal with attacks from above, below or on level. There were another ten working at the bottom, and twenty on deck, but they only had sidearms and were distracted by their cargo work.

It was an army, but one that was half-blind and with an arm tied behind its back.

"Radulf, I owe you for this bullshit," the Argentine neo-Nazi commander snarled under his breath.

Automatic submachine gun fire suddenly erupted from the bottom of the hold, and Genoveva whirled, bringing up his FMK3 machine pistol. The cacophony of bullets striking metal was a blood-chilling jolt, jarring the Argentine crew from their current task. The gunners on the catwalk responded in unison, pouring lead toward the hold's bottom hatch.

"Get down there! Move!" Genoveva bellowed to be heard over the racket that threatened to hammer the eardrums out of his head.

One of the balcony crew turned toward the hatch between this hold and the other, calling for reinforcements. That brought eight more men to the catwalk to back up the force already present.

Genoveva's lip curled up into a sneer. "What are you doing? Get back and guard the jammer!"

A brain-squeezing thunderbolt of an explosion sent a spike of agony through Genoveva's head, and every other working set of ears in the hold. One of his men who had been descending a ladder lost his grip and plummeted twenty feet to fold his spine over the side of a shipping container. He died instantly, but the rest were not so lucky. Genoveva pulled his hand from his cheek, finding it sticky and red.

He screamed out his order to return to the jammer,

but the supernova of concentrated sound that reverberated through the echo-chamber-like acoustics of the hold had wrecked everyone's hearing. Genoveva wasn't even certain that he was doing more than breathing hard and frothing over his lips as he mouthed words. His hand dropped to his radio, but he remembered that the jammer was still active.

Now most of my army is wholly deaf, he thought disgustedly.

At least the remaining guards on the catwalk had split into two groups, one dropping to the floor to deal with the intruders, the other half in sniper positions to act as a support team.

Vibrations rocked through Genoveva's feet, and he paused in his stride to join his AJC elite soldiers. It was another spike of…what? Noise? Genoveva waved frantically at two of the men on the catwalk. He needed them to get back to the radio jammer before it was knocked out.

The contents of his burst ears pouring down his neck, Genoveva remained ignorant as the radio clipped to his belt hissed with static, followed by a desperate request.

"Commander Genoveva! Please respond! What happened to the jammer?"

CHAPTER ELEVEN

Stony Man Farm

Barbara Price jolted in her seat as an incoming signal interrupted the silence that had previously engulfed Tokyo. While Able Team's two contingents had reported in from their actions, Calvin James was out of contact and surrounded by enemies on an Argentine cargo ship. The same cargo ship had been the source of a powerful jamming signal that smothered wireless, cellular and radio signals across the city.

Subsequent backup attacks had destroyed a dozen key nodes where hardwire communications such as telephone and DSL could reach the world beyond.

"Do you read me?" James asked at the end of a hiss of static.

Price wiped her mouth, trying to erase the smile that crossed her face. "Cal!"

"Tokyo should be back online now," James said. "We took out this giant transmitter."

"They're still only working on a few frequencies," Price returned. "Saboteurs cut several trunk lines throughout the city."

"Damn. Listen—the cargo ship brought in more than a transmitter. We've got chemical weapons being off-loaded," James said.

Price sighed. "Can you confirm?"

James's PDA transmitted photographs of the shells. Thanks to the excellent digital camera Schwarz had designed for the combat microcomputer, Price could make out the artillery shells on her monitor. They were definitely chemical-payload rounds.

"Any sign of field guns to use them?" Price asked.

James sighed. "If there are, they must still be in shipping containers. But since when does artillery need to be fired anymore? If there's one thing we've learned from Iraq…"

"IEDs," Price muttered.

"Improvised Explosive Devices. Some C-4, a cell phone and one of these shells, you've got the means to disperse nerve gas even if you left your howitzer at home," James answered.

"What's the situation on board?" Price asked.

"A good chunk of the enemy are deaf, but not all of them," James said. "I've put some force multiplication into play, though. Gotta go—things to do, people to kill."

"Good luck," Price got in before James signed off. She turned to Kurtzman. "Aaron?"

"Already trying to get Tokyo emergency services into action to deal with violence that flared up during the communications blackout," Kurtzman answered. "So far, it looks just like the explosions were the nodes going down."

Price pulled up a map of Tokyo. "Aaron, give me an overlay of where the sabotage occurred."

With a few keystrokes, Kurtzman transmitted the new map that superimposed itself over Price's image of Tokyo. The Stony Man cyberchief swallowed hard as he looked at the results.

"How to transport dozens of improvised explosives throughout a major metropolis without being seen, lesson one," Price said. "Look like you belong."

"Utilities repair crews will be scrambling all over the place," Kurtzman agreed. "Their trucks are large and they travel in packs. With the right uniforms and decals, the Fist of Heaven can put their vehicles everywhere in the city."

Price brought up her communication link to James in the field. "Aaron, look for Tokyo utility trucks near the dock where James is. We might not have enough time…"

James wasn't answering his PDA.

Price fired through a priority text message to him, knowing that James and John Trent were fighting for their lives, and likely wouldn't survive to read it.

Tokyo Harbor

CALVIN JAMES DUCKED BACK a moment before a spray of rifle fire sparked off the steel beam he was behind. To his right, John Trent fired his TMP machine pistol in response, the ninja's spray of autofire running long, but finally connecting with a target.

That flurry of shooting was bait enough for the Fist of Heaven's Argentine troopers to rush right in front of one of James's radio-controlled booby traps. As they were there, James pressed the firing stud on his detonator, and a cone of fire and force vomited off the wall. Three men were crushed under the hammering blast wave, while two more were knocked to the ground, writhing in pain. The cloud of the plastic explosives' combustion hung in the air, obscuring the corridor farther down, but the bomb had served good purpose, taking out a number of enemies and stopping the advance of the rest.

James's PDA vibrated in its pocket, and the Phoenix Force medic sighed.

"I love you, Barb, baby, but I'm going to have to keep you on hold," James whispered to himself. He motioned to Trent to retreat a little further, to the safe spot marked past the next ambush mine. The Chicago badass then spent half of his TMP's magazine, emptying it through the obfuscating smoke. Through his electronic earplugs, James picked up screams of pain as 9 mm rounds sliced through flesh. He hadn't counted on hitting any of his targets, so that was a bonus to his plan.

He retreated, staying ahead of the chatter of enemy weapons snarling in retaliation. The PDA pulsed again, indicating that he had received an urgent text message from Stony Man Farm. James tucked into a safe spot to watch the hallway, his brain working to anticipate what the message was about, but he couldn't come up with any alternative other than Price had found out how the chemical weapons were being transported or dispersed. One more dreadful thought came to mind, that Price, through satellite cameras over Tokyo, had seen the deadly artillery shells disembarking from the docks, headed for their targets.

There would be time enough for that later. The electronic buds hooked into his ears served two purposes, both specifically designed into them by Hermann Schwarz. The first was as an electronic noise filter, topping out high-intensity sonic impulses at a sedate and relatively painless eighty-five decibels. The second was a sound amplifier, like the squeak of hatch hinges in the ladder tube above he and Trent.

James pointed upward, and Trent nodded. The ninja wore the advanced hearing protectors under his hood, so he could cut loose with the 9 mm Steyr with impunity, even in the confined spaces of the ship's bowels. Trent held down the trigger, riddling two men on the ladder with a salvo of slugs before stepping back to avoid their plummeting carcasses. James fired another burst at their pursuers to draw them out.

This time, one of them rushed forward by himself, separating from the pack that had stacked in the shadow of a buttress beam that would protect them from James's autofire. The Phoenix Force veteran made a show of reloading his partially empty submachine gun to provide an excuse for letting the scout "slip past" without harm. The Argentine neo-Nazi fired a blast from his AK-47 to keep James's and Trent's heads down as he advanced even farther. That allowed him to hopscotch forward as his allies advanced to the position he'd determined was safe.

James knew the drill, as it was the strategy of trained soldiers to be more conservative in advancing in the wake of an explosive ambush. Once the scout's AK stopped chattering, James thumbed the detonator once more. Acoustic electronics smothered the thunder of the second blast down to a more manageable level, and the filters allowed him to hear screams of agony erupt in concert with the explosion.

The Argentine scout paused and looked back toward

the source of the explosion, leaving him unprepared for James and Trent firing at him in unison. The Fist of Heaven neo-Nazi collapsed in a bloody heap, joining his dismembered comrades in eternal darkness. The TMPs having crossed their streams of Parabellum devastation on one target, their users spread the fire out, sweeping the corridor with savage brutality. It was a ruthless tactic to fire upon opponents who had been stunned by deafening sound and shock waves, but the Phoenix fighter and his ninja companion were heavily outnumbered and working on an encroaching deadline.

James pointed to Trent and motioned for him to go up the ladder. He was going to take a parallel access ladder to get up on deck. Trent nodded and slid up five rungs. The ninja slowed only to hook up a fishing line linked to a detonator's pin. In the darkness, the enemy wouldn't see it, even if they shone a light on it. Anyone climbing would yank the pin on a hand grenade's fuse. Once the enemy recovered and advanced far enough, James had calculated that Trent and he would be well past the deadly blast radius of their booby traps.

He reached the other ladder in a fast run, then scurried up to hook his own mine in place. Now it was time for a climb, up fifty feet of ladder in a close, dark tunnel. He knew that the grenade tripwire wouldn't protect him if the Fist of Heaven riflemen decided to trigger their AKs upward. His only hope of avoiding being gunned off the ladder was their hesitancy to rush after him and Trent. That still left the deck and the neo-Nazi boat crew who had been put on high alert by the battle below them.

Undoubtedly, they knew where at least one hatch

was, and would be waiting for Trent, which was why the ninja had volunteered to use that particular ladder. James hadn't liked the idea, but John Trent had one convincing argument to reinforce his volunteer action.

"My answer is two words. Want me to repeat them again?"

"Ninja yadda yadda yadda," James droned in response.

Trent chuckled, though the Phoenix vet didn't know what his friend and sensei had in mind, but the confidence with which Trent had spoken had ensured his position on that ladder.

James grunted with exertion, his muscles screaming as he climbed as fast as he could. He didn't dare stop, and felt the extended stock of the TMP bump against projections around the ladder. If the weapon snagged on something, James would either have to wrestle it free, taking precious time, or cut the gun's sling, depriving him of a primary weapon. At least he'd still have a handgun, which would give him the opportunity to fight his way to a more powerful firearm. He couldn't imagine Trent climbing faster than he was, especially with his sword and martial-arts gear adding to his combat load.

And even if Trent did reach the top, James worried about what would happen when the Fist of Heaven's defenders saw him.

THE GUARDS AT THE TOP of the hatch, after pulling aside one of their wounded comrades, had closed the lid and surrounded it, keeping their eyes and rifle muzzles trained on the trapdoor. The intruders in the bowels of the ship had claimed four lives with their automatic weapons, two killed instantly by bullets to the head, two bleeding to death after being dragged from the hatch opening. Angry frustration filled them, and itchy fingers rode triggers, waiting for a chance to cut loose with a blast of grim revenge.

A squeal of rusty metal hinges resounded from the trapdoor and one of the gunmen clenched down on his trigger, spraying AK-47 rounds at the heavy metal lid. Another of the sentries screamed, blood gargling up into his throat as a ricochet punched through his sternum and churned one of his lungs into foam. Two more of the guards lunged at their partner, trying to stop his panic fire, but it was too late. Another man was dead, and the tense gunman had spent his rifle's payload.

"Maricon!" one of the Argentine neo-Nazis snarled. "Open it before they get away!"

As one, the remaining uninjured, unoccupied guards fell upon the hatch, tearing it open, muzzles aiming down into the darkness. The men triggered their weapons, streams of AK lead pouring parallel to the ladder. If there was a man anywhere on it, he would be dead, riddled with slugs.

Distant gunfire rattled at the bottom of the boat, return fire sizzling and punching through the forehead of one of the neo-Nazis. His head was cleaved open, a V-shaped furrow gouged through his skull. Rifles chattered angrily down the hole in retribution for another death.

Something exploded below, and two guards at the top looked down. Inky blackness stared back at them, and they turned to their leader.

"Did you see anyone on the ladder?" he asked them.

"No, but you saw them shoot back," one of the two guards said.

"Glkk!" the other blurted as a brass ball swiftly orbited his throat. Five stunned pairs of eyes locked on their comrade as the tether attached to the sphere lost its slack and their ally was yanked backward. His fingers flew to his throat in an effort to loosen the biting cord, but the back of his head cracked wetly against the edge of the opening, his body stiffening for a moment. Five pairs of desperate hands clutched at their friend's legs, trying to keep him from being pulled into the merciless darkness. It was too late, because John Trent's meteor hammer had broken his victim's neck the same time it cracked open his skull.

"Don't let him go!" the leader of the squad bellowed. "Don't let him—"

A small white sphere erupted through the open trapdoor, seemingly homing in on his face. The Justice Coalition officer tried to raise his hand to block the small egg when it burst against his cheek, releasing a cloud of what seemed to be eye-roasting fire.

The truth was, it was a simple *tetsubushi*. One of the fabled pieces of ninja equipment, it was nothing more than a wad of packed pepper, this particular one filled with flash powder. While the powder was harmless, producing only the slightest of burns on skin, the Fist of Heaven enforcer's agony was endless as hot capsicum extract splashed into his eye's mucus membranes, causing instant inflammation. The flash powder's low-temperature burn didn't even penetrate the patina of tears that normally kept the orb lubricated and safe.

Trent's burning cloud spread quickly, in the space of a heartbeat. The other four Argentine gunmen experienced varying degrees of blindness and pain as eyes and nostrils became the resting place for pepper powder. Capsicum was the primary component that induced the painful burn in spicy, peppery foods, but it was also the main ingredient in tear gas. With mucus membranes and sinuses burning and swollen, the Fist of Heaven defenders barely had a chance to see the American ninja climb onto the deck.

One of the gunmen, less affected than the others, swung his rifle up to cut down the walking shadow that had erupted from the darkness. Before he could pull the trigger, Trent's sword whistled through the air and connected with the Argentine's neck. Though this sword hadn't been pounded down and honed to a near monomolecular edge like the greatest swords of the samurai, Trent had forged it to be more than sufficient to slice through bone. He missed the man's neck vertebrae, so he couldn't tell if it would affect a living person the same way it parted a rack of beef ribs. Arterial spray fanned out from the opened throat, and the rifleman dropped back, no longer having the strength to stand or to use a weapon.

Another of the Fist of Heaven crew fired blindly, his vision too blurred to make out more than color and vague shape. Unfortunately for the guard's comrade, in the darkness and through pepper-powder-burned eyes, an Argentine neo-Nazi looked identical to an American ninja. A flurry of 7.62 mm slugs ripped his fellow Justice Coalition trooper from crotch to face, splitting him open as if someone had tugged on a zipper that held in his entrails. The mostly blind rifleman didn't have a chance to learn that he'd killed one of his own men as Trent slashed through his torso with the sword.

Having caught the gunner under one of his arms, then sliced out through his back, Trent had taken out the Argentine's brachial arteries and spine in one swing. The sword dragged for a bit when it carved through sacral vertebrae, but not enough that Trent didn't have the blade drawn back and held in a close retention grip.

The leader of the group gasped for air, having breathed in the choking pepper. His throat threatened to swell shut, but he still fought to gurgle commands in Spanish. The other neo-Nazi turned his rifle around and swung it wildly like a club. Trent brought up his sword to keep the AK's wooden stock from taking his head off, but the enemy's clumsy flailing struck his forearm rather than the spine of his sword. Trent backed up, grimacing as the blade clattered onto the deck, his right hand numb from what he knew was a fractured ulna.

The blinded guard chuckled at the sounds, and from the look on his face, his vision was clearing. "You're dead now!"

Trent saw the enemy's rifle swing down once more, but with his left hand, he drew his *sai*. The forked bludgeon caught the stock of the weapon, preventing the wood from crushing Trent's skull. A swift kick destroyed the neo-Nazi's left knee, and he fell to the deck, giving the American ninja a chance to disengage the *sai* from the AK's stock. The Argentine officer had one hand clamped over his eye, the other plunging to his holster to draw a pistol.

It was a lightning-quick decision, and John Trent ignored the hobbled gunman to deal with the more pressing threat. Weaving like a cobra, Trent felt the heat of a bullet singe the air near his ear. He ducked his head and swung under the squad leader's shifting aim, the gunshot's intense sound pressure mitigated by his electronic hearing protectors. Trent managed to get another step closer, and he drove the *sai*'s blunt steel rod into the neo-Nazi's sternum. Bone splintered under the impact, sharp shards puncturing the Argentine's heart and aorta. Trent pulled back and whirled, driving his heel into the dying man's kidney to throw him to the deck, pistol barking reflexively into empty air.

The last of the guards over the hatch crossed his forearms in front of his face, screaming in horror at the midnight wraith that had torn through superior odds like a reaper's scythe through chaff. Trent took the opportunity to retrieve both his sword and his meteor hammer.

With a wince, he took his other *sai* and wound a length of cord around the weapon as an improvised splint. It was the same cord he'd used to make the hatch's wheel turn while he took cover in an indentation off to the side of the ladder. Tucked into a small space, he'd been out of the crossfire between the two ends of the ladder. Trent didn't know what caused the explosion below, but he made an educated guess that it was more likely a stray bullet striking the grenade, rather than anyone attempting to climb the ladder into the line of fire.

With the *sai* cinched to his forearm, he tested his fingers. They moved, but pain burned in his forearm as he did so. Trent heard the rattle of automatic fire, and transferred the Steyr machine pistol to his left hand.

Calvin James had made contact with other members of the Fist of Heaven crew. The battle for this boat wasn't over. Trent would just have to fight with an injured arm.

JAMES LOWERED HIS STEYR after he reloaded its partially spent magazine. He'd cleared out some of the enemy at the bow of the ship, and he was alone for now. He plucked out his PDA to check the urgent message that had come through.

"Look for Tokyo utility trucks. Trucks = weapons transport."

The Phoenix Force commando grimaced as he realized the Fist of Heaven's strategy. He didn't need a map of the city to understand that the sabotage Price had mentioned would pinpoint perfect locations to release nerve gas. The whole city wouldn't be poisoned by the invisible weapon, but thousands would still die horribly. James had seen the effects of chemical weapons too many times to be under the assumption that nerve gas wasn't one of the most horrific ways to die. He jogged to the rail overlooking the dock and leaned out, looking for signs of vehicles parked there. Unable to see anything with his bare eyes, he fished in his load-bearing vest for his night-vision monocle.

As he brought up the pocket telescope, a dark shape

lurched into view, blocking the lens. James stepped back, reaching for his H&K pistol in its holster. Just in time, he recognized John Trent.

"Damn near stopped my heart," James muttered.

Trent looked back over his shoulder. "Wouldn't be the first tonight."

"How'd it go?" James asked.

"They had the hatch covered, but they weren't ready for a few dirty tricks," Trent answered.

James's gaze settled on the *sai* splinted to his sensei's forearm. "You did take one hit."

"It was a lucky swing," Trent replied. "What was that message from the Farm?"

"We've got to stop any utility trucks from leaving this shipyard," James answered. "That's where they want to put the shells."

Trent frowned. "I saw them trying to get a couple of dollies full of shells down the gangplank on my way over here."

"Then we don't have much time," James said. "You up to stopping a convoy of murder?"

Trent nodded.

James led the way, Trent following on his heels.

If even one truck escaped, Tokyo's worst nightmares would begin.

THE ERUPTION OF GUNFIRE on the deck of the freighter grabbed at Tadashi Takeo like the talons of an eagle sinking into his cheek, whipping his head toward the gangplank. Two of Genoveva's neo-Nazi riflemen tumbled off the railed ramp in bloodied heaps as they were stitched by full-auto salvos. Tadashi whirled and pointed to some of his Masa Minori soldiers on hand for the weapons transfer.

"Hold the line! Don't let anyone else down that plank!" Tadashi snarled.

"But we've only got enough shells for three trucks!" one of his drivers reported.

"Three is better than none!" Tadashi growled, heading toward one of the trucks that already had its deadly payload. "Keep that ship bottled up, by any means necessary!"

The Masa Minori leader scrambled into the cherry-picker bucket mounted on the back of one utility truck. The organization had managed to purchase or steal twenty-four utility trucks from various sources. Many had been retired from service due to rust or battered fenders or had reached the end of their service life and had been on their way to the wrecking yard to be recycled. Their disappearances went unnoticed as most of them were trash, allowing Tadashi's true believers to repaint them and run rudimentary repairs by salvaging parts from junkyards to get them all running.

Tadashi had planned for two trucks per operation, one to actually carry the nerve gas shells, and one to ride escort. The murder cult leader's cherry-picker ride was an escort vehicle, the bucket allowing him a good vantage point to rain down sheets of autofire from the Ultimax 100 light machine gun he had stashed in the bucket. The Singapore-built weapon carried handy, easily reloaded 100-round drums, which would keep him in any fight for a long time. "Mount up, people! We're going now!"

The drivers of the six readied vehicles and their

gunners looked at Tadashi as he stood over them in the podium provided by the cherry picker, then at their allies who were rushing to the bottom of the gangplank. They had been ready to put their lives on the line to turn Japan into a monarchy with Tadashi as the new emperor, the voice of the gods upon the face of the Earth. Now that there was the unmistakable evidence of lethal opposition to their holy crusade, there was a moment of doubt among them.

Tadashi saw their hesitation, then shouldered the Ultimax. He pushed aside the temptation to shoot a few of the slowest of his followers, knowing he needed everyone at his back. Tadashi swung the muzzle toward the top of the gangplank and cut loose with the light machine gun. Gunmen twitched and danced as hypersonic 5.56 mm rounds slashed through their torsos, leaving churning tunnels of ruptured tissue and shattered bone in their wake.

"You are my immortal champions and you outnumber them! Fall upon the enemy like locusts!" Tadashi bellowed.

The engine of his truck snorted as gears ground. Tadashi slammed home a fresh 100-round drum and fanned the deck of the freighter once more as the utility vehicle lurched forward. Out of the corner of his eye, he could see something big and bulky loom over the railing of the deck, something ominous that whipped out of his peripheral vision before he could focus on it. The man who would be the new emperor of Japan felt a cold knot of dread in his stomach, even as dozens of his armed fanatics lurched up the gangplank.

"Drive, damn it. Drive as fast as you can!" Tadashi urged.

CHAPTER TWELVE

John Trent winced as the remnants of the on-deck defenders cornered him and Calvin James on board the ship. Blazing autofire tore through the air, ricocheting bullets screaming too close to his ears for comfort. He looked toward James for direction.

Had James been able to cut through the red tape of customs with the usual package of Stony Man forged identification, the ex-Navy SEAL would have had access to his preferred combat package. The Steyr TMP was a fistful of firepower, but with the odds this tight and with the distant rumble of trucks filling the air, James would have preferred his M-16/M-203 rifle-and-grenade-launcher combination. A charge of 40 mm high explosive would have been more than enough to cut down the odds. As it was, James knew that there were still enemy gunmen in the hold and inner corridors of the ship, and it wouldn't take long for them to burst into the open and surround the Phoenix warrior and his partner.

Something caught James's eye, and he had a surge of hope. One of the small forklifts had been left idling as he and Trent had made their assault. There was also a glimmer of hope in the stacks of chemical weapon artillery shells left at the top of the gangplank, ready to be hauled down to the dock where the Fist of Heaven's utility trucks were waiting.

"Most of the shells still appear to be on deck," James said.

"So the damage might not be that bad," Trent said.

"Several hundred to thousands if even one goes off," James replied. "Good news is, we've got the equivalent of a one-man tank right there."

"Give me some cover—I'm going to get some heavier firepower," Trent said, reaching into a belt pouch.

James nodded, accepting a handful of the ninja's *testsubushi* eggs. Trent gripped the Steyr with his good hand, then motioned for James to begin his assault. The Chicago badass kept in good form with grenade training, the manual kind without a big 40 mm tube, and though the pepper-loaded capsules were lighter, he was able to throw the first one with stunning accuracy. The shell exploded against one Argentine neo-Nazi's face, flash powder flaring brightly and sending men scattering, thinking they had come under grenade attack.

Trent moved with blinding speed, sliding his injured arm through the slings of two of the enemy's assault rifles, the knife in his unhurt hand slashing bandoliers of ammunition off dead men. James continued to hammer the Fist of Heaven sailors with the pepper eggs, in between one-handed sweeps of autofire with his Steyr machine pistol. The American ninja looked over the bodies, but he couldn't see any hand grenades on them. He rushed back to James's side as the Phoenix Force commando kept heads down or burst open with a salvo of 9 mm slugs.

"Went shopping. You like 'em?" Trent asked, handing over one rifle.

James nodded. The Argentines who had the luxury

of working on deck, away from the closed quarters of the corridors below, were equipped with Brazilian IMBEL rifles. He checked one of the spare magazines, and saw that it was in 5.56 mm, but he didn't know the gun's designation. It didn't matter; the rifle was a vast improvement of firepower.

"Know how to drive one of those things?" James asked.

Trent looked at it. "One lever to turn left, one lever to turn right and both forward to advance, right?"

"Good enough," James answered.

"Why?" Trent asked.

"Because you've got an ulnar fracture, so you can't shoot a rifle and hang on to the back of a miniforklift at the same time, and there's no room for two people in one of those little cages," James explained. "So you drive. I ride shotgun."

Trent nodded, and James once again provided cover for him as he jumped into the cramped cab and looked at the controls. They had been designed to be simple to use, and he was surprised to see a small steering wheel on this particular model. He grabbed what he thought was a gearshift. The arms of the miniforklift rose, bringing up a pallet of artillery shells that blocked his field of view.

"Shit!" Trent hissed when he felt the weight of his Phoenix Force ally land on the back of the little workhorse.

"Don't worry about that. The fuses are facing toward us, and they aren't armed," James said. "They have a lot of steel, so no dinky little .22 is going to punch through them."

"You sure?" Trent asked.

"Go! Go! Go!" James bellowed.

Trent threw the forklift into Reverse, backing up enough to turn it toward the defenders when both men saw the Fist of Heaven soldiers assailed by a wave of light machine-gun fire. "Backup?" Trent asked.

"Or some dumb shit who doesn't know who his targets are," James replied. He shoved the IMBEL toward the enemy and added his own heat to the conflagration, supersonic bullets disrupting internal organs and pulping muscle mass with brutal efficiency.

Trent accelerated toward the gangplank as James acted as an ersatz machine gunner atop the vehicle. The forklift wouldn't win any records on a race track, but its motor had plenty of pep, revving up to twenty miles per hour. The steering felt sluggish, and a course correction around an obstacle on the deck made him think that he was going to flip it over, spilling nerve-gas-filled explosive rounds onto the steel structure of the ship, or dump it into Tokyo Harbor.

Something impacted against the front of the pallet, a fine mist of red droplets spattering against the Plexiglas windshield of the cab. Wheels thumped over limbs with a crunch accompanied by a scream, all while James ripped off short bursts from his Brazilian assault rifle.

"One truck's moving!" James bellowed. He glanced down the gangplank, then grunted.

"What?" Trent asked.

"Company coming up," James answered.

Trent didn't wait for the obvious command, and he stomped on the forklift's gas, speeding down the ramp.

He felt the stubby little construction vehicle pick up more speed with the assistance of gravity. The barreling forklift seemed as if it were in a free fall, a moment of weightless motion that made Trent imagine that he was flying. The forklift shuddered as its lifting arms and the heavy mass of wood and steel hammered into the bodies of Japanese fanatics, crushing bones and throwing bodies into the water. The wheels rumbled over torsos and limbs, death cries and howls of agony assaulting his ears between the staccato rips of rifle fire that James poured on.

The forklift reached the bottom of the ramp with a bone-jarring bump. Blood-slicked wheels skidded on wood. Trent fought to keep the construction vehicle under control, but the pallet was too heavy. He was hurled against the roll cage inside the cab as wood splintered and steel rang out against each other.

Trent's head was swimming in the wake of the upheaval, but he could move all of his limbs easily. All of them except his tightly bound right wrist, though it was in a splint.

The side door was ripped open, and he looked up to see James straddling the cab entrance, brass somersaulting out of the breech of his rifle. "Come on, John!"

Trent lurched and pulled himself up. The dock was a scene of mayhem, bodies strewed about. Many of them looked relatively normal, obviously put down by streams of bullets, but some were flattened and twisted at odd angles. Those were the leftovers of a half ton of speeding machine and cargo, whatever hadn't been knocked into the brackish harbor waters between the freighter and the boardwalk. Trent scooped up his rifle, pushing the images of human wreckage out of his mind.

These were people who intended to murder thousands with poison gas, he reminded himself. Don't be queasy just because they were smashed like the bugs they are.

"How many trucks left?" Trent asked, dropping to the dock, James right behind him.

"Two," James answered. "But we've got a ride."

Trent turned and saw four sets of windshields starred and punctured by rifle fire. Their engines idled, headlights glowing like abandoned dragons in the night. He and James rushed to one of the trucks. Trent yanked a dead driver out of his seat and slid behind the wheel as James kicked out the broken windshield so they could see better. Trent tromped the gas, knowing that it was going to be the same setup as on the forklift. He'd drive, and James would ride shotgun.

Two hard kicks knocked off the old truck's passenger door as Trent sped out of its parking spot. James looked back to see the door skid on the boardwalk, then turned his attention to the two sets of red taillights fading in the distance.

Wind blew through the rectangular slot that used to be the windshield, and Trent ripped his hood off to keep flapping fabric from distracting him. To the east, the sky began to glow orange with the coming dawn. He looked over at James, who perched in the passenger seat, his IMBEL rifle resting across his thigh like a high-tech lance.

"What kind of firepower were we looking at with the people who owned these trucks?" Trent asked.

"They looked like Type 89s, standard Japanese Defense Force issue," James answered. "That's what I thought, though the guy riding in that cherry picker seemed like he had some kind of Tommy gun on steroids."

"Anything that can knock out this engine?" Trent asked, keeping the pedal to the metal to close the distance with the escaping Masa Minori vehicles.

"Normally I'd say no for a 5.56 mm, but we don't have any safety glass, and this tub of rust sounds like it's already wheezing its last breaths," James told him. "Not that a windshield did any good for the first two guys in these seats."

"Damn the torpedoes, eh?" Trent asked.

James nodded. "Full speed ahead."

TADASHI TAKEO, the man who would be the new emperor of Japan, saw a pair of headlights burning in the distance, trailing his and the other truck as they slowed at the gates to the dock. With the wind whipping past his ears, he couldn't tell the results of the battle back at the freighter. Only the occasional sputter of gunfire stretched to reach him. He fumbled in the bucket and brought up a pair of binoculars. As the sky brightened with the rising sun, he took it as a good omen.

"The rising sun ascends to greet me, the emperor of its land," he said, despite the fact that no one could hear him as the truck shuddered and bounced on a pockmarked road. It felt good to make that pronouncement.

Since they had turned, Tadashi was no longer in line of sight with the approaching vehicle, but given the speed that it was closing with them, he'd be able to get a good look in no time. Still, niggling bites of paranoia inspired him to identify the other truck's occupants before they came too close. His hand tightened around the grip of his Ultimax 100. Fear impelled him to reload the light machine gun, working another 100-round drum into the breech.

"Sire?" the Masa Minori soldier riding shotgun called out. "I don't get a response on the radio!"

Tadashi's mouth curled down into a frown. He brought up the binoculars, but he didn't need the eyesight of an eagle to see how the pursuing truck screeched into a drifting turn out of the gates, the rear of the truck fishtailing until it was almost coasting sideways on the road. Somehow the enemy driver brought it back under control, gunning the engine to eat up the ground between them. "Full speed ahead! It's the enemy!"

He looked over to see the other vehicle, the one that had a 500-pound shell, lined with military plastic explosives, on board. Tadashi had the radio detonator in his pocket, and he thought about what would happen if the Japanese authorities tried to stop him.

If the emperor could not claim his land, then he would deny the enemy the pleasure of incarcerating him. But that would be only his last resort. Tadashi was armed and prepared to fight for his supremacy. It didn't matter that dozens of his followers were likely dead. He only needed his force of will to bring others to serve him. The delusional pawns that called themselves the Japanese government would know his power if even one shell detonated, smothering the lives of thousands with its invisible toxins.

Tadashi shouldered the Ultimax, aimed at the enemy

truck and held down the trigger, roaring as he unleashed a wave of lightning and thunder at those who would try to usurp him.

TRENT FOUGHT the temptation to hit the brakes as he saw the muzzle-flash erupt from the bucket of the crane on the back of the other truck. The gunner had loaded tracers into his machine gun, and he saw sparks of light bounce and waver, spreading wide around the glassless windshield. He glanced over at James, who leaned forward in his seat, as if stretching his neck would somehow make the vehicle go faster.

"He's not hitting us," Trent said.

"We're too far, and this road's too bumpy," James explained. "I'm surprised that he's even able to hang on to that thing."

"But if we get closer…" Trent said.

"He'll have a better chance at hitting us," James concluded. He brought up the IMBEL, flicking the selector switch to single shot. Full-auto wouldn't give him much more than an empty magazine. He'd need his trained trigger finger to have any hope of connecting with any part of the enemy truck.

Timing the bounces of his ride and the shooter's, James tapped the trigger moments before the jumpy front sight crossed the other vehicle. Actually, he thought to tap the trigger. By the time the nerve impulses made his finger contract, the muzzle of the rifle was nearly in line with his target. Another brief moment of delay as the gears between the trigger and the firing pin ignited a 5.56 mm bullet, and the barrel was pointed straight at the truck. At 3,200 feet per second, the projectile crossed the hundred feet between the two vehicles in an instant.

It was all a matter of timing, a factoring of instants between will and action, and James was rewarded as he blew out a taillight with one shot. He'd fired five rounds quickly, working his timing to make sure he hit something, but at this range, he couldn't tell if he'd struck any part of the vehicle less spectacularly fragile than the taillight.

James could see the bucket gunner duck down, an arm swept over his head.

"How did you do that?" Trent asked.

"Phoenix Force," James answered with a grim smile as he triggered the rifle again, spacing out shots to twice a second. Rubber burst on a rear tire, the rim sparking violently as steel met the road, creating a flaming comet that trailed after Tadashi's ride. "It's like that ninja crap, except shit blows up real good!"

Trent grinned and tromped on the gas. "Can't argue with that!"

The gunner worked to lever the light machine gun over the lip of the crane's bucket, and triggered. The Ultimax's muzzle flared again, but this time, rounds flew high over the truck cab, a symptom of firing blindly with the barrel of the weapon resting on an angle. Trent shifted, trying to milk as much out of the engine as he could.

"Ignore that guy," James said. "The other truck's driving with some purpose."

Trent looked at the second vehicle pulling away from the first. James had a point; that truck had room for a payload, as opposed to the one with the cherry picker.

As James's target sped along, the other driver swerved to block Trent, naked rim spitting a blazing spray as it swung in front of them.

James crawled out of the cab, hanging on by the roof support strut. His IMBEL hung on its sling, traded in for the Steyr TMP, which could be used more easily with one hand. Marksmanship at range between two speeding trucks was next to impossible without the expertise and experience to compensate for an unstable shooting platform. However, at a range of a few yards, the close-quarters chatterbox was more than accurate enough to easily rain fire on the other vehicle. The hammer-shaped machine pistol vomited a tongue of flame that raked across the side of the Masa Minori truck.

The limping enemy transport screeched as its driver reacted to the sudden splash of hot lead. James hadn't put any bullets into the cab, but the rapid-fire staccato against the driver's door threw fear into his gut, eliciting a reaction. The Japanese cult vehicle slowed as it bled off velocity in lateral movement, and Trent aimed for an open patch of road that would put him on the other truck's tail.

James bellowed a warning, unintelligible even with the power of the electronic hearing protectors. There were too many sound sources fighting for dominance in Trent's hearing. Still, the warning was enough for Trent to brace himself as the enemy truck slammed into theirs. Metal crunched on metal as James leaped onto the hood in front of Trent, fingers locked on to the lip where the windshield used to be. Trent grimaced and returned the favor to the Masa Minori transport, swerving into it and taking some grim satisfaction in the squeal of crumpling fenders.

"You okay?" Trent bellowed.

"Just drive!" James returned. He had lost his rifle and machine pistol in the leap out of the way. While it was an inconvenience that put him at a disadvantage, it was far better than becoming the meat sandwiched between two slices of Japanese trucks.

James managed to pull his knees up onto the hood, and then finally braced his waffle-treaded boots on the front of the truck to get into a crouch. Trent could see the black man's knuckles whiten around the roof strut and the top of the dashboard. James looked over his shoulder toward the other truck, and his whole body tensed, like a spring compressing for a launch.

"You're not…" Trent said.

"Get me closer," James ordered.

Trent laid on the gas, shifting the gears as high as he could to catch up with the nerve-gas-laden vehicle. It made sense that James would have to make the leap. While mere handgun and carbine bullets wouldn't rupture the steel case of an artillery shell, it was entirely possible that a crashing truck would produce enough trauma to release the deadly poison payload. James had to take control of the other transport and put on the brakes.

The hood closed with the back of the other truck, and James's legs snapped open, hurling him onto the side of the utility vehicle. There was a railing at the top that he'd barely managed to snag with one hand. Trent grimaced as James's feet flailed in the wind. The Phoenix warrior's body was swung through the air parallel to the ground. James got his other hand on the railing and folded himself up to brace his knees against the side of the truck.

The Fist of Heaven soldier who had been riding shotgun threw open the passenger-side door and leaned out of the cab. He tried to bring up the Type 89 rifle that Masa Minori had stolen from a JSDF depot. At the contact range, Trent knew that the automatic weapon would saw James in half if the Japanese cultist got it on target. James twisted himself on the rail and stabbed both of his feet forward. The double-kick caught the rifleman in the chest, breaking his grip on the seat that kept him on the truck.

Trent had to hold on to the wheel tightly as the cultist's corpse was ground under his tires. In his side mirror, he was able to see the gory smear of splintered bones and burst flesh on the road behind him. Though he didn't need to keep up with the enemy now that James had gotten on board, Trent wasn't about to let his former student get too far away from him.

A shadow lurched in Trent's peripheral view. A less trained man wouldn't have noticed as, mentally, he would have been locked in to tunnel vision. Trent, however, as part of his martial-arts training, had taught himself to exist in the moment, every sense spread out, cast like a net around him so that he wouldn't be caught by surprise. The shadow wrenched himself into the cab beside the ninja—he must have leaped onto their truck when Trent was busy trading paint with the other Masa Minori vehicle.

Instinctively, Trent brought his injured forearm up, slamming it against the shadow's wrist. Pain spiked through the fractured bone, but it had spared the ninja a bullet in the head as the Japanese madman had been a moment from pulling the trigger on his handgun. His opponent lashed out with his other hand, fingers clawing at Trent's face. Though agony burned through his wounded limb, the ninja slammed his hand into the guy's face in an effort to push him off.

The handgun in the man's fist swung back toward Trent. One squeeze of his finger, and Trent would be dead. The ninja clawed out, grabbing his opponent by the neck of his shirt, and yanked him forward. The attacker was thrown off balance, and now the handgun hung out the driver's-side window.

"You will not deny me my destiny!" he exclaimed now that the two men were face-to-face in the front seat. "I will be emperor!"

Trent snapped his forehead into the face of the man who would be emperor. Hot blood spattered all over the ninja's face, salt stinging his eyes. His opponent stunned, Trent shoved him out of the way so that he could see the road. Steering was next to impossible with the Japanese cultist's body between him and the wheel. The man struggled to sit up and return to battling Trent when the American ninja saw that they were looming on a parked van.

There would be no time to stop, so Trent wrapped his arms around the man, hanging on tightly.

The impact felt like a hammer blow from the gods.

CALVIN JAMES WATCHED in horror as John Trent drove their truck into a collision. He knew that the vehicle was old enough that it wouldn't have airbags, and that his former sensei wasn't wearing his seat belt. The rear of the truck rose into the air as it came to a sudden, violent stop.

It may have been too late for his friend, but James knew that many more lives were at stake. He drew his pistol from its holster, and swung into the cab, pumping bullets into the Japanese driver. The man was dead instantly, giving James the chance to grab the wheel to stabilize it. He wrenched back on the emergency brake, rubber vaporizing from the sudden friction. The ugly tarry smell assaulted James's nostrils as he was thrown against the dashboard, but he never let go of the steering wheel.

His shoulders sagged once the vehicle was stopped. James ripped the key from the ignition and mopped smeared blood off his face from where the driver's gore-splattered corpse had slammed into him. He crawled out of the cab, out of breath, and looked to see a figure limp from the accident site a hundred yards away. James didn't have any guns left, so he pulled his knife, just in case he was looking at a Fist of Heaven terrorist.

Trent waved to James. He, too, was covered in blood, and he staggered more than walked. James put his blade away.

"How did you survive?" James asked. "And if you say that one more time…"

Trent shook his head. "The freak with the machine gun from the cherry picker got on our truck. Before we crashed, I pinned him to the steering wheel. Turns out, for a mass murderer, he made a pretty good airbag."

James sighed with relief, fumbling in his pocket for his PDA.

Time for Stony Man Farm to arrange for the cleanup of a stockpile of dangerous nerve gas.

CHAPTER THIRTEEN

Lomié, Cameroon

The other four members of Phoenix Force had reunited in Yaoundé, the capital city of Cameroon. Rather than directing the team to one of the two relatively unstable nations that were the Republic and the Democratic Republic of the Congo, Barbara Price had sent Phoenix Force to the generally stable Cameroon. Cameroon wasn't perfect, but international sexual slavery and forced labor were evident in every country in Central Africa. Despite strong presidential control, Cameroon was slowly edging into full representative democracy, as well.

Phoenix Force had reassembled in Yaoundé simply because it had an international airport and an American Embassy. The American Embassy was of vital importance to the Stony Man strike team, because they had rushed to Africa ahead of any diplomatic pouches or forged credentials that would grant them the ability to bring high-tech military weapons past local customs officials. Luckily, Barbara Price had managed to speak with the diplomatic security service contingent for the embassy in Yaoundé. A care package of SIG-Sauer P-229s and Colt M-4s with M-203 grenade launchers was ready for Phoenix Force. Knowing Gary Manning's preference for powerful revolvers, a Smith & Wesson Model 19 Combat Magnum had been drawn from old inventory, giving the brawny Canadian a six-shot .357 Magnum to make up for the lack of a designated marksman's rifle. McCarter, rarely a fan of double-action autopistols, had been presented with the gift of a Colt 1911 from the U.S. Marine Guard captain of the Embassy.

A note had accompanied the package.

"Let's see a travel agent whip up this kind of firepower inside of ten hours."

Currently they were unpacking their gear at a small rural airport. To call it an airport was an exaggeration, as it was a grassless field where single-prop planes and utility helicopters sat while their pilots worked on engines by themselves. There was a fueling station, as well, and their borrowed Sikorsky H-34 helicopter was in the queue to fill her parched tanks.

McCarter opened the weapons cases and saw a slip of paper with a printout. He read the note, then narrowed his eyes, glaring at T. J. Hawkins. "You ruffled Barb's feathers again, didn't you?"

Encizo grinned, speaking up for the embarrassed Hawkins. "He said that if we didn't raise a ruckus now and again, she'd only be buying us tickets to get around the world."

McCarter leaned forward and rapped his knuckles gently on Hawkins's forehead. "Knock, knock! Is anyone at the wheels up there?"

"All right, let's all have a good laugh at the only member of the team not eligible for the seniors' discount," Hawkins replied with a sneer. He defused any real animosity with a wink, and the elder members of the team managed a chuckle.

"He said you get a seniors' discount, Rafe," McCarter said with a grin and a light punch on the shoulder.

Encizo groaned and shook his head. "No fair, switching gears between rookie jokes and old-people jokes. He meant you guys were ancient, too."

"Speak for yourself, Rafe. I'm ageless," McCarter replied with a wink.

Manning let out a sigh, the look on his face indicating that it was time to set the comedy aside. "We have two American operatives lost in that basin, as well as a launch facility putting orbital bombardment weapons into space."

McCarter rolled his eyes. "What else are we going to do while we're waiting for the tank to top off? I've got my course plotted, and our gear has been triple-checked."

Manning checked over the map, frowning. "I know you've set the course so that we can cover the likeliest angles that Carmichael and Arcado would take to get back to base, but there should be something else we can do to make certain we can locate them."

McCarter looked where Manning was looking. "I hate to say this, but short of getting Gadgets to try out some of his paranormal research, we're not going to get any better than our asses in that flying eggbeater and our eyeballs in the sky."

Manning nodded. "At least Akira was able to get a good idea where the launch pad was supposed to be."

"Thanks to your wind-pattern calculations putting that seed in his head," McCarter added.

Manning's frown deepened. "According to the diplomatic security service back in Yaoundé, Carmichael and Arcado made the approach into the Congo from here."

He was referring to Lomié, the city they were in. This part of the country was the seat of Cameroon's forestry industry, about the only activity in the vast untracked areas that had barely been dented by subsistence farms. The wild jungle that snarled up this corner of the country provided a porous, hard-to-control border. With the conflict between the Democratic Republic and the Republic of the Congo, those two countries didn't have an interest in watching their northern approach.

Not that any army would be able to cut through the thick forest without carving a two-hundred-mile road across terrain that had resisted civilization's advances for centuries. Two men on foot, keeping to game trails, could have made the crossing with relative ease, but no invasion would have had a chance. Phoenix Force would have made the excursion as easily as Carmichael and Arcado, but it would have been a trek spanning days.

Days that the two Department of Defense agents didn't have.

That was why Phoenix Force had the old, rusted Sikorsky. The helicopter could cover more ground and make the search easier. Phoenix Force would find the two men who had risked their lives to put an end to a pipeline of human beings sold into slavery. And they would then be in position to destroy a launch site that had been responsible for over ten thousand murders.

Too much suffering had emanated from a hidden spot on the Congo.

It was time for McCarter and his men to drop the hammer on them.

JOHN CARMICHAEL SLIPPED in the mud as a torrent of rain opened up from the heavens above. That fall and crash to the ground was the only thing that had saved his life as a rifle round exploded the trunk of a nearby tree. Carmichael cursed and rolled, tucking his weapon to his chest to protect it from getting clotted with debris. If it had been an AK-47, Carmichael could have poured oatmeal down the barrel and into the magazine and it still would have worked, but the AR-15 platform was generally more sensitive to grit and sludge. He could trust a few M-4 variations to be chokeproof in a downpour, but he didn't know which truck this clean rifle had fallen off of.

All he could do was hope that gravity did enough to drag him out of the line of fire as he slid downhill. Leaves and branches slapped at him, and he could feel the mud smearing under his clothes and against his skin. After the chewing he'd received from the rainforest insects, the sludge was actually a soothing salve.

He took a deep breath as he landed in a crouch at the bottom of the slope. Big raindrops the size of bullets slapped Carmichael in the face as he looked toward the top to see if anyone had wanted to follow him over the edge. The M-4 carbine was aimed right where he was looking, so if he saw a human being, it would catch a bullet in the head. In the meantime, he crawled backward, retreating into the taller bushes and longer grass to get out of sight. Being caught in the open had nearly gotten his head blown off a few moments ago. He wasn't going to repeat that error.

Not when Arcado spent his life buying Carmichael some time. As he roosted in the shadows of the foliage, he heard voices speaking in a rough, guttural language, a tone that didn't belong in the heart of darkest Africa. Carmichael had spent time in Germany, and though he hadn't learned more than a few phrases and words, the sound of it was unmistakable.

Sure, he and Arcado had seen a blend of Europeans and Africans lording over enslaved Congolese people, but the two men had assumed that the whites had been South Africans or perhaps retired Russian military men who had become expatriates. Carmichael tried to narrow down who exactly would have brought Germans into central Africa, but there was nothing that made sense.

The American soldier frowned, then looked around for an escape route. Lying in the shadows, hidden by thick foliage, was good for the time being, but his pursuers would see exactly where he'd come down and follow him into the undergrowth. These men were man trackers, and even if he moved off course, they would eventually see that he left no trail and return to the last spot that they'd had his scent.

Carmichael had left behind some false leads on this chase across the jungle, but these trackers were thorough and capable. He saw one of the men as he perched atop the slope, scanning.

They were in communication. The hunter wore a hands-free radio headset with a boom microphone extending along his jawline. The man's eyes were, even at this distance, a bright, shockingly clear blue. He was either shirtless, or he wore a tank top under his load-bearing vest, because his arms were bare and thickly muscled. Tattoos flowed down the powerful limbs to his wrists. They were not a thick blue tapestry like Carmichael'd seen on American inmates, but clear, distinct skin tags that didn't have to be hidden from prison guards, symbols meant to jump out and proclaim the purpose of the ink.

Lightning-shaped runes. Swastikas. The Iron Cross.

Carmichael's jaw clenched at the sight.

He was being hunted by twenty-first-century neo-Nazis. Loathing rose within him, a rage that would have hurled him at the man had he less discipline or awareness that he was outnumbered and outgunned.

Arcado's words echoed in his mind. Fight smart.

Getting emotional now would end up with his corpse decomposing, entering the circle of life as he was demoted from human to maggot shit. They were close, hot on his trail, and right now, he couldn't do anything without bringing the rest of the tracker's team down on him.

The hunter reached into his belt and pulled out a flare pistol, aiming it skyward. Carmichael was pushed to the point where he had two choices.

Remain still and be hemmed in by a determined enemy, or pull the trigger and still draw their fire.

Carmichael snapped off a shot at the neo-Nazi, but the rustle of the M-4 rising from the bushes caught the hunter's attention. Rather than coring the bastard through his skull, the American soldier missed him.

The flare popped into the air, streaking up and trailing a wake of smoke, reminiscent of the rocket he'd seen only two days ago. The sudden downpour had finished as quickly as it had started, and though the skies were still thick and gray, the flare was a bright star. There was no way the other hunters could have missed it.

"Fuck," Carmichael cursed.

The hunters knew where he was, and no cavalry was on the horizon to rush to his aid.

RAFAEL ENCIZO SAW THE PUFF of a flare in the distance, the smoky column it rose upon originating somewhere over the horizon, and he immediately keyed his radio as he watched out the starboard side of the H-34.

"We've got a flare!" Encizo called. "Four o' clock!"

The ungainly, bulbous Sikorsky yawed as David McCarter swung the big bird in the direction that Encizo had noted. While the old, battered remnant of the sixties didn't have the pep of the newer, sleeker Blackhawk UH-60, the veteran bird still flew smoothly, making the turn easily. Its 1500-horsepower engine revved higher, propelling Phoenix Force toward the fading trail of the flare.

"Is it Carmichael asking for help?" Hawkins asked as he moved from his position on the H-34's port side. "Or is it some hostile locals?"

"Either way, we're going to take a closer look," Encizo proclaimed grimly. It had been a frustrating two days. Certainly there had been plenty of progress in the hunt for the conspirators who had left two cities in chaos and wreckage, but the Cuban Phoenix veteran hadn't had much to do with it. He took a rappelling rope and hooked it in the doorway of the Sikorsky. A quick snap through the carabiners on his harness, and he was ready to drop from the sky.

Hawkins quickly prepared for his jump as Manning crawled down from the copilot's seat in the cockpit situated above the passenger and cargo cabin. He scooped up the M-4/M-203 that had been stowed at the bottom of the stairs, as the cockpit was too small to fit much more than himself and McCarter. Encizo braced his feet against the doorway, holding his rappelling line taut. While it would have been quicker to hang out the door, braced the same way, Encizo wasn't thrilled with the prospect of exposing his back to enemy gunmen on the ground. A quick leap, and he'd still be on the way down, though he had to keep his rifle cinched and relatively useless to keep it out of his way. Hawkins was in a similar position, and Manning hunkered down to act as door gunner, just in case of trouble.

"We'll be on target in thirty seconds," McCarter announced.

"Gary? Can you see anything?" Encizo asked, looking over his shoulder.

Manning swept the ground, looking through the scope on his carbine. The Canadian's sniper-trained eyes were sharp and he could scan a hundred square feet in a heartbeat. His skill as a hunter and outdoorsman gave him a further advantage, so that few things could hide from him in any forest from the Arctic Circle to this steaming, muggy tangle of jungle in Africa.

"Lots of movement," Manning said. "Between four and six people down there. Two factions, a group chasing a lone man."

Hawkins spoke up. "Chasing. Sounds like our side, then?"

"We'll see on the ground," Encizo replied.

"David! Evasive action!" Manning bellowed over their com link. Encizo winced at the Canadian's roar, but before Manning had even completed his first syllable, the Sikorsky veered sharply.

As the jungle spun below them, Encizo could see the bright stars of two assault rifles' muzzle blasts. Small-arms fire and an old helicopter were more than sufficient reason for McCarter's wild maneuvering, but there was no guarantee that the enemy wouldn't have something more than a Kalashnikov to knock them out of the sky.

"I'm dropping you and T.J. off a little ways back," McCarter said over the com. "It'll let me sit still long enough for you to fast rope down. We'll have the forest canopy covering us."

"Sounds good to me," Encizo replied. "I'm itching to get dirt beneath my feet anyway."

"I'm jealous. I still have to ride with this maniac," Manning muttered.

"Bloody back-seat drivers," McCarter snarled as he brought the Sikorsky to a steady hover. "Go!"

Encizo and Hawkins didn't need to be urged on. They had kicked themselves through the door of the helicopter even as it had come to a halt in the air. Nylon rope smoked against the tough soles of Encizo's rappelling gloves as gravity pulled him back into the arms of Mother Earth. His boot treads hit the mud and the Cuban flexed his knees to absorb the impact of his descent, bleeding off the momentum. Encizo broke open the clasps that kept his harness around his hips and lower back, freeing him from the helicopter.

The Phoenix Force veteran pulled his M-4 down on its sling, then drew it to his shoulder, ready to fight. Hawkins had been only a half second behind him, and now crouched at his side, sweeping the jungle for enemies. The lines that had deposited the pair into the forest slurped up into the sky as McCarter pulled the Sikorsky higher and back to keep away from the gunmen on the ground.

"Gary's rifle doesn't have the range to give us fire support," Hawkins drawled. "We're on our own."

Encizo nodded. "We also don't have a clue if it was the good guys or the bad guys who fired on us."

"Them's the breaks," Hawkins replied. "Split up, or do we hopscotch it?"

"Split. Keep low," Encizo answered tersely. "And give me a heads-up if any of you see anything."

"I was just going to do some bird-watching up here. Thanks for the suggestion," Manning retorted over the radio. "Movement to your east. Estimate one man."

Encizo hand signaled for Hawkins to stay put and cover him. With that, the Cuban Phoenix veteran stalked off into the undergrowth. The ex-Ranger nestled behind a tree trunk that provided both protection and concealment, M-4 at the ready to rip through any hostiles.

With the speed and stealth of a jaguar, Encizo moved with confidence that could only be provided by his Phoenix Force allies at his back and years of jungle fighting experience under his belt. It was foolhardy to charge into an unknown situation alone, but the Cuban wasn't stumbling blindly into the forest. His every sense was acutely honed now, and his brothers were watching out for him. A man walked into view, and Encizo knew that it wasn't one of the two DOD investigators who'd come down from Cameroon. They had been an African American and a Latino, and this man was blond and blue-eyed, with tattoos on his arms all the way down to the wrists.

Encizo tensed, ready to leap on the man when an instinct urged him to turn and stop an attack. With a spin, he brought up his forearm to collide with the wrist of a hand that held a knife. The assailant's limb was chocolate-brown, and wild, dark eyes met Encizo's as both men grunted. Encizo forced himself to mentally pause as he pitted his strength against the other man's, not wishing to inadvertently cause harm to one of the agents he'd come thousands of miles to rescue. It was hard to tell if the attacker was a native African or had been born in the States.

A clawed palm rose to meet Encizo's face, but he pivoted his forearm, grabbing hold of the black man's wrist. The Cuban's upper-body strength was more than enough to drag the opponent off balance, and by stepping back and twisting, Encizo had avoided the punch. The Cuban fired a quick boot toe into the back of the other man's knee and he clamped a strong hand over his mouth. The very fact that Encizo hadn't been able to flip him ass over head thanks to a solid stance showed martial-arts training. The palm-heel stroke was the icing on the cake, a simple punch borrowed from kung fu for Rangers hand-to-hand training, something Encizo had seen Hawkins use plenty of times.

John Carmichael tried to thrash free, but Encizo

slipped his other forearm under the American's chin. The Phoenix Force warrior clenched his fist and pressed it hard under Carmichael's ear, pulling the man's head against it. With incredible pressure slowing the blood to Carmichael's brain, the sleeper hold had immobilized him. Encizo now had the advantage over the stunned American to pull him farther back into the brush.

The speed of the interaction made all of the assault take place in the space of a second and a half, long enough to attract the blond hunter's attention, but swift enough that Encizo was able to drag Carmichael out of the way of the Fist of Heaven tracker's hasty gunshot.

"Free-fire zone!" Encizo shouted as he rolled over on top of Carmichael as a human shield.

T. J. Hawkins didn't need much impetus to open fire, and as soon as he heard Encizo's first word, he tracked the neo-Nazi killer's muzzle-flash and unleashed five rapid shots. The ex-Ranger's supersonic bullets streaked through the forest and forced the enemy to duck for cover. Hawkins knew that his opening salvo merely had a suppressive effect, but his goal was to buy Encizo some space to do whatever he had to.

The Phoenix Force operatives had planned ahead of time for this instance, and once one of the team had managed to get both members of the DOD investigation probe out of the line of fire, then the others would be able to engage anyone still walking around. Hawkins didn't want to think of the implication that Encizo had likely only encountered one man in the brief moments since he'd taken to the thickness of the forest, but the mental image of a dead fellow American soldier rose unbidden. With a grimace, Hawkins looked for more signs of movement, keeping his anger bottled until it could find a target to explode against.

Two rifles cracked from a copse of jungle trees, and Hawkins was glad for the trunk he'd chosen to fight from. Their bullets chopped into wood, but only produced small gouges in the ancient tree's form. Hawkins opened fire, two shots to the muzzle-flash on the left, three for the one on the right, rewarded by a dying scream from his right-hand target. It could have been a ploy, but the sudden spray of autofire from the gunman on the left was accompanied by an enraged bellow.

With the trigger held back, the angry rifleman had no control, recoil throwing his aim off so that even if Hawkins had been exposed to incoming fire, nothing would have hit. The enemy rifle clunked empty, its bolt locked back.

"Scheissen!" came a frustrated curse.

Hawkins wasn't about to let the man reload or pick up his fallen partner's weapon. It was a ruthless action, but the youngest Phoenix fighter pumped four quick shots into the Fist of Heaven hunter's fleeting shadow. There was a strangled gargle of pain, meaning that he'd scored a hit, and Hawkins nearly poked his head out to confirm his assessment.

Instincts froze Hawkins in place, and he instead pressed himself hard against the old tree trunk, feeling the rapid drumming of enemy bullets smacking into his cover. It had been the one who'd tried to gun down Encizo.

Hawkins spun around the other side of the trunk, ready to unleash a stream of hot lead, when he saw his Cuban partner pounce from the undergrowth, a Cold

Steel Tanto locked into his brawny fist. The blond man turned and threw his rifle up as a shield against the ice-pick stab Encizo had opened with. Hawkins thought that his partner had underestimated the Fist of Heaven enemy, but Encizo simply used his knife as a hook to rip the neo-Nazi's weapon out of his hands.

Hawkins turned back to look for the rifleman that he'd wounded, confident that Encizo was in fine shape. The ex-Ranger was rewarded for his quick decision by seeing a limping man lurch toward a fallen corpse. The Fist of Heaven trooper's hand was open, clawing for a rifle that was in the brush, and he moved with the swiftness to make him a threat.

Hawkins took off most of the neo-Nazi's head with two swift gunshots, both rounds producing massive cavitation. Stringy brain matter and torn rugs of brown-haired scalp flew as the bullets' supersonic passage forced incompressible fluids to detonate the neo-Nazi's head.

"T.J.!" Manning called from above on the radio.

Hawkins dived behind a bush instants before a storm of enemy lead chopped at him.

Encizo had gotten the blond hunter's rifle out of his grasp using the spine of his chisel-tipped Tanto knife, and swiftly lashed out with an uppercut. While Encizo's knuckles missed the Fist of Heaven terrorist, the six-inch straight blade of his stainless-steel knife parted the man's shoulder down to the bone. A growl of pain issued forth, and the tracker whipped his machete from its scabbard in a bid to return the favor. The long chopper swept through the air, and Encizo only barely deflected the blade using his Tanto as a forearm guard.

The Cuban shrugged the machete aside and stepped in close, pivoting his left elbow up hard into the corner between the neo-Nazi's nose and upper lip. Cartilage crunched and teeth cracked out of his upper gum line from the impact, giving Encizo another few moments of uninterrupted assault. The dazed Fist of Heaven hunter was oblivious to the razor-sharp chisel of steel that punched through his lower ribs, crushing bone aside to spear deep into his heart. Encizo gave the knife a twist, eliciting a torrent of blood, which flooded out of the neo-Nazi's mouth.

The Cuban slipped his knife out of the dead man's chest and shoved the lifeless sack of meat to the forest floor, attention turning to see if there were any more opponents coming. A stream of autofire opened up, but Encizo wasn't the target. He saw Hawkins strike the ground, however, and a mixture of rage, panic and concern spurred Encizo to quick-draw the SIG P-229 from his thigh holster.

No safety levers to disengage, and ready to go with a pull of the trigger, Encizo hammered off two fast shots at the space just behind the enemy muzzle-flash. There was a grunt, and Encizo ducked to one knee, laterally moving to the other side of a thin tree trunk as the barely seen opponent fired again. Encizo fired three more times, and this time, there was the unmistakable sound of a body crashing through the branches of a bush.

"T.J.?" Encizo asked into his radio, voice edged with concern.

"I'll live. You?" Hawkins asked.

"*Sí*," Encizo answered. He looked back toward Carmichael, his breath returning to normal.

So would one of the men they'd come to rescue.

CHAPTER FOURTEEN

Tokyo

Flavio Genoveva had the hearing return in one ear, but the other one felt as if it had been stuffed with cotton after someone had trapped a feedback-screeching speaker in the aural canal. His head pounded, and he poured half a bottle of aspirin into one hand before raising it to his mouth. The bitter tablets crunched into powder, and he washed it down with the tap water some genius decided to package and sell for profit. The gritty leftovers still stuck in his esophagus made him cough, and one particularly hard convulsion ended with him experiencing the unique hell of a sharp chunk of a pill come through his nose.

Sitting in the Toyota compact he'd hot-wired, he wiped the tears from his eyes, then checked himself in the mirror. A trickle of blood issued from where the shard of tablet had damaged his sinus membranes on its way out of his respiratory system.

"Fucking pills are supposed to make the pain go away, not cause bleeding," he muttered.

Genoveva had a South American knockoff of a Smith & Wesson .357 Magnum resting on the seat next to him, the only weapon he'd managed to stuff into his waistband before he hurled himself over the railing and into the brackish waters of Tokyo Harbor. He hated abandoning his brothers, the few remaining men who hadn't been cut down by gunfire from the intruders and that idiot Tadashi, or those who hadn't been torn apart by explosive pitfalls set by the enemy. He'd come to Japan with a force of 150 men, and somehow, chaos and confusion had turned two marauders into an unstoppable army.

From the end of the dock, Genoveva could see the flashing lights of Tokyo police and he could also make out the bright yellow sacks worn by hazardous-material teams. Drenched and miserable in the front seat of his car, he kept an eye out for one of the two who had gutted the Argentine Justice Coalition in the space of an hour. It had been a long shot; he didn't believe that an operator like the one who'd unleashed carnage on the freighter would stick around for cleanup.

He leaned back on the headrest. In the mirror, he could see that his right ear was seeping again. Genoveva searched through the car once more. His first sweep of the dashboard had provided a bottle of aspirin. Maybe he could find a paper towel or napkin that could be rolled up to absorb the leaking fluid from his irreparably damaged ear.

The Argentine neo-Nazi commander found a small package of facial tissues, and he sighed with relief. The softness of the tissue would be a godsend. He twisted a corner into a rat-tail and gently pushed it into the shell of his ear.

One more look at the assembled cleanup crew, and Genoveva realized that he was in absolutely no condition to strike out in vengeance now. He would have to wait, sneak out of the country and heal before he could hunt down the men who had wrecked his chance for advancement in the Fist of Heaven. He reached for the exposed ignition wires and twisted them.

Nothing. Not even the stinging spark of electricity through the wires.

Genoveva's heart began to pound. "No. No, no, no!"

He opened the car door and limped around to the hood, releasing it. Nothing seemed wrong with the engine, and he tightened the leads on the battery. He looked closer at the big wet cell that should have had the Toyota purring. The battery was dead. Unable to contain his disgust, he slammed the hood of the car down and stalked toward the passenger-side door to retrieve his .357 Magnum.

Genoveva untucked his shirt, then stuffed the barrel and cylinder in the gap between his waistband and his stomach. He'd have to get rid of the handgun eventually, but there was no way that he would be caught unarmed this close to the ship. He limped toward the other entrance of the dock. With one destroyed eardrum, he wasn't feeling too steady as he walked, so he had to take his time. Concentrating on each step had absorbed so much of his attention that he didn't hear the footsteps of the man jogging up to him until it was too late.

Genoveva turned and looked at the person as he came to a stop. It was an African, maybe an African American. The man was tall and slender, wearing a white pullover sweater and jeans. Genoveva was fully conscious that he looked like a freshly drowned rat.

"Perdo'neme, por favor," the black said in good Spanish. "Are you all right? You don't look well."

Genoveva took a deep breath. "It's nothing. I heard some shooting before and dove into the harbor to get out of the way."

The Argentine paused, his eyes meeting the black's, realization cutting through the dull haze of his battered brain. This man had spoken to him in Spanish, when very little of Genoveva's appearance gave the impression that he was Hispanic.

"Don't go for that pistol under your shirt," Calvin James said grimly. Genoveva looked down to see that the black Phoenix Force warrior's hand was wrapped around the grip of a weapon tucked into his pants, as well. "You'll never be able to outdraw me."

Genoveva nodded and lifted the hem of his shirt with both hands. James looked at him for a long moment, then stepped forward to pluck at the revolver's stocks. As soon as he did so, Genoveva pushed down hard and snarled the fabric of the shirt around James's wrist, pinning his arm as he gripped the Argentine's handgun. It was only a temporary measure, and he released the hem and clamped both hands around his enemy's wrist.

James grimaced as Genoveva's weight hauled him off balance. He would curse himself for falling for the neo-Nazi's trick later, provided he survived this combat. With a twist, Genoveva had extended James's arm straight. The Argentine threw himself sideways, and James knew that the weight of the other man would break his arm or dislocate his elbow and shoulder. Rather than try to pull free, James shoved himself tight into Genoveva to keep his weight off the trapped arm. The Phoenix pro braced his feet on the ground and pushed back against his opponent to uproot Genoveva.

Momentarily airborne, the Argentine's grasp loosened and James was able to pry his arm loose. A swift pivot turned James around as he speared his knee into Genoveva's side just under his ribs. Wracked by pain from the kidney kick, the neo-Nazi collapsed to his hands and knees.

"I'm not going to be taken prisoner," Genoveva rasped.

James snaked his arm under the man's chin and shoved both of his fists under the corners of Genoveva's jaw. It took only a minute, but the Phoenix pro had rendered the man unconscious.

"Yes," James panted, "you are. And we're going to find out who you're really working for."

The Congo River Basin

DAVID MCCARTER DEBRIEFED John Carmichael as his teammates formed a bucket brigade to transfer spare fuel in cans to the thirsty engine of the Sikorsky H-34. While the helicopter had a near two-hundred-mile range, the team intended to extend that as much as possible with a supply of jerry cans that provided an alternative to nonexistent external storage tanks for the bulb-nosed, high-cockpit aircraft. The Sikorsky had been bought from the neighboring nation of Katanga by a Cameroonian logger when the province had been reabsorbed into the Democratic Republic of the Congo.

The Phoenix Force commandos were not under the illusion that they would be flying out under their own power, not if they hoped to take decisive action against the Fist of Heaven's African stronghold. Either they'd have to abandon the aircraft, in which case they might not find it, or they'd have to fly it over the launch site and subject it to antiaircraft fire.

Once the old bird was gassed up, the other three members of Phoenix Force checked on McCarter and the American agent. McCarter handed Manning a map.

"You were right," McCarter said. "Satellite launch on a conventional rocket into low orbit. He didn't get a good look at the platform, but we're not looking at Houston Aerospace."

Manning looked at the location that Carmichael had indicated on the map, then nodded, not feeling satisfied by the correctness of his calculations. "How big is this place?"

"This is a mostly camouflage facility. All I know is that they had a refugee camp of over a thousand Congolese men, women and children," Carmichael answered. "They have the facilities for about twice that, and according to one of the people I talked to, they had brought about five thousand in."

"Packed in like sardines," Hawkins grumbled. "Fuckin' bigots."

"Life is too damn cheap in Africa," Encizo said with a sigh. "Castro sent enough of my cousins to be killed in the Angola wars. It seems that once someone sends people over here, they don't give a damn anymore."

"Barb gives a damn about us, and we give a damn about John and his mate David," McCarter countered. "And I give a big fat damn about those poor people that these neo-Nazis worked to death."

"If you let me come along, I'll show you how much I'm willing to give," Carmichael added.

"Damn straight we're bringin' you with us, sunshine," McCarter said. "It's not like we've got enough petrol to drop you off at your mum's and come back to kick some ass."

Hawkins smirked. After years of working with Americans and traveling the globe, the Phoenix Force leader, a former member of the SAS, had managed to let his old neighborhood Cockney accent fade enough into a generic British brogue that McCarter altered to suit the situation and his cover story. However, now the Briton had his dander back up, and the Cockney street-fighting ire rose in his words.

"What's got you smirkin'?" McCarter asked.

"Seeing a guy that these two told me I'd never see, now that you're all respectable and leaderlike," Hawkins said.

McCarter managed a grin. "You've got a lot of cheek, haven't you?"

"I've got enough," Hawkins replied. "I've been through this continent before, back when I was wearing a uniform for Uncle Sam. At that time, I heard the term 'Africa wins again.' I heard that the best strategy was to let her sink."

"Yeah, they told me that, too," Carmichael agreed. "You don't care, you're not disappointed when the people you're sent to protect end up murdered by slave traffickers."

"Fuck that noise," Hawkins said to the former Green Beret.

"So we've got a pack of heavily armed Nazis to deal

with," Encizo spoke up. "We just fly across some of the densest, most inhospitable jungle on this side of the Atlantic, enter a covert launch facility developed by a rich and powerful organization, free one thousand slaves and figure out where their mission control is, all before they send the next satellite up with a payload that can flatten a city."

McCarter thought about it for a moment, then gave Encizo a thumbs-up. Hawkins nodded in agreement. The Cuban looked to Manning, who merely raised an eyebrow.

"I'm in," Encizo said.

"Show us the layout of this facility again," McCarter ordered Carmichael.

Phoenix Force and their ally circled around the map.

Stony Man Farm

WITH ABLE TEAM BACK at headquarters, ready for deployment, the War Room felt especially cramped and crowded. Barbara Price pinched the skin between her eyebrows as Carl Lyons and Rosario Blancanales hovered over Hermann Schwarz's shoulders, looking at his screen.

"Don't you two have guns to field-strip?" Price asked Lyons and Blancanales.

Price could tell immediately that Lyons was in a mischievous mood when the big ex-cop's face took on an innocent expression. "Actually, no. We've got Cowboy running maintenance on our gear. Isn't that correct, Rosario, old man?"

"Quite concise, my dear Carl," Blancanales answered.

Price closed her eyes briefly, and she could feel the wrinkle lines creasing her forehead. "Give me strength."

Schwarz looked up and gave her a wink, but his tone was serious. "Carmen made a list of U.S.-based white-power movements, and I'm checking it twice. Trying to see what kind of money has been flowing through the organizations," he explained.

"So they took in more cash than they were spending?" Price asked.

Schwarz nodded. "I'd run those numbers already. If anything, some of these groups are spending a little more than their means."

Schwarz put a graph of several groups on his monitor. "Since Carl's done a lot of looking at these crazies, he's been thorough. Not only does he know their major meeting places, but he understands how their finances work."

"Lyons is trying to nail them à la CPA?" Price asked.

"An accountant was able to bring down Al Capone," Schwarz answered. "And the man not only was a beat cop, but a detective. I'm not saying we'll see him poring over ledgers all night with a pencil and a scratch pad, adding numbers, but he knows the day-to-day costs of these kinds of groups. He's researched where they're vulnerable, thanks to a few anti-white-supremacist groups trying to sue these Klan spinoffs out of existence."

"The trouble with those lawyers is that they can catch

a lot of lead," Price said. "How many death threats has that one received?"

"Not sure about death threats, but actual organized assassination attempts number about five at this time," Schwarz said. "We'll be there to hand the crazies their asses for try number six."

"Because the only time Carl's willing to do his math homework is so that he can be in position to open fire on a right-wing death squad," Price said.

Schwarz nodded, then squinted at something on his computer screen. "All right, this is interesting."

"What?" Price asked.

"The United Legion of Messianic America has a few tax write-offs," Schwarz said. "Construction supplies listed for repairs to their regional headquarters in Tennessee."

"ULMA?" Price exclaimed. "Those blowhards? They were one of the first groups we looked at, as well as the Amalgamated Klans of the United States, with their Kentucky fortress."

"You implying that ULMA has a fortress of their own?" Schwarz asked.

Price thought about it. "I'm not sure off the top of my head. I'd have to—"

"Carl!" Schwarz barked, cutting her off.

Lyons leaned over Schwarz's shoulder. "What?"

"ULMA—fortress or no?" Schwarz asked.

"Fortress in Tennessee. Right about the Appalachians," Lyons answered.

"Sure it's not Kentucky and the AKUS?" Price asked.

"Augustus Hammersmith tried suing AKUS for

taking his idea of a secure stronghold," Lyons said. "The Southern Legal Defense Guild offered to take the Klans' side, but they wanted to see their accounting records. The suit was dropped, but once in a while, you see biker gangs associated with both sides shoot the fuck out of each other."

"That's the one. Lawyer Roauld Dees is the SLDG leader who had those assassination attempts on his life," Price said.

"Carl has the cyberteam keep an eye on Dees's health," Schwarz explained. "He gets so much as a stubbed toe, the Ironman plans to drop the hammer of Thor on AKUS."

Lyons shook his head. "The hammer of Thor would be too swift and merciful. I want them to suffer."

Price sighed. "Doesn't Stony Man have enough to do without babysitting an antibigot crusader?"

"Yes," Lyons said. "But when it comes to protecting the enemy of our enemy, there's nothing better to do. If the Klans do decide to start getting uppity…"

"Klans…uppity…nice," Schwarz interjected with a thumbs-up. Price rolled her eyes.

"Thanks, Gadgets. If the bastards do decide to start wiping out everyone who's given them a headache, Dees is our early-warning system," Lyons said.

"Early warning. You mean, he'll be bait," Price said.

Lyons shook his head. "I had Dees hire two security consultants to do the actual babysitting."

Price raised an eyebrow. "Two? Who? Gadgets's and Pol's Able Group Investigations?"

"Technically," Schwarz answered. "We certified

them under our detective agency. And we know they can handle themselves. They've kept up with Striker and us on a few occasions, actually."

"Former blacksuits," Price muttered.

"So when the Klans come a-knocking, they'll run into someone who can knock back," Lyons said. "So what about the ULMA fortress? Anything on it?"

"Bought a lot of construction supplies and wrote it off on their taxes," Schwarz said.

"An antigovernment group paying taxes?" Lyons asked.

"How better to keep us from being interested in what they're doing?" Price contended.

Lyons nodded. "What about electronics?"

"Computers, servers, telecommunications equipment," Schwarz said. "A lot of phone repairs."

"It'd make sense. ULMA has one of the largest white-power websites on the net," Lyons added.

Price frowned. "It might make sense, but why even keep books about that?"

"Plausible deniability," Lyons answered. "They show up at the IRS offices with big boxes of receipts and phone bills and bury their agents in forensic accounting."

"It provides the perfect smoke screen for anything else they're buying and whatever else they're doing with this internet technology," Schwarz said. "'Oh, we're just here to buy a new server for Hatechildren-dot-com.'"

"Why even list this stuff on their books, though?" Price asked.

Lyons didn't look amused now. "Because they're trying not to look like a criminal organization. They want to be the legitimate face of their twisted little hate breed so that they could go to court and launch lawsuits against groups and federal agencies. They managed to get an injunction against the Tennessee State Police for illegal search and seizure of one of their transport vans. Any evidence that the cops found was thrown out, and without that evidence, the Tennessee police had to hand back fifty *real* assault rifles, not the stuff sold over the counter that only look like the shit that can do full-auto, to a group who advocates a coming civil war."

Price took a deep breath. "I remember something about that. The Bureau of Alcohol, Tobacco and Firearms wanted a piece of that, too, didn't they?"

Lyons nodded. "ULMA screwed the TSP on that case, and left the BATF with their hat in their hands, begging the attorney general for help. But since there was now legal precedent…"

"Federal prosecutors were now gun shy, pardon the pun," Price concluded. Her eyes narrowed. "You three don't need warrants."

"All we need is a road trip to Tennessee," Lyons answered. "Once Gadgets does his thing to give us some clear pointers."

Schwarz nodded. "We'd hate to engage in an armed assault on the wrong gun-toting white supremacist militia."

"Especially since they're lobbing weapon platforms into orbit," Lyons added.

Price nodded. "Even when I'm willing to let you guys off your leash, you have more restraint than I credit you for."

"Not restraint," Lyons said. "We just don't want to

waste ammo on something that's not immediately behind a plot to drop kinetic darts on innocent civilians."

"Pragmatism, not the milk of human decency," Schwarz quipped.

Lyons pointed grimly toward the image of Augustus Hammersmith on Schwarz's monitor. "When I find him, decency will not be in the room with the two of us."

CHAPTER FIFTEEN

Tokyo

Calvin James and John Trent sat in the hotel room, the American ninja's arm wrapped in a cast. James hovered over the laptop as he finished transmitting the video, audio and transcripts of his scopolamine-assisted interrogation of Flavio Genoveva. Over the high-speed Stony Man satellite hookup, the information dumps transpired at blinding speed, but James still felt a gnawing impatience.

It wasn't as if the information he'd pried loose from the Argentine neo-Nazi had been of earth-shaking value, but he had some names. Names would give the Farm enough information to start looking in the right corners of the white-supremacist underground to get details on how far and wide the Fist of Heaven conspiracy had stretched.

Barbara Price's face popped up on the laptop monitor. "We've got your transmission. Can we get a summary?"

"I've got a couple of names, one of which I recognized instantly," James answered. "Niklaus Radulf, of ODESSA."

"Radulf?" Price asked. "He's been around awhile as

a second stringer, but I thought he'd been taken out by Katz in an operation in France."

"The same one where Rafe had his hair parted by a 9 mm slug," James confirmed. "Thing is, we were in a hurry to get out of the resort they had used as a base. Katz took enough photos to confirm the identities of officers, but it's possible that Radulf was playing possum. Stony Man has been hearing whispers of activity on Radulf's part."

"Rumors are one thing, but we like to have harder evidence," Price said. "Radulf could have just been a ghost to keep Interpol wondering who was behind a lot of hate crime in Europe."

"Genoveva wasn't lying, not under that much scope," James said, referring to the truth serum he'd utilized on their Fist of Heaven officer. "He'd met Radulf face-to-face in Argentina."

"That's across the ocean from Africa," Price mused. "Maybe the Fist of Heaven set up all of its operation south of the equator?"

"No. Radulf was simply there to arrange for the sale of a stockpile of stolen American chemical weapons to Masa Minori," James explained.

"They're done now, right?" Price queried.

James nodded.

"What's the other name you got out of Genoveva?" Price asked.

"Darius Dispenza," James said. "While I was doing the upload, I did a little web surfing on my PDA. He's the webmaster for ULMA."

"How did his name come up?" Price asked.

"Dispenza has been facilitating communications

between Japan and Argentina," James said. "Genoveva has talked with him quite a bit."

"It gives us another link between the Legion and the Fist of Heaven, but did Genoveva say that he was working with ULMA, or was Dispenza moonlighting?" Price asked.

"Any communication went solely through Dispenza. The bastard kept his trail covered so that he wouldn't implicate his extended Klan," James explained.

Price grimaced. "Did you hear that, Gadgets?"

"Yes," came a voice from across the room. James recognized Schwarz, who popped up in another sub-window on his laptop screen. "What's up, Cal?"

"The body count in Tokyo harbor," James answered. "Any joy in the States?"

"We've had a few skirmishes, but you gave me the hook we need to pin 'em down for the knockout," Schwarz replied.

"Is this info that good?" Price asked.

"Dispenza's been on Aaron's radar for a while," Schwarz told her. "And every hacker has a particular style that can be tracked, if you're good enough."

"That's why we hired people like Akira, Hunt and Carmen," Price countered.

Schwarz nodded with a smile. "Thanks, Cal. I owe you."

Schwarz disappeared from the screen, and James turned back to Price. "Any word on David and the others?"

"They're fine. They've found one of the agents who disappeared in the Congo," Price replied. "We've got confirmation of the launch facility's location. They're ready to hit it after a quick recon."

"Wish 'em luck. I'd love to be there," James told her.

"I know," Price answered. "But they'll do their best. Farm, out."

Not usually a praying man, Calvin James sent one anyway to his brothers in arms.

The Congo River Basin

DAVID MCCARTER HAD FLOWN the H-34 Sikorsky as close as he dared to the Fist of Heaven rocket facility, knowing that the international conspiracy would likely have some form of early detection radar around their perimeter. He'd flown the old bird so low that the stationary landing gear clipped branches on the forest canopy in its passing. That was the only way he could keep the aircraft from being seen with its half-century-old design.

It was enough. They'd gotten within five miles of the facility, giving McCarter the room to find a clearing to set down the bird. Once they'd landed, Phoenix Force made one more check of their gear. Each of the four Stony Man warriors had lent John Carmichael some extra ammunition so that he could assist them in the Fist of Heaven takedown. The team burned their new loadout into their memories, so that they would conserve their firepower. With their awareness locked in, none of the team would make the mistake of reaching for a magazine that was not there, leaving them vulnerable as they came up empty in midreload. Phoenix Force and their ex–Green Beret ally were going to be hard-pressed against a security force sufficient to keep thousands captive in slave labor, so every ounce of mental acuity and preparation was as important as every bullet they carried.

Just before McCarter landed the helicopter, they'd received word from Stony Man Farm about the information that James had picked up in Tokyo. At least one part of the Fist of Heaven operation had come under the purview of ODESSA, one of Phoenix Force's most virulent adversaries. Rafael Encizo tried to contain his sneer at the mention of the group's name, his fingers absently rising to his hairline to feel the scar where one of their neo-Nazis had shot him in the skull. Only the rounded dome of bone and the angle of the enemy shot turned a fatal bullet into a temporarily debilitating concussion.

The news of ODESSA's involvement had other implications, as the organization boasted ties in Europe, South America and in the nation of South Africa, as well as Rhodesian expatriates. Though apartheid had ended years ago, there were still plenty of new recruits from younger generations of white South Africans to join Radulf's neo-Nazi revivalists. There weren't enough to stage a coup in Johannesburg or Soweto, but there were still plenty of pairs of boots to stamp the faces of thousands of slaves in the Congo.

Five miles was still beyond the horizon from the launch facility, even at treetop level, so Phoenix Force didn't know what the camp was doing, or if their sentries were on alert after having lost contact with their hunting team. The Stony Man team moved as quickly through the jungle as they dared, Gary Manning taking point. One of the finest outdoorsmen on the planet, as well as a veteran of jungle warfare, the big Canadian had the others fall in step in single file behind him as he cut the trail for Phoenix Force. His senses were keenly attuned to the natural and artificial dangers that could be hidden in the thick darkness of a forest. The team moved in Manning's footsteps, confident in his skill at avoiding dangerous fauna, uncertain terrain and looming mines and booby traps.

McCarter's ears perked up as a low rumble permeated the air, a vibration that rose through his boots and pressed on his ears. The omnipresent sound was familiar, and the rest of the team paused as they heard it, too. McCarter knew it couldn't be thunder. From the Sikorsky, he'd been able to see far enough into the African skies to know that there was no storm front, even if he couldn't see conditions on the ground.

This part of the continent was geologically stable and it was unlikely that there would be an active volcano or fault in the Earth's crust for the ex-SAS commando to consider the ever-increasing roar to be seismic activity.

There was only one thing that could account for the noise. The Fist of Heaven was launching.

"Oh, no," Carmichael whispered as he cast his eyes skyward.

The first smoky spear rose into the sky, its engine nozzles burning like a miniature sun as the massive rocket's motors converted liquid oxygen into expanding, superheated gasses. McCarter grimaced as he looked at the unfettered might of 9,700,000 joules ripping the massive shaft free from Earth's hold.

"Bugger all," McCarter growled as he saw a second then a third rocket rising into view, their ascending paths bracketing the first of the rockets. He urgently pulled his PDA from its pocket, dialing in Stony Man Farm. There was no point controlling the edgy concern turning his voice to a rasp. "Barb! Have you got eyes on the site?"

"Negative," came the response from Price. "What's that racket?"

"Three bloody liquid fuel rockets pushing God knows how much firepower into Earth orbit," McCarter answered.

"Three?" Price exclaimed. She must have turned away from her microphone, because McCarter couldn't make out her words over the PDA's speaker.

"If she's asking for the potential wipeout damage from those things, we're looking at six cities' worth of kinetic darts," Manning told McCarter.

"Six cities," McCarter repeated. "In other words, they can drop shit in the member nations of the G8 that haven't been hit already."

"Not good at all," Hawkins said. "What now?"

"Now we kick down their door," McCarter answered.

A worried Price transmitted loud and clear again. "David, Gadgets just told me—"

"Six cities are going to be hit," McCarter cut her off. "Gary told me."

"We're going to alert the remaining member nations,"

Price said. "But we have to cut off this problem at its root."

"I know," McCarter answered. "We're on our way in."

"And what about the thousand potential hostages?" Carmichael asked, reminding the Phoenix Force commander of the slaves still held in their labor camps.

"I haven't forgotten them. Why do you think we're not calling in a bunch of supersonic strike aircraft down on that dump?" McCarter returned. "We're a precision instrument, sunshine."

"I was worried for a moment," Carmichael said.

McCarter nodded. "Rafe and Gary, on me. T.J., you help Carmichael effect the release of the prisoners. We can use the extra manpower, if possible."

"And if not?" Hawkins asked.

"If they can't fight, at least they'll be out of our bloody way," McCarter told him. "Come on, lads. We've got to save the world."

"Again," Encizo added.

Phoenix Force split into two and stalked into the forest as fast as they could.

NIKLAUS RADULF'S EARS PERKED UP as he heard one of his men shouting as the three Atlas-style rockets faded into the sky above. He turned to see the technician pointing at his screen.

Radulf marched over to the workstation and saw a small blip on the map.

"We picked up an encrypted signal," the tech told him. "Communications close to us, and not on our approved frequencies."

"It means that they have come," Radulf said, nodding sagely.

"Who has come?" the communications officer asked him.

"Those who would follow the two Americans who previously violated our privacy," Radulf explained. "We will be dealing with an assault force in a short time. I want the entire facility on red alert."

"Sir!" the communications officer answered.

Radulf touched the scars that surrounded his eye-patch, remembering the battle in France and the man who had left his face torn, his eye hanging out on its nerve stalk. Unfortunately for Radulf, the old man had been Yakov Katzenelenbogen, one of the five most experienced combatants on the planet. Though past middle age, Katz was a more than capable fighter. What the neo-Nazi had thought at the time was a cripple who had no place on the battlefield was in fact a warrior who turned his handicap into a platform for a whole new weapons system. The clawed prosthesis he wore could carve flesh and gouge bone easily, as Radulf had discovered.

He'd clutched his torn features as Katz had turned to retrieve his Uzi. The stutter of the Jew's submachine gun was accompanied by a half-dozen impacts that Radulf had felt, even through his Kevlar body armor. Knocked onto his back, the neo-Nazi had faded from conscious-ness, only to awaken to the deathly quiet of an empty, snow-bound hotel. The cold and his heavy clothing must have made it seem as if he lay dead.

For a while, ODESSA had made him wish he had been killed in conflict with the mysterious force that thwarted their attempt to overthrow France. The enmity of his masters didn't last very long. A short while later, another conflict with the unknown marauders had wrecked a large chunk of the hierarchy of the neo-Nazi organization. Short on experienced officers, Radulf was once more accepted, the destruction of his face providing the excuse for his exoneration in the face of failure.

Radulf still felt the sting of their admonishment, but like a good soldier, he'd remained quiet. His job was to travel the world, recruiting from the shadows, seeking out like-minded men, such as Augustus Hammersmith from Tennessee.

With the formation of the Fist of Heaven union, Radulf was overly pleased to escape the stifling desk job he had been saddled with. He had been able to scour the globe to cull the best and the brightest of the white-power movement for the project. His disillusionment with the half-measures taken by ODESSA grew exponentially as he discovered other movements who had surpassed the ancient, tired ODESSA group in zeal and scope.

Now, the Fist of Heaven had a chance to avenge the accident of history that had laid the Third Reich low. For all of Radulf's talk of not wishing to emulate the failed legacy of Adolph Hitler, the neo-Nazi had an undeniable urge to correct the mistakes of the past and return legitimacy to the unending empire. The world had already shaken at the first words of the Fist of Heaven, which had triggered riots around the globe, cast fear into nations and shown that the governments who had succeeded into this modern century were helpless to protect their people.

It was only the strong, steady hand of those like Hammersmith and Radulf that would guide humanity to its next great steps of evolution, cutting the chaff of the lesser races to ensure the ascension of mankind to its rightful place in the universe.

Yes, it was possible that the nightmarish men who had crushed ODESSA's operations so completely might have been lurking in the jungles beyond the perimeter of the Fist of Heaven launch pad. But Radulf had an army of the finest soldiers from Europe, South America and Africa at his command, men who were equipped with the finest state-of-the-art weaponry.

Let the interlopers come. They would find only the bitter ashes of defeat in this stronghold.

Washington, D.C.

THREE HUNDRED FEET beneath the White House the President was ushered off the elevator by his cordon of Secret Service agents, the men as grim as their midnight-black suits and dark sunglasses. He'd been brought down here on only a few rare occasions, mostly for security, but this time there was a crackling, electric urgency buzzing in the air. From where he was being escorted, he could see most of his cabinet already on hand, as well as the leaders of several intelligence agencies, including Hal Brognola.

Brognola was the burly old veteran from the Justice Department who had told the President that there was a weapon available to the United States government that could be called upon in the direst of emergencies. Things didn't become much more urgent than riots spreading across the globe like wildfire, with two cities smitten from space by dangerous orbital weapons technology. The leader of the Free World watched as Brognola excused himself from the agency heads and made a beeline toward him.

The Secret Service agents closed ranks, forming an inscrutable, impassable wall between the President and the big Fed. Brognola knew the drill, and stopped in front of the group, raising his arms. One of the President's bodyguards went over him with a metal detector wand, sweeping him for weapons. The preliminary scan showed nothing, but the executive protection detail was on a level of alert that approached abject paranoia. Another one frisked Brognola by hand, a thorough pat down.

Declared completely harmless and escorted to the President's personal office, only then was Brognola allowed to speak with the President. The Man slipped behind his desk and peeled off his jacket as Brognola pulled a cigar from his shirt pocket. The tobacco wrap was dented and slightly bent from his frisking, but Brognola clamped it between his teeth anyway.

"What have you got for me, Hal?"

"Sir, as you already know, we intercepted an attempt to attack Los Angeles with a dirty bomb yesterday," Brognola answered. "As of a half hour ago, one of our strike teams in Africa had a confirmed sighting of three rockets launched into Earth orbit."

"Three rockets. Multiple warheads?" the President asked.

"Our technology experts have confirmed that the

three orbital vehicles have sufficient payloads to engage six cities. It's no coincidence that there are six member nations of the G8 that have not been struck yet," Brognola said.

The President rubbed his forehead. "This is just their introduction, isn't it?"

"One wave to raise awareness—that would be London and Moscow," Brognola agreed. "The second wave will be a larger, widespread assault, showing their ability to simultaneously destroy even more enemies."

"What about the threats to Los Angeles, Tokyo and Washington, D.C.?" the Man asked.

Brognola took a deep breath. "We believe that Tokyo was especially designed to inform us that they had more than just kinetic darts."

"How many chemical weapon shells were recovered?"

Brognola checked his notebook. "Thirty. Four of them had managed to get a half mile from the freighter before our man in Tokyo stopped them."

"That's in addition to the communications blackout, correct?" the President asked.

Brognola nodded. "Tokyo was a test bed. We had lesser displays of radio jamming here in America. Los Angeles never got off the ground, but Washington, D.C., was in the dark for ten minutes."

The President counted off the crisis points. "Two teams in the U.S., a team in Southeast Asia and now one in Africa? Did you recruit more people?"

"No," Brognola answered. "Los Angeles and Tokyo were dealt with by one Stony Man operator apiece. Their teammates were spread out, the remainder of Able Team ending the Washington blackout, while we had Phoenix Force subdivided two more times. As it stands, Able Team is reunited and ready to move on a hardsite in America, and four members of Phoenix Force are staging an assault in Africa."

"I can imagine that your teams are spread pretty thin," the President said.

"Law-enforcement agencies in eight nations are running themselves ragged dealing with riots orchestrated by this group, the Fist of Heaven," Brognola explained. "If anything, our boys are right where they need to be."

"And you've confirmed that this is an international amalgamation of white-supremacist groups?"

"There's a violent Christian identity organization in the U.S. called the United Legion of Messianic America," Brognola answered. "We have also encountered elements of ODESSA, the Jakkhammer Legacy, the Justice Coalition of Argentina and a Japanese pseudo-Christian cult called Masa Minori."

The President sighed. "All those crazies would have to come out of the woodwork on my watch."

Brognola managed a weak smile. "They say the caliber of a man is judged by the scope of his enemies."

"Is that a good thing or a bad thing with all these psychotic bigots?" the President asked.

Brognola looked out the window of the office, his gaze settling on the map of the world. The President waited a moment before the big Fed heaved his shoulders with a sigh, returning his attention to the conversation. "Ask me after this is over, sir."

Brognola left the President alone in his office to contemplate the worldwide crisis.

CHAPTER SIXTEEN

ULMA headquarters, Tennessee

Augustus Hammersmith looked at the lime-green tarp that had been hung along the wall in front of the video camera and sighed.

"One more time in front of the green screen before we film, sir," Wallace said meekly. Hammersmith looked down on the pederast with some disdain, but not as much as the sniveling weaklings in the mainstream media would have assumed. Wallace had denied his sexual urges of late, under Hammersmith's guiding hand. With the message of God's purpose for his pure-carved children, Hammersmith had awakened the convicted kidnapper of his worth to the cause.

So long as Wallace did not cast a lustful eye upon the fair-skinned, blue-eyed youth, then Hammersmith could easily forgive the man's depravities. Indeed, because the child predator had only brought harm to mud people, Hammersmith saw a place for him after the decadent leaders of man were torn down and replaced by those who followed the Messianic principles.

"All right, sir," Wallace spoke up. "You show up in front of the background without image bleed. No one will be distracted by pixels showing up through your body. Black and red were a good choice."

"Of course they are," Hammersmith answered. "Was there ever any doubt?"

Wallace shook his head. "Dispenza will be ready to broadcast in five minutes."

The founder of ULMA, the mastermind who had unleashed the Fist of Heaven upon a heathen world, smiled and took a seat at a table just off camera. He scanned his legal pad, though he had already memorized his speech. He had fashioned it specifically to put the fires of inspiration into the hearts of those who loved his God of gods, but also laced it with the provocation necessary to turn the impure barbarian hordes who had soiled America and Europe into the seething, uncontrolled savages that they were.

He had been troubled by the loss of the Tokyo operation, but it had been a calculated risk. Radulf had told him that it was foolish to side with the Japanese, no matter how much they proclaimed to share the same beliefs as Hammersmith. The ULMA founder hadn't expected a surefire victory in any case. This was the Fist of Heaven rattling its saber, showing that it had far more than one form of weapon in its arsenal. Even though the Scorpion Bombardment Satellites were nearly undetectable and brutally effective, Radulf could only launch so many at a time.

Even now, the African launch site was preparing another three rockets to follow the other trio into orbit. Once Hammersmith had made his ultimatum, the world would be galvanized into action. It wouldn't take long for the enemy governments to mobilize military excursions into Africa to destroy the launch site, so Radulf and his force were going to be working around the clock, firing high-tech arrows into the cradle of space so that the Fist of Heaven would have the firepower to punish those who dared oppose his new world order.

Already Radulf had sent word from the Congo that there was a team in the vicinity. Hammersmith didn't think that it was a large force, but to hear the ODESSA commander speak, it was as if the Americans had summoned a group of devils to tear down their space program.

"If these are the men I assume they are, this battle will be magnificent," Radulf had said over their secure satellite link.

"How large is this attack force?" Hammersmith had asked him.

"They number between four and eight," Radulf replied.

Hammersmith bit his tongue to hide his skepticism, though considering the harassment that the Fist of Heaven had received in the past two days, Radulf might have had a point. A small, mobile, highly skilled commando unit would have been the logical choice to seek out and sabotage the launch facility. The dispatch of an army would have drawn too much attention and been impossible to sneak into Africa on such a tight timetable. Meanwhile, a handful of men could have been flown around the globe and deployed with stealth.

Hammersmith wondered how such a conflict would be called "a magnificent battle," but then he remembered how the Reich Highwaymen and the Maryland manse had disappeared without a moment's notice. Had a federal agency dropped a platoon of jackbooted SWAT troopers on either of them, the attack teams would have been noticed immediately. As it was, the manse had sent out a brief, urgent warning that it was under attack by a small group. The California operation disappeared completely with no cry, and yet Dispenza's monitoring of the LAPD and federal agencies showed no mobilization, save for the enhanced security for the President in Los Angeles, at least until Wallace heard the dispatch of a nuclear energy security team to handle the radioactive waste.

"With but a few men, much can be accomplished," Hammersmith mused softly. "An army of deer led by a lion is more to be feared than an army of lions lead by a deer."

"Richard the Fifth?" Dispenza asked.

"Philip of Macedonia," Hammersmith corrected him. "The father of Alexander the Great, the man who nearly conquered the world."

Dispenza nodded. "Something we may accomplish this very day?"

"We will be taking the first steps on the road to victory," Hammersmith said. "But the mud people have infested this world too completely for our conquest to come quickly."

Dispenza looked at the video camera, then checked his watch. "What is coming quickly is the broadcast. Does the slide show have your approval, sir?"

Hammersmith nodded. Behind him, on the green screen, would be projected a series of images of inner-city squalor, Muslims protesting in the streets and images of the recent, Jew-engineered economic crash that had allowed the Kenyan-born to be elected to the highest post in America. Each photo had been picked for sheer insult to those Hammersmith opposed, and to shock the scales from the eyes of white Americans and Europeans.

The speech he was about to give was going to be the shot heard around the world.

The ULMA commander stood and walked in front of the green screen, his heart hammering with excitement.

Stony Man Farm

HUNTINGTON WETHERS WAS normally a calm, dispassionate man outwardly. The only semblance of excitement he generally displayed was his intense concentration on exploring the finer details of research and combing through code with intimate, loving dedication. But right now, as Augustus Hammersmith was displayed on the War Room wall, ten feet tall and framed by some of the ugliest images of racial inequality in American history, Wethers's teeth clenched and snapped the stem on his trademark pipe.

Carmen Delahunt spoke up. "Hunt, you don't have to listen to this shit."

Wethers had to tear his gaze from the black-uniformed Aryan on the screen. "Trust me, Carm. I want to hear every vile syllable put out by this reprobate. It's going to make things feel so much better when Carl comes back from Tennessee wearing this moron's brains on his knuckles."

Delahunt swallowed, never having heard her compatriot speak so vehemently before. Indeed, she struggled to remember a time when she'd heard a foul word escape the quiet, educated man. Then again, the grinning ape who was broadcasting himself around the planet was someone she'd call names that would make sailors blanch.

Price watched the speech, her face an impassionate mask, only the wrinkles between her eyebrows displaying the fury bubbling from within.

Hammersmith turned on the screen to point to an image of a crescent with a star between the horns, the typical symbol of Islam. "Though the current abomination that is in charge of our beloved land claims not to be a Muslim…"

"Despite going to a Christian church for decades and having a blatantly Christian wife and children…" Price interjected.

"…he has bowed before the leaders of those heathen nations. As well, he is on good terms with the traitorous government of the United Kingdom, a sniveling pack of cowards who buckle to pressure to have two laws in their land, the law for white Christians, and the sharia law of the savages. None in that pack of jackals dare to stand up to this warlike cult to say that no church but the true church and no God but the true God shall be obeyed.

"This is why London suffered so soon. Moscow, with their pandering to the psychotics running Azerbaijan and Kazakhstan, with their history of giving the heathens in Syria weapons of mass destruction, were the very first. But do not consider the rest of the G8 to be without their sins against Heaven and Earth. Today, we reach down from the skies with the fists that God Himself has granted us, and we will bury the blasphemers and the unrepentant under their monuments to their false idols."

Akira Tokaido turned up the volume on the heavy metal music that coursed through his MP3 player to drown out the madman's words. Trembling with pent-up tension and fury, he turned in his chair to look away from the screen.

Kurtzman paid only enough attention to see what he could glean from the broadcast. Unfortunately, the green screen behind the white-supremacist mastermind hid any details. The transmission had been bounced off several satellites, and while he and the rest of the cybernetics team worked diligently, the origin of the signal was elusive. It didn't help, however, that the rantings of this maniac were drilling under their skin.

"Any reaction to this maggot's speech yet?" Price asked.

"South Central L.A. just turned into a shooting gallery," Delahunt said. "Black and Latino gangs have declared open season on the LAPD."

"Any casualties so far?" Price pressed.

"A few injuries. Luckily the cops there wear body armor," Delahunt explained. "Damnation. Chicago and Atlanta are adding to the mix."

"It'll reach Washington, D.C., soon enough," Price muttered. "You've got entire poverty-laden communities in the shadow of the highest halls of this nation. With a history of coke-snorting mayors and inept attempts at crime control, you've got breeding grounds for disenfranchisement."

"That may be, but traffic control says that the Beltway is packed," Tokaido spoke up. "Washingtonians know what happened to London and Moscow, and they realize that they're going to be at ground zero for the Fist of Heaven's next show of force."

"Maryland and Virginia state police are mobilizing, but the Beltway has turned into a parking lot," Wethers added. "I don't want to think of what would happen if those murderers lobbed a line of kinetic darts along that road."

"Hunt, run the numbers on what would happen if one of those things struck the bunker under the White House," Kurtzman said. "We might have to evacuate the President to a backup Continuity of Government shelter."

"On it," Wethers answered. Finally, the erudite, brilliant scientist had something to focus on rather than the venomous bile spewed by Hammersmith.

"New York City's also going nuts," Delahunt observed. "There's violence in the housing projects, and all the bridges and tunnels out of Manhattan are congested."

"Like it or not, a lot of New Yorkers think that they are the most important city in America. And while the White House might be a tempting target for these Nazi bastards, there's no more blatant evidence of a multicultural melting pot than the Big Apple," Kurtzman explained.

"I wouldn't put it past the Fist of Heaven to make us wonder which city will be hit," Price said. "Don't forget, there's also the United Nations Building, which has hosted its fair share of G8 and G20 conferences."

"You've got citizens thinking about that," Kurtzman said. "Let me check something."

Price gnawed on her knuckle as she worked the main screen controls to minimize Hammersmith and put up the map of the U.S. "You're looking at NORAD's response?"

"Yeah. The USAF and Navy have put up a lot of fighter planes to perform civilian air patrol," Kurtzman said. "But that's wishful thinking. Those missiles are going to be coming in too fast for even an F-15 to intercept."

"They're going to do their damnedest," Price said. "General consensus among military pilots is that if there's going to be another attack on the U.S., they'll put themselves and their planes in the way of anything heading for a city."

"Any deflection will be minimal unless the jets hit them at the proper angle of approach," Wethers explained. "That's if they can even maneuver into position."

"Less negative thoughts, Hunt," Tokaido growled.

"I can't help it," Wethers said. "That man's inside my head. And I use the term *man* in the loosest of possible definitions."

"He's called down Carl and the gang," Kurtzman promised. "He might as well have tried to punch God in the balls, because there's nothing that's going to stop Able from inserting his head up his own ass."

"Normally, I abhor the concept of primal vengeance, but in this instance, its cathartic value offers me consolation," Wethers noted.

There was some therapy in angry bravado, but the presence of six weapons platforms maneuvering in Earth orbit gave everyone pause.

Right now, Able Team and Phoenix Force were the only ones in any position to stop the deadly satellites from unleashing high shock-power death from above.

Tennessee

CARL LYONS HEARD Augustus Hammersmith's speech over his headset as Charlie Mott pushed their Bell JetRanger through the sky at nearly 200 miles per hour. His gear bag was at his feet, and what he didn't have already stuffed in various holsters around his body was zipped up inside, chamber hot, safety on. He had his AA-12 automatic shotgun in the carryall, bandoliers of 12-gauge ammunition weighing the satchel down. That plus his MP-357, his snub Python and his Centennial were going to be his main gear for this hit.

The one concession that Lyons made for this assault was the addition of the H&K M-320 grenade launcher under the barrel of the riflelike, magazine-fed shotgun. A bandolier of high-explosive, dual-purpose shells would feed the big 40 mm cannon.

Blancanales and Schwarz performed one last communications check as the JetRanger screamed over the treetops. Lyons grunted as they asked him to sound off, his attention still focused on the white supremacist's screed of spite and scorn for anyone who didn't have the same lack of pigmentation that he had.

Lyons had never been the target of that kind of prejudice, but scum like Hammersmith had brought anger against the big blond ex-cop. Not only was he the blue-eyed, golden-haired ideal that had been the Nazi dream of inbreeding, but Lyons had also been with the Los

Angeles Police Department, considered by many in the urban sprawl to be just one step removed from the SS stormtroopers of World War II. The Able Team commander had struggled against those prejudices all of his life, guilt winnowing through his gut that he shared the same appearance as the froth-mouthed fanatics who called for the lynchings of mixed-race couples and civil war against any state that proclaimed equality for all.

Hammersmith and his ilk were cut from the same cloth, and with the flesh-shredding power of the AA-12 and its grenade launcher, the Able Team commander intended to unravel that rotted fabric one gore blast at a time.

The Congo

THE FABRIC OF THE TENT parted under T. J. Hawkins's blade while John Carmichael covered him. With a heave, Hawkins stuffed the corpse of a white South African expatriate into the slit he'd made and then held the opening for Carmichael. It had only taken a moment for the two men to stuff the throat-slit sentry out of sight and achieve a good hiding spot in the forced labor camp.

The dead guard had patrolled a little too close to the section of fence that the Phoenix pro and his comrade had opened up, and had to be taken down while Carmichael effected a temporary repair on the chain link to keep their point of entry secret. Pulling his flashlight, Hawkins swept the tent. It was too small to be anything more than storage, but the stench of stored lye burned his nostrils enough that he pulled a kerchief over his face to filter it out. Carmichael did likewise.

"Lye isn't a part of any space program I can think of," Carmichael said.

"No, but do you think these bigots are going to bury Africans?" Hawkins asked with a snarl.

Carmichael's forehead wrinkled at the realization. "They dissolve the corpses before they rot and stink up the place."

"The Nazis have the gall to consider other people as human trash," Hawkins added. "Look for something we can use."

"Like what?" Carmichael asked, skirting the sacks of lye as if they were hyenas hungry for human flesh.

"Something we can use to make a distraction," Hawkins said.

The former Ranger struggled to keep his anger under control. He had served in Africa before, Somalia to be exact. The youngest member of Phoenix Force had sacrificed his military career to prevent the murder of a village at the hands of a warlord. He nearly had sacrificed his life, standing up to the predatory African, but he had been quicker on the draw. As it was, the incident, thanks to the interference of a UN major in a peacekeeping force, had been the end of Hawkins's tenure in the Delta Force, discharged honorably. It was for his willingness to stand up to bureaucracy and violent inhumanity that Hawkins had been selected for Phoenix Force.

Human life, most of it, was precious to the commando. Only those who sought to harm others had revoked their right to live out their days, and Hawkins

vowed to use every ounce of his skill to hunt down killers, torturers and tyrants to protect the helpless from
their depredations.

"Oy, *keffir,* what you doin' in heah?" The voice was
laden with the unmistakable accent of a South African,
and Hawkins swung around a stack of supply crates to
see a gunman staring down Carmichael in the shadows.
Only the African American's setting down of his rifle
had hidden his purpose in the unlit tent, but once the
sentry's eyes acclimated to the darkness, the ruse would
be over.

Hawkins didn't have time to draw his knife. He
stepped quickly up to the Fist of Heaven slavemaster
and punched the man hard in the kidney. Jolting agony
ripped through the guard and he bent backward, face
twisted into a hideous mask. Hawkins looped his arm
around the white supremacist's head, folding his forearm up under his neck. With a wrench of his shoulders,
Hawkins was rewarded with the sickening crunch of
shattering vertebrae. The corpse dropped backward onto
a crate, head dangling on a distended tube of muscle
and skin.

"You okay?" Hawkins asked, ignoring the flopped
head swinging like a pendulum.

"Heart's hammering, but I'll live," Carmichael said.
"Quick thinking."

Hawkins booted the carcass off the crate, and ex-
amined the writing on the box. For the first time in
a while, he managed a smile. "Blasting caps. But no
regular explosives."

"Would you pack detonators and the stuff they blow
up together?" Carmichael asked.

Hawkins shook his head, agreeing with Carmichael's assessment. "We won't need a lot of explosive power. These might be just enough to blow out a section of barbed wire."

"I'll cover you. Get into that fucker's uniform to set things up," Carmichael suggested.

Hawkins set to stripping the corpse. He paused, looking at the triangular symbol of a South African terrorist organization. He wrinkled his nose at the foul patch, but pulled the battle tunic over his load-bearing vest anyway.

At a glance, he looked like a fat man, especially with a belt cinched around his waist. That disguise wouldn't last under scrutiny, however.

"I didn't see any of the guards packing grenade launchers, so take my M-4," Hawkins said. He took the dead man's weapon after making the handoff. "Besides, I want you to take out the sentry towers as fast as possible."

There were two forty-foot-tall, camouflaged platforms where Fist of Heaven soldiers manned machine guns and spotlights. In the daylight, there would be no need for the floodlights, but the machine guns were an ever-present threat. If the white supremacists thought that they were going to lose their slave force, those weapons would sweep the camp, pouring death from above.

Carmichael looked at the pivot-barreled launcher, then pantomimed a fast reload. "This automatically ejects?"

Hawkins nodded. "Direct a 40 mm parcel to each of those machine gun nests. And don't miss."

"I won't," Carmichael answered. "Just don't accidentally get in the way while wearing that crap."

"I'll pull this off as soon as the balloon goes up," Hawkins said. "Don't let them pin you down here, either."

"Brother, I had most of the same training you have, by what I've seen you do," Carmichael said. "I know what to do."

"We don't train until we get it right once, brother," Hawkins returned. "We train until we never get it wrong. Forgive me for stating the obvious…"

"But sometimes, in the heat of the battle, we forget the obvious," Carmichael concluded. He extended a hand to his fellow Ranger alum. "Thanks, if we don't meet again."

Hawkins took the offered hand, shaking it firmly. "We'll meet. Be it the exfil rendezvous or the big mess tent that all warriors go to in the sky. Just try to make it to the helicopter if possible."

With that, clad in the uniform of the enemy, Thomas Jackson Hawkins stepped out of the tent, heading toward the barbed-wire perimeter where a thousand innocent lives had been subjected to hell. He would deliver them from this evil, and repay that hell to the monsters who'd made them captives and slaves.

CHAPTER SEVENTEEN

Tennessee

Augustus Hammersmith, born Augie Hansen, watched the aftermath of his declaration of war upon the governments of the world. News networks struggled to put his words into a context that fit their lies about how the world should be while their military experts tried to downplay the threat of the Rods from God that the Fist of Heaven intended to spear into their cities. He knew that his father, a man who had lost his job at the auto plant because he'd called a spade a spade, literally, was smiling down on him from the afterlife.

The Arabic news network displayed incensed Saudi, Syrian and Pakistani leaders decrying the insults that Hammersmith had thrown against their prophet, Mohammed, and their religion. The streets of those heathen nations were clogged with angry fanatics who burned American flags and shouted epithets at the Christians of the world. U.S. embassies through the Middle East were inundated, and Hammersmith knew that it would be only a matter of time before violence erupted as the American warriors stationed there grew tired of their ranting. He had pulled the pin on religious enmity, and the fuse would burn swiftly.

"For we shall grow stronger through the persecution of our faith," Hammersmith said.

"Was that one of the letters of the New Testament?" Dispenza asked.

"It is mine. All mine," Hammersmith answered. "The godless desert dwellers are beside themselves with the truth that I have lain bare before the world."

Dispenza nodded. "Just to let you know, we're making course adjustments for the Scorpions. The first platform will be ready to fire in twenty minutes."

Hammersmith checked his watch. "Which Scorpion will fire first?"

"Washington, D.C., just as you directed," Dispenza answered.

"And the White House will be ground zero," Hammersmith said.

"GPS has two darts locked on target. Allegedly, the President will be in a nuclear-proof bunker, but the kinetic darts are meant to induce seismic trauma. One dart can easily punch through a hundred feet of bedrock. Two should collapse even the toughest underground lair like a house of cards," Dispenza said.

"One hopes that the animal will stay put, but undoubtedly, his protectors will be aware of the kinetic damage potential themselves," Hammersmith said. "The bunker was designed for a nuclear airburst, not a ground-penetrating weapon. He'll flee like a monkey with his tail between his legs."

Dispenza chortled. "Maybe he'll go back home, where Radulf will greet him?"

"We should be so lucky," Hammersmith answered. "But by the time the smoke settles, the armies of the world will have unleashed their full might against the Congo, regardless of collateral damage against the savages they consider so sacrosanct."

Hammersmith turned to Dispenza. "Speaking of which, how is the second wave of launches shaping up?"

"They'll be ready in—" Dispenza turned on the cameras at the launch facility "—give it fifteen minutes."

"A few more rounds to be fired into the breach," Hammersmith mused. "We must take everything we can get before we lose that resource."

"They'll come for us soon enough," Dispenza said. "You should go to your helicopter now."

"I am leading a war," Hammersmith countered. "Let me see the destruction I'll wreak, and then I shall retreat."

Hammersmith and Dispenza remained quiet about the reason for Dispenza's urgency. The fortress had an addition that no living member of the organization was aware of. Planted under twenty feet of soil was a two-megaton nuclear bomb. Here in rural Tennessee, secure and isolated from the rest of the East Coast, the blast radius wouldn't be enough to damage more than a few one-stoplight towns, but that wasn't the purpose of the explosive.

Since the nuke was embedded in the Earth, it would throw up thousands of tons of irradiated dirt, scattering it into a cloud that would stretch from Tennessee to Newfoundland. The fallout would render thousands of square miles uninhabitable, and radioactive particles would strike down hundreds with debilitating sickness. In the wake of the kinetic-dart assault on Washington,

D.C., the fallout would blacken the sky with an enormous cloud of airborne death.

According to Dispenza's figures, two million would die as weather patterns smeared the radioactive mass across a dozen states. Another thirty million would be sickened and rendered homeless. Since the Reich Highwaymen had failed to dispose of Los Angeles, the liberal strongholds on both coasts wouldn't fall, but at least one flank of the United States would be scoured clean of the stench of race mixing.

The world would be changed today, and Hammersmith would be elevated to godhood as the prophet of a new world.

Hammersmith wasn't going to allow everyone in the Messianic Legion fortress to disappear in a flash of nuclear fire. Essential personnel and loyal soldiers would escape, while a small contingent of local bikers and extremist militiamen would be left on hand to make this stronghold appear worth taking. The irony of an army of federal agents dying trying to secure a two-megaton warhead was delicious. Their heathen masters would not miss them, but law enforcement across the rest of the country would soon learn that they were expendable pawns. With that knowledge, they would turn on the Zionists and the Communists who had crippled America, turning their allegiance to the Messianic Legion's just and true laws handed down from God.

Alarm klaxons blared suddenly, and Hammersmith heard a distant rumble beneath their wail.

"What's going on?" Hammersmith barked.

Wallace looked up from his workstation. "Antiaircraft defenses are attempting to knock out a helicopter that invaded our airspace. The helicopter fired back, taking out one of our guns."

Hammersmith and Dispenza looked at each other.

"Only one helicopter?" Hammersmith asked.

"Yes. And it's a civilian model, but there are gunners in the doors," Wallace answered.

"Someone is on the ball," Hammersmith snarled. His guards were prepared for the attack. He didn't have to issue orders. All they had to do was to hold out until the Scorpion fired its deadly payload at Washington, D.C. The rest would be academic, secondary sites picking up the slack to bring down the wrath of the Messianic Legion.

"Now should we leave?" Dispenza asked.

"We hold our ground," Hammersmith said. "This isn't an all-out assault by our enemies. No black-clad stormtroopers are kicking down our gates. We can protect ourselves from the occupants of one aircraft."

A security camera on Wallace's monitor turned to snowy static, a hissing punctuation to Hammersmith's hollow boast.

The Congo

DAVID MCCARTER, Gary Manning and Rafael Encizo threw themselves flat as they reached a berm where they could look at the facility, even though it had been disguised from the air by camouflage netting. What couldn't be hidden, they noticed, were three more giant launch vehicles being pushed into position by bulldozers. The rockets were settled atop flat train cars, and McCarter made note of four burned-out hulks that had been tossed into a ditch to the side of the conning towers. Upon liftoff, the rolling platforms were immolated and reduced to charred slag. However, without the bulk of the giant missile on top of them, it would be easy for bulldozers to shove them off the tracks, and new rockets to be pushed into position.

The three veteran warriors used their binoculars to scan the work force around the site as the rocket vehicles and their platforms were locked into place. In the distance, outside of the fire blast area, another six Atlas missiles stood. There was no doubt that each of them had orbital weapons satellites loaded into their noses.

"No sign of slave labor handling the bulldozers or the rockets," Encizo said. "Thank goodness these bastards think so poorly of Africans that they can't be trusted to work the heavy machinery."

"It gives us an option or two," McCarter said. "Sometimes bigotry does have a silver lining."

"We're weapons free," Manning agreed. "What are we going to do about the rockets? From my calculations, it will be only a few minutes before they hook up the control cables to fire them into orbit."

"Too bad we don't have serious rifles," McCarter said. "That trick we pulled in China would be just what the doctor ordered. A .223 at five hundred yards isn't even going to scratch the paint on a liquid oxygen tank."

"We'll need to get closer," Encizo mused.

"Company's on the way," Manning warned. "Two jeeps full of... Gentlemen, our problem may be solved."

McCarter turned and saw that one of the jeeps,

actually a pickup, had a heavy machine gun mounted on top of the cab. The other jeep was open-topped and bristling with riflemen. The Fist of Heaven convoy wasn't acting as if it was reacting to their presence here, but the gunmen inside were on alert. McCarter looked down at his PDA and sighed.

"They heard me call the Farm," he admitted. "Now they're aggressively patrolling for us."

"We can use it to our advantage," Manning said. "A 5.56 mm might not scratch the paint on a tank, but it can pop the skull of a driver at two hundred yards."

"I want the technical," McCarter whispered. "Rafe, you and me take out the jeep."

"High explosives or bullets?" Encizo asked.

"They know we're around. Might as well give them a bloody show," McCarter growled. "Make sure we can use that pickup. Especially the machine gun."

"Do you mind a scratch or two on the fender?" Manning asked.

"Bloody do it and stop showing off," McCarter snapped.

Manning pulled the trigger and the technical skidded wildly, its rear tires spewing up rooster tails of dirt and sand that flew into the jeep right behind it. McCarter and Encizo pumped out two 40 mm shells that arced into the Fist of Heaven transport as it swerved out of the cloud put out by the pickup. The twin high-explosive eggs struck the bulk of the vehicle, impact fuses going off within milliseconds of each other. The enemy jeep crumpled like an empty beer can against a jock's forehead, save for the mangled, separated limbs that spiraled from the flaming wreckage.

The technical was still rolling, and the machine gunner atop was unable to fire as the vehicle jerked and bounced wildly. All he could do was hang on as the driver slammed on the brakes. The pickup twisted into a sideways skid, its fender grinding against a tree trunk before it whipped 180 degrees. The machine gunner was torn out of his position by centrifugal force, and his scream stretched out as he flew, then cut short as his back folded over a jutting roadside boulder.

The man who had been riding shotgun in the pickup staggered out of his seat, dizzy from the rapid spin and stunned from where his scalp split against the passenger-side window. He made an effort to raise his rifle, but Manning ended his confusion with a single round that plunged through his right eye and burrowed deeply into the man's brain.

The driver also got out of the technical, but he was without a weapon and clutched a shattered arm.

"You shot out his driving hand?" McCarter asked.

"Left him his other to control the steering, and he could work the brakes," Manning said. "And since you said you didn't mind a scratch on the fender..."

"I said nothing of the sort," McCarter answered.

"You two old married biddies want to wait until later to discuss this?" Encizo asked. "The patrol on the other side of the launch site just turned around, and there's a bunch of other vehicles taking off from inside the perimeter."

"I'll drive," McCarter announced, slipping behind the wheel.

"I don't know who should be more scared," Manning said. "Us or the Fist of Heaven?"

"Let's give the terror to them. At least we know David's the worst driver on the planet," Encizo answered as he and the Canadian crawled into the bed of the pickup. Encizo took up the controls of the heavy machine gun, a 12.7 mm Soviet leftover with several boxes of ammunition. Manning tossed Encizo some rope to strap in, then tethered himself to where he could fire out of the back of the vehicle.

"You girls all set?" McCarter asked.

"Hit it, David!" Encizo replied.

Divots of earth exploded a hundred yards short of the technical. Encizo spun the weapon around and aimed high, taking range and bullet drop into account, thumbs stabbing down at the spade trigger on the heavy machine gun. The weapon roared, spitting out its big, empty brass after chucking a dozen half-inch-wide bullets toward an onrushing jeep. The engine exploded as the juggernaut rounds tore into it, and the jeep flipped end over end, the Fist of Heaven crew inside flattened beneath the weight of the tumbling vehicle.

"You're going to have to get me closer to those rockets," Encizo called.

McCarter threw the pickup into gear, stomping on the gas. The clutch crunched loudly as he worked the shift to rapidly accelerate.

Phoenix Force had only minutes to ground the flight of Fist of Heaven rockets before the deadly conspiracy doubled the weapons it had in orbit. The three men vowed that nothing else would lift off from Africa. Spitting thunder from the big cannon on top of its cab, the Phoenix Force technical charged off road into battle.

Tennessee

LYONS EJECTED THE EMPTY 40 mm cartridge from the M-320 grenade launcher and stuffed another shell into the breech. Blancanales and Schwarz, on the other side of the JetRanger, did likewise. Below them, a trio of machine gun nests smoked from where Able Team had dumped high-explosive cartridges into them. Charlie Mott pushed the helicopter for all he could milk out of it, swinging through the skies at top speed.

Though local law enforcement had categorized the ULMA compound as a fortress, Lyons had attributed the description to hyperbole until he'd had a chance to study aerial photos of the facility. A half-dozen anti-aircraft-capable machine-gun emplacements stood on parapets around the Messianic Legion's castle. Augustus Hammersmith had been busy over the years, turning his headquarters into a hardsite that was second to none.

"And we thought DiGeorge had a hell of a setup," Schwarz said.

"You talking about the place that chewed up eight of your old buddies?" Lyons asked.

"None other," Blancanales said. He triggered his M-4, sweeping a line of autofire along a section of wall-top walkway. A pair of Fist of Heaven riflemen had rushed out to add their weapons to the defense of the castle, but they were riddled with bullets for their efforts.

Lyons grimaced. "I don't mean to speak ill of the dead…but you didn't have me with you back there."

To punctuate his point, Lyons leveled his AA-12 and burned off a 20-round drum of FRAG-12 high-explosive shotgun grenades into a bank of windows that was alive with muzzle-flashes. The special-purpose blast rounds chewed glass and brick into a swirling cloud in the wake of his course of fire. The JetRanger pivoted in midair, and Lyons glanced over his shoulder through the helicopter's cabin. The remains of a dozen men were left twisted in the gaping wound torn through the fortress.

Blancanales and Schwarz triggered their M-320s in unison, their 40 mm shells punching out ten-foot craters in the wall below the bank of windows. The building shuddered under the double hammerblow, and Lyons's two Able Team partners followed up with full-auto bursts into the holes they'd cut in the fortress. Lyons dumped his empty drum and fed in another. He'd packed sixty rounds of the FRAG-12 grenades onto the helicopter, and it was his intent to soften up the opposition from the air with each shell that he had. He flicked the selector switch on his Atchisson to single-shot and looked for more targets as Mott swooped the helicopter over the walls.

A blossom of an explosion curled up into the sky to one side, and Lyons could see the remains of the last machine gun nest smoldering after being smacked by 40 mm of high-explosive punishment.

"Charlie, ease up on the throttle," Blancanales shouted into his headset microphone. "Those MGs are down."

"The MGs are down, but you've got all these assholes running around with rifles," Mott answered. "You jokers are going to have to clear out an LZ for me to put you down."

"One scorched perimeter coming up," Schwarz replied. His M-320 burped, spitting a payload of white phosphorous into a courtyard. The shell detonated, spraying a sphere of smoky, white-hot metal into gunmen who had assembled on-site. White phosphorous melted through clothing, flesh and bone as if it were a hot ember on snow. Screams of horror erupted from the Fist of Heaven defenders, and Lyons popped off three of his FRAG-12s into clots of agonized survivors of the initial WP blast. Lyons's shotgun grenade struck a gunman in the torso and cavitated it, leaving only back muscles and shoulders connecting his head to his legs. A white supremacist standing next to him collapsed as a jagged length of rib was embedded in his neck, arterial spray squirting under high pressure.

Blancanales batted cleanup, hosing down the last of the opposition with the M-4 before switching to his grenade launcher to pump a buckshot shell into a corridor that opened out into the courtyard. Dozens of pellets bounced off concrete, ricocheting off brick walls, eliciting wails as deformed lead balls shredded human flesh.

A balcony looked over the courtyard, and Lyons fired four more of his shotgun grenades into the doorway leading out to it. He'd shot just in time, as an arm clinging to the pistol grip of an assault rifle spiraled into the air before plummeting to the ground.

"So much for the plan of hammering these jackals from the air," Lyons said.

"I'll give you a few more seconds to empty that drum if you want," Mott said.

"Nah," Lyons answered. "Put us down. I'll save the high explosives for room clearance."

Schwarz peeled off his bandolier of grenade shells

and dismounted the H&K M-320 from its spot under the barrel of his carbine. Lyons did the same, but Blancanales kept his grenade launcher in place. Like Lyons, he wanted the option of tearing a huge hole through a wall without waiting for Schwarz to place a breeching charge. The JetRanger's landing skids touched the courtyard floor for only a moment, and the men of Able Team exited the helicopter.

Mott pulled the bird high into the air after giving the Stony Man warriors a salute.

Lyons scanned the corridor that Blancanales had hit with his swarm of buckshot and saw a half-dozen men strewed across the floor. None were a threat, so Lyons unleathered his snub-nosed Colt Python and took the opportunity to refill his partially spent revolver, then exchanged his half-empty AA-12 drum for an 8-round box of conventional buckshot.

"How big of a force do you think they've got in here?" Schwarz asked.

"Unless every damn bigot in North America is on station here, it's not enough," Lyons replied.

"If there were, we sure as hell didn't bring enough ammunition, Ironman," Blancanales told him. "I'd calculate we've still got between one and two hundred left to tackle in this dump."

Lyons scowled, then took the lead position in the group. "Remember, Phoenix reported that they put six platforms into orbit. We have to find mission control and shut it down. Anyone gets in your way, put them in a grave. We don't stop for prisoners—we don't stop for anything."

"Just another day at the office," Schwarz said.

"Roll out!" Lyons ordered.

Three grim warriors strode among the broken dead who had been the first line of defense for the Fist of Heaven. They would not be the last corpses that Able Team stepped over, not if they hoped to stop an apocalypse from crashing into a half-dozen cities.

Stony Man Farm

HAL BROGNOLA WAS ON the line to the Farm's War Room, and Barbara Price was on point in the conversation.

"The President refuses to evacuate the city," Brognola told her. "He says he's not going to leave the American people without leadership."

"That's brave of him, but we're looking at weapons designed to take out fortifications akin to NORAD Mountain," Price replied. "The kinetic darts pack more than sufficient energy to turn any underground facility into a cave-in."

"Which is why I'm hoping that Able Team and Phoenix Force can do their job," Brognola said.

"You're not evacuating, either," Price concluded.

"I've never left a President in the lurch in all my years running the Farm. I'm not about to start now," Brognola replied. "He's going to be a leader, and that means he's going to bolster the people, even if it makes him a target."

"More power to him," Price said. "Able Team and Phoenix Force are on-site and engaged."

"Here's hoping that will be enough," Brognola said grimly.

CHAPTER EIGHTEEN

The Congo

Rafael Encizo hung on to the grips of the 12.7 mm machine gun for dear life as the technical crashed violently through undergrowth on its way to reach the rockets on the launch pad. He had tied himself in place in the truck bed, because he knew that with David McCarter at the wheel and thousands of lives at stake, there was no way that the pickup was going to take any terrain nice and easily. If it hadn't been for the high clearance of the Toyota, Encizo was certain that the truck would have bottomed out at least twice on their mad charge through the forest.

The grille and hood of the vehicle were dented from striking support poles for camouflage netting, and striking more than a couple of Fist of Heaven personnel who had rushed to head off the intruding vehicle. Encizo was tempted to rake huts and supply tents with the powerful cannon, but he wanted to save his ammunition for the Fist of Heaven rockets.

"We're in range," Manning shouted, patting Encizo on the back.

Twisting the massive weapon on its mount, the Cuban Phoenix Force veteran raked one of the mighty liquid fuel rockets with a prolonged burst of automatic fire.

At 600 rounds per minute, the Soviet blaster spit out half-inch-wide armor-piercing slugs that ripped an ugly line across the bottom of one of the launch vehicles. Encizo wasn't sure if he'd scored any critical damage when jets of white steam burst through the holes he'd made in the missile.

McCarter slammed on the brakes, putting the Toyota into a fishtailing skid, and Encizo fought to keep the big weapon on target. Once the Phoenix Force leader had bled off enough momentum, he pushed the truck into gear, grinding the clutch into dust before roaring parallel to the line of enemy rockets. Encizo triggered another burst of 12.7 mm devastation toward the first ruptured rocket, and a hot tracer round burned from the barrel and into one of the hissing spouts of liquid oxygen.

Ignition was instantaneous, the stream of air turning into a river of flame that arced out of the shell of the big missile. Burning sheets of camouflage netting tore loose from their support poles and fluttered wildly. Men touched by the blazing fabric screamed wildly before they, too, were bathed in fire, skin and bone melting.

"You bloody bastards! Talking about fists of heaven!" McCarter bellowed out the driver's window. "You want to know a cleansing weapon! Fire! That'll make you pure!"

"Eyes on the road, damn it!" Encizo snapped. "You can yell at their corpses later!"

Something thundered behind them, and Encizo whipped his head around to see that the convoy of Fist of Heaven technicals and jeeps had caught up with them. Or they would have been right on top of their stolen Toyota if Gary Manning hadn't planted a 40 mm high-explosive charge into the driver's compartment of an enemy pickup. Driver and passenger blasted into oblivion, the enemy pursuit vehicle traveled only a few yards before it crashed into a hut and spun into the path of two jeeps following it. Metal screamed and crumpled as dying howls split the air.

Manning wasn't usually a grenadier, preferring to utilize his demolitions skills in a more hands-on manner, but he had taken Encizo's rifle-and-launcher combo to use the weapon to its maximum effect. If anything could stop a jeep or a technical cold, it was the six-and-a-half ounces of military-grade explosives launched from the 40 mm tube of an M-203.

Encizo returned his attention to the two remaining launch vehicles on the pad, and noticed that the first Atlas-style rocket had bent over, its metal skin flowing like melting rubber. The vehicle's immolation was nearly complete, and scattering guards and rocket scientists scrambled out of the path of the toppling, flaming mass. The scene reminded Encizo of old film footage of the Hindenburg disaster, right down to the swastikas emblazoned on the rocket's burning fins. It was a grim and grisly display, and a hot wind pushed the stench of cooking human meat into the Cuban's nostrils.

He thumbed the machine gun's trigger again and wrenched the muzzle like a hose. Instead of water droplets, thumb-size bullets ripped out of the barrel and cut a lethal swath through the air before punching into the fuel section of a second rocket. Encizo held down the trigger, feeling the bone-jarring vibration of the massive weapon's bolt travel up his arms. The Toyota skidded

again into a sideways drift, and Encizo found himself
sweeping a Fist of Heaven jeep with his machine gun's
arc of fire. The driver and his crew were helpless as
heavyweight slugs vaporized the jeep's windshield and
mashed skulls and chests into mists of blood and bone
splinters.

"Concentrate on the rockets! I'll take care of our
pursuit!" Manning snapped.

"Totally unintentional!" Encizo answered as
McCarter wrenched the pickup around and drove it right
down the enemy's throats.

The Cuban trusted his commander to keep them all
alive while he tore a path of destruction through the
liquid-fueled rockets on the pad. There were few better
ways to unnerve an opponent than pushing a two-and-a-
half-ton truck at them at around fifty miles per hour. If
McCarter's insane game of chicken wasn't sufficient to
send the enemy convoy into disarray, Manning followed
up with another 40 mm grenade into their midst.

The Cuban Phoenix Force pro leaned on the trigger
and poured more ammo into the two remaining missiles,
tracer rounds sinking into the frozen oxygen tanks. The
burning bullets raised the temperature of the liquid fuel
to flash point, and the ground shook all around them.
Encizo grimaced as he realized that it wasn't the ground
that shuddered under the twin detonations; McCarter
had sailed the Toyota over a berm and they were still
airborne. The air itself quaked under the force of the
detonation.

Burning panels of metal cartwheeled into the camp,
slicing through camouflage netting, tents and prefab
structures without preference. Encizo saw one of the

whirling, flaming guillotines split a neo-Nazi defender down the centerline of his body. His two separated parts flailed, lungs wheezing in unison in an attempt to scream, but with his larynx bisected, all that came out was a frothy spray of foam from the two air sacs. The doubled corpse collapsed back against itself, the two halves of torso leaning against each other before a blazing tendril of camouflage netting landed on the dead man and incinerated it.

"Can you see if the other rockets are intact?" McCarter called through the rear window of the cab.

"At this point, it's academic!" Manning answered. "Do you honestly think anyone is going to try to push anything else onto the launch pad?"

"Do you think we can get out of this place before we end up roasted?" Encizo asked.

McCarter swerved, pulling away from the launch pad, and Encizo balked at the sight of a wall of fire looming behind the pickup. He swallowed hard as he felt the sweat evaporate on his skin, flesh drying out instantly.

"David!" Encizo bellowed.

"Not now, I'm busy!" McCarter called back. The burning cloud lurched toward them, swallowing people, huts and vehicles as it pursued them. Encizo was about to complain about how slow their truck was going when acceleration forces shoved him hard on the ropes. Manning reached out a branchlike arm to hold the Cuban still and the two men could see that their technical had left the ground, once more taking flight.

Camouflage netting that hadn't been ignited stretched around them as the pickup leaped through it. The strands snapped as the multiton truck was too much for it to hold back, and Phoenix Force was suddenly out of the launch camp. The waving tendrils of net flashed as it burst on fire before the cloud crashed like a wave on the shore.

The wheels of the Toyota struck the ground and Encizo felt the jarring impact all the way up to his hips. Later on, he'd complain about a minor back ache, but at least he would be alive to feel the hurt. Had not David McCarter's driving been so aggressive, Encizo could see himself reduced to a charred briquette.

No, Encizo told himself. Phoenix Force would not have to rise from the ashes on this day. They had escaped the fires of hell licking at their heels, surviving to continue their duties.

McCarter slowed the truck and looked in the back. "You two all right?"

"A little dried out by that fireball," Manning answered. "How about you?"

"Good. We might even be able to drive this thing back to the old Sikorsky," McCarter said.

"That would be a relief," Encizo added, taking his knife to the rope harness that had strapped him to the truck bed. A thump resounded in the distance, an all too familiar noise to his trained ears, and on instinct, he lunged for Manning, pushing him over the tailgate.

A thunderbolt crashed into the ground, flipping the Toyota upside down.

Then darkness descended on the stunned Cuban, almost blotting out the shapes of several men approaching him and his fallen teammates.

As THE ROAR OF EXPLOSIONS and heavy machine gun fire filled the air in the distance, T. J. Hawkins had to give his commander credit. The man knew how to send up a signal.

He and John Carmichael had been expecting something loud to occur, but the sentries who surrounded the slave camp were caught unaware. A dozen pairs of eyes turned toward the sound of conflict, giving Hawkins the opportunity to lay three sacks of blasting caps at the bases of posts that were strung together by barbed wire.

Congolese and Liberian prisoners watched as Hawkins laid his charge down, and instinct told them that something was going to happen. The stronger helped the weak along, pulling them back and beyond the blast radius of the satchel charges, and the ex-Ranger moved back, as well. Gary Manning had lent him a few small blocks of C-4 and radio detonators, which Hawkins had placed among the blasting caps. It wasn't going to be the neatest or the most focused of demolitions work, but it would be more than sufficient to bring down a barbed-wire fence.

He glanced back toward the tent where Carmichael was waiting and gave a quick wave of his hand.

The African American Green Beret pushed aside the flap of the tent and leveled his grenade launcher at one of the guard towers. With a pull of the trigger, his explosive package spiraled through the air and slammed into the raised nest. The minibomb detonated on impact, an air-splitting roar cracking through the sky as crushed bodies and two twisted machine guns were thrown to the ground forty feet below.

Hawkins thumbed the radio detonator and three rapid booms sounded in quick succession. Posts tumbled and barbed wire snapped under the weight of falling timbers, creating a gap fifty feet wide in the prison compound. The thunder of close explosions had drawn attention, and Hawkins whipped up his SIG P-229 from its holster. The sleek 9 mm barked out its lethal message as the Phoenix Force pro ripped off double taps into the three closest Fist of Heaven sentries as they turned to see the slaves throwing tables and cots across the barbed wire to protect their barefoot companions.

Three neo-Nazis collapsed in the dirt with two bullets in each of their faces. Hawkins's swift reaction had bought the Congolese kidnap victims more time to escape their confines. Another rifleman was about to drop the hammer on Hawkins when Carmichael blew up the second machine gun platform with a grenade. The crash of the explosion caused the Fist of Heaven slave lord to wince and flinch, giving Hawkins all the time he needed to bring up his SIG and punch two rounds into the man's evil heart.

"Move it, people!" Hawkins bellowed, counting on the Africans who knew English to urge their fellows onward.

Two brawny men burst from the flood of humanity and rushed toward the corpses of their former captors, scooping up weapons.

"Thank you, sir!" one of them shouted in heavily accented English. "Who's rescuing us?"

"Just two friends from across the ocean," Hawkins answered. "The less you ask, the less I lie to you."

"Friends is good enough!" the English speaker

answered as he tossed a rifle to another African who had come to join him. "Just two?"

"We're hoping that you can handle yourselves while we keep these bastards busy," Hawkins said. "Guard your own until we clear the area."

The former slave nodded. "Just say the word, and we'll help you kill—"

In the distance, the launch pad erupted in a gout of flame.

Hawkins tossed another African a rifle and tore off his stolen tunic. His pistol wasn't going to be much, but the escapees would need firepower. He tossed spare magazines to anyone who wanted some. Gunfire erupted around the perimeter as the freed Africans started fighting for themselves.

Hawkins could see that the guards, suddenly faced with armed opposition, weren't going to stick around to receive their just deserts. Fist of Heaven sentries ran for the tree line as angry bullets zipped through the air after them. Carmichael lobbed a third grenade toward a clot of neo-Nazis that shredded four men.

A thunderous explosion ripped the air at the launch pad and Hawkins whirled to see an ever-expanding cloud of flame flood across the ground. He tensed, realizing that his friends and partners in Phoenix Force were right in the path of fire.

"Damn it," Hawkins growled. "John, see any wheels around here?"

"A jeep, right over there," Carmichael said.

"Come on!" Hawkins shouted. "This doesn't look good."

Carmichael said nothing as the two men rushed

toward the jeep. Liberated Congolese shouted in victory as the last of the neo-Nazi guards either collapsed with bullets in their backs or fled into the jungle.

Hawkins had done his job, now he had to look after his friends.

NIKLAUS RADULF TILTED UP Encizo's chin as the Cuban returned to consciousness. The scar-faced, one-eyed ODESSA officer sneered down at him, McCarter and Manning, all of whom were bound hand and foot while they had been out cold.

"I recognize you three," Radulf said. "Remember a cold winter night in an isolated resort?"

"I don't know what you're talking about," McCarter spoke up defiantly. "You must be confusing me with one of your old boyfriends."

"Did he keep you warm that evening?" Encizo added to the taunts.

"Humor," Radulf said. "The three of you weren't in the company of an old, one-armed Jew?"

"Not a clue," Manning said. "You two—"

Radulf swung a kick into Manning's stomach, bending him over. "I'm good at remembering faces. And you, muscles, carried this little brown greaser past me as I lay near death and frozen in the snow."

"Muscles, eh?" Encizo asked. "You're as creative with your nicknames as you are…"

Radulf backhanded the Cuban across the jaw. "Quiet, you sniveling little spic."

"Try that shit again, luv," McCarter snarled. "I'll bite your other fucking eye out, even with my hands tied behind my back."

Radulf snorted. "So where is the old Jew? Retired to Florida to rot in the sun?"

Manning glared up from the ground. "You keep repeating the word *Jew* as if it were some kind of insult, Nazi."

Radulf looked down on the Canadian, then looked around at his remaining ODESSA troops. There were five of them, and they all had assault rifles leveled at the captive Phoenix Force members. McCarter spoke a good game toward the cyclopean Fist of Heaven leader, but he knew that with all three of them bound, any action at all would be ended quickly. Whether it be by bullet or rifle stock to the head depended on how long Radulf was willing to spend treating the three Stony Man warriors to a lesson in pain.

"Gunter, you can take the burly one. Hans, have fun with this little brown piece of refuse," Radulf said. He turned to McCarter.

"You and I, Englishman, we'll see how sharp your tongue is when I use a pair of pliers to rip it out of your jaw," Radulf warned.

The two men that Radulf had called to action set their rifles and gun belts aside. McCarter could see the delight in the neo-Nazis' eyes at the prospect of letting their cruel fantasies of revenge run amok. He could also see Encizo weakening his bonds with the razor blade he kept between two bandages at the small of his back for situations like this. Manning's fists flexed behind him, and the Phoenix Force commander knew that his Canadian friend's muscles were bulging with enough force to break, or at least stretch, the cords that held him captive.

McCarter took a deep breath. Sure enough, he was going to have to deal with Radulf as he had said—with both hands tied behind his back. McCarter's only concern was with the three riflemen who were behind them. The Fist of Heaven troopers would hesitate to open fire, for fear of hitting their compatriots, but any delay wouldn't be long. His only hope on that front was T. J. Hawkins and John Carmichael, if they were finished freeing the Africans held in the slave labor camp.

McCarter saw the ropes around Encizo's wrists go slack. He'd gotten his hands free, and he noticed the glint of the razor blade's edge between his fingertips. It wasn't much of a weapon, but the sharp edge would at least give Encizo something to fight with.

"Well, you bloody gimp geezer, you gonna look at my pretty face all day, or you finally gonna whip your dick out to jack it?" McCarter taunted.

Radulf started to chuckle. "You think too much of yourself, Englishman. But don't worry, I'll give you some humility."

A gunshot cracked and Radulf's attention was drawn to the figure of one of his riflemen. The guard staggered backward, a quarter of his skull torn from the rest of his head. His twitching legs finally stopped receiving jolted messages from a misfiring spinal cord and folded beneath him, brains spilling out into the dirt.

Even as that neo-Nazi had collapsed, a 9 mm handgun barked four times in rapid fire. McCarter didn't need to confirm if the shots struck the other two sentries. Hawkins was one of the few people on the team who could come close to challenging him in pistol speed shooting and accuracy. The 9 mm SIG-Sauer that Hawkins fired would put the bullets right where the ex-Ranger wanted them, and his marksmanship was sufficient that, even with ball ammunition, he'd bring down two armed gunmen with four shots.

The chatter of weapons was enough of a cue, and ropes snapped in time with the gunshots as Manning burst free of his bonds.

Gunter was a large man, a half head taller than Manning, and having approximately fifty pounds on him. By all rights, the ODESSA strongman's battle against the stunned Canadian should have been no contest, and it was. Manning swung both fists around in slashing arcs that connected with the German's ears. Gunter howled as his eardrums burst under the twin hammer blows of the Canadian's fists, and he staggered backward. Manning pushed off his knees, sinking his fingers into Gunter's shirt to help himself rise to his feet. The Fist of Heaven muscleman flailed his arms wildly and helplessly, jerked into the air by the Phoenix Force brawler's superior strength and leverage.

With a surge, Manning spun and hip-tossed Gunter face-first into the ground. The neo-Nazi's chin stopped when it struck the dirt, but his shoulders and the rest of his body continued onward with the unmistakable sickening, wet crunch of a shattered neck. Gunter's carcass was a limp puddle of meat on the forest floor, not even a twitch remaining in his lifeless nervous system.

Rafael Encizo pistoned a hard punch into Hans's groin, doubling the sneering neo-Nazi over with an explosion of fetid breath. Now that Hans and Encizo were face-to-face, the Cuban brought up his hand with the razor blade pinched between his index and middle fingers. The sharp edge jutted like a single talon, and Encizo sliced it behind the ODESSA thug's ear, sinking deep into the flesh of his neck. Hans gurgled in surprise at the hot flash of pain that licked at his throat, then saw a fountain of arterial blood arc into the air, his carotid artery turned into a hose that dropped his blood pressure to nothing in the space of a few seconds.

Exsanguinated in a few moments, the Fist of Heaven man toppled backward and Encizo turned to check on McCarter.

Wrists firmly bound at the small of his back, McCarter decided to use his head. He whipped the dome of his skull up and into Niklaus Radulf's nose with all the force that he could muster. A head butt was one of McCarter's favorite surprise moves in combat, and with the right timing and the proper angle, it would be all that he needed.

The ODESSA commander heard the ugly crack of his facial bones, but that was all the outside indication he ever received from his senses about the killing blow that struck him. Radulf felt no pain as splinters of skull were driven right into his brain. He crashed to the earth, felled by a single blow from an otherwise helpless enemy. Had Radulf possessed any consciousness, he would have been embarrassed that this was the second instance where underestimating an opponent had cost him dearly.

"Untie me, Rafe," McCarter snarled, looking down at the corpse at his feet. Encizo's razor sliced through his bindings and finally the Briton's hands were free. "T.J., lend me your SIG."

Hawkins handed over the handgun. "What for?"

McCarter checked the load in the magazine, then emptied the ten remaining cartridges in the pistol into Radulf's slack, lifeless face. He pulled the trigger even after the dead neo-Nazi's features had been pounded into a wet puddle of gore in the dirt. McCarter knelt and felt for a pulse, then nodded with confirmation.

"Making sure this prick doesn't come back for a third dance," McCarter explained.

He turned to his team and to John Carmichael and sighed. "Come on, mates. Let's find John's partner, and then it's time to head home."

CHAPTER NINETEEN

Tennessee

With a snarl of rage, Carl Lyons let his AA-12 drop on its sling, its 8-round box magazine spent, bolt locked back after putting out a swarm of full-auto buckshot. Five of Augustus Hammersmith's assembled Messianic Legionnaires staggered, mortally wounded from a dozen double-buck pellets apiece, some of the copper-jacketed lead balls having sliced through two men before coming to a sudden stop. For all the firepower Lyons had laid on, there were still two more gunmen who were up and fighting, their handguns blazing in response to Lyons's assault.

A 9 mm round struck the Able Team commander in the chest, stopped cold by Kevlar and chain-mail mesh armor. With one hand, Lyons pushed the empty shotgun out of his way, the other plucking his MP-357 from its holster in a lightning-fast, practiced speed draw. The Smith & Wesson's sights aligned, letting Lyons know that he was on target for one of his opponents, and he triggered the powerful handgun. A 125-grain jacketed hollowpoint screamed through the air between Lyons and his opponent, its nose cavity filling with cloth, blood and flesh to the point that it burst open, peeling back like a deadly flower in bloom. Deformation did little to slow its forward momentum, and suddenly the bullet was three-quarters of an inch across, dragging its leaden petals through organ tissue and blood vessels before it struck the white supremacist's spinal column. Though it had been stopped cold, the hollowpoint had done its butcher's job, and the Fist of Heaven defender's legs buckled before he stumbled against his comrade.

Distracted by the weight of a dead man slamming into him, the second gunner's shot went wild, giving Lyons the opportunity to pump out another .357 auto slug that bit into his forehead. At thirteen hundred feet per second, Lyons's second shot punched through heavy skull bone easily. The impact flattened the bullet, tearing off its copper jacket and long splinters of fractured skeletal material. Suddenly in two distorted pieces and accompanied by a dozen smaller shards, Lyons's round whipped the American fascist's brain into a fine froth, ending his days of hatred instantly.

Lyons pulled himself back behind a corner, peering around it to evaluate the kind of opposition that was still awaiting Able Team.

"Moving up, Carl," Blancanales called.

"Come on up, Pol," Lyons said.

The eldest member of the team and Schwarz advanced, Blancanales kneeling at Lyons's side with his M-4 at the ready. "Go ahead and reload."

Lyons dumped the partially spent magazine on his Smith & Wesson, despite thirteen rounds remaining inside of its boxy walls. He put a fresh one into the grip, not wanting to come up empty in the middle of a future gunfight. He dropped the empty shotgun clip and fished another stick of eight shells from his vest.

With a rack of the autoweapon's bolt, the AA-12 was live again, ready to shred more enemy gunmen.

"What's the countdown at, Gadgets?" Lyons asked.

Schwarz didn't even have to look at his PDA's screen. "It's taken us eleven minutes to fight this far into their fortress. I'd wager that we've got anywhere between four and eight minutes left before the first satellites are in position to fire."

"I don't want Vegas odds. I want real numbers," Lyons said.

Schwarz retrieved his PDA and looked down. "Even with the best software Stony Man can design, this system is keeping us out of the Fist of Heaven's data feed. I'm going to have to enter the system directly at mission control."

"Once there, you'll be able to stop the satellites from firing?" Lyons asked.

"Provided we don't wreck the place getting inside," Schwarz told him.

"No blowing up computers. Check," Lyons said.

"That's my brother," Schwarz replied. The electronics genius looked down at the screen of his pocket computer, frowning as he did so. He held the PDA up to better pick up a signal when his eyes slipped past the unit and through an open door.

"What's wrong?" Lyons asked.

"TV studio," Schwarz noted.

Lyons stepped in, seeing the green tarp hanging from the wall and the camera in front of it. "Gadgets, get in here. Is that an ethernet cable?"

Schwarz was in the room beside Lyons in a heartbeat. "Absolutely, Ironman."

"And usually, you hook up a camera to a USB cable. I don't see as much as a laptop in here," Lyons noted.

"That means the camera is connected to whatever server system this place has," Schwarz confirmed. "Keep this up, and you might be mistaken for a twenty-first-century crime fighter."

"Knuckles and 12-gauges have their place in any era, Gadgets," Lyons returned. "Think you can use that ethernet connection to get into the main computer?"

"With my PDA, no," Schwarz answered. He pulled a USB cable out and connected the pocket computer to the camera.

"But Stony Man can use the PDA as a portal to break in to the system," Lyons concluded.

Schwarz clucked his tongue. "I'm going to have to start keeping technological secrets from you again, bright boy."

"Stow the comedy and get the gang to hacking," Lyons growled. He returned to the doorway to the studio. Blancanales stood guard outside, eyes open for signs of trouble. "Anything?"

"I'd have opened fire if there were," Blancanales answered. "If Gadgets and the cyberteam can break into their mainframe through their network, we might be able to stop the satellites without ever having to hit mission control. Then we can hightail it out of here and just call in an airstrike to flatten this cesspool."

"That'd be interesting, but I've got a few more plans," Lyons said.

Blancanales raised a quizzical eyebrow. "What do you have in mind?"

"Hammersmith threw the world into a panic with

his broadcast," Lyons explained. "The only way to defuse things is to show everyone that he's no longer a threat."

"That means capturing him and putting him before the camera," Blancanales surmised.

Lyons nodded. "Of coursè, we have to decide if we should execute the fucker for millions and millions of people to see."

"Barb would give birth to a litter of kittens right in the War Room, even if we hid our faces behind the surest disguises on Earth," Blancanales said.

Lyons smirked. "So you don't see a downside to popping Hammersmith's head on live TV?"

"That's a brutal plan, even for you, Carl," Blancanales told him. "An unarmed prisoner? Mack would never approve."

"I'm not looking for approval. I'm looking for a way to calm the planet down, demoralize the racist scumbags inspired by this shithead and teach the world to sing in perfect harmony," Lyons replied.

Blancanales tilted his head in confusion. "Wait… What?"

"Just seeing if you were paying attention with that last part," Lyons said. "We have to finish this crisis off decisively and publicly."

"We'll burn that bridge when we get to it," Blancanales answered.

The two Able Team warriors heard the sound of movement down an adjacent corridor and aimed their weapons at the intersection. Blancanales wrapped his hand around the M-320's grip and Lyons flicked the selector switch on his AA-12 to 3-round burst. Shadows loomed into the hallway, rifle barrels poking around the corner to get the drop on the Stony Man pair.

Lyons and Blancanales fired in unison, the 40 mm buckshot charge and a 3-round burst of double-buck pellets ripping through the corridor, creating a scythe of hurtling pellets that scoured the walls and elicited death screams from gunmen who had poked their heads out to aim at the two warriors.

"Damn it!" someone shouted, and a hand grenade bounced into the hallway. Lyons grabbed Blancanales and dived into the Fist of Heaven's studio. The fragger's thunder rumbled down toward them, loud enough to leave their ears ringing, but neither man had been hit by shrapnel.

"Nice save," Blancanales admitted.

Lyons checked the hall with a pocket mirror. The enemy was being more careful now, timid and literally gun shy in regard to the firepower they potentially faced. Lyons dropped his magazine and emptied the AA-12's chamber to replace it with the drum of FRAG-12 special-purpose warheads.

"You like those things, don't you?" Blancanales asked.

"They're just a tool," Lyons replied. "A cool tool that makes Jackson Pollock paintings out of people, but a useful tool."

The Able Team leader once again consulted the pocket mirror and saw a line of Messianic Legionnaires creeping toward the studio, weapons at the ready. "Keep an eye on Gadgets here. I'm going to meet the neighbors."

"Good shooting," Blancanales offered.

Lyons sidestepped into the open, AA-12 jammed to his shoulder, sights centered on the leader of the human snake as it advanced. The white-supremacist troopers froze at the sight of the furious, brawny blond with a monster of an assault weapon, surprise giving Lyons all the advantage he needed. A 3-round burst of FRAG-12 shells ripped down the smooth bore of his shotgun, punching a fist-size hole through the chest of the lead rifleman before it exploded in the face of the legionnaire behind him. The second grenade threaded the needle of the sucking chest wound and burst the second man's rib cage like a balloon, turning his skeleton into shrapnel that peppered the gunmen behind him. Recoil had pushed the third FRAG-12 up and into the ceiling above the group of white-power soldiers, detonating violently and cratering the concrete above their heads. The blast's shock wave hammered the Fist of Heaven team from above with pebbles, scattering them.

That gave Lyons the opportunity to fire another 3-round burst into the enemy crowd, the special-purpose shotgun grenades neutralizing the opposition.

The wave of defenders was devastated, corpses littering the floor. Lyons turned to Schwarz through the doorway. "Have you gotten into their communications?"

"Yes," Schwarz answered. "You and Pol put them to rout. Hammersmith is calling for them to regroup for another attack, but the captain of the guard isn't buying it. He's lost sixty men so far."

"How's everything going with the hacking?" Lyons queried.

"Glowingly," Schwarz returned. "Since all four of

the cyberteam can access through my PDA acting as a router—"

"Gadgets, you're already worried that I can follow too much of your computer jargon," Lyons cut him off. "To the point!"

"They're digging into the system like your last family reunion tore into a fresh mastodon kill," Schwarz said.

Lyons licked his lips, watching the hallway. "Mom always did make good mammoth steaks."

"Focus, Carl," Blancanales admonished.

"I'm focused," Lyons snapped. "We've got time while these idiots are regrouping."

"I'm not sure," Schwarz announced. "Hammersmith just called to the hangar. His helicopter is being readied for a quick exit."

Lyons turned to look at his partner. "Quick exit?"

"Yeah, he wants to get to—damn—minimum safe distance!" Schwarz exclaimed.

"Another fucking nuke," Blancanales cursed. "You'd think we'd captured or neutralized the whole Cold War output by now."

"Pol, stay here and keep the Nazis off Gadgets's ass. I've got a flight to catch," Lyons ordered.

"Go!" Blancanales called after him.

The Able Team commander burst into the hall, backtracking the way they had come.

Hammersmith was not going to escape.

AUGUSTUS HAMMERSMITH CHARGED out into the courtyard off to the side of his fortress. The stench of cooking meat assaulted his nostrils even before he saw the bodies of his slain legionnaires. Their twisted, burned and bullet-riddled forms steamed from where white-phosphorous shrapnel continued to burn inside their carcasses. It would take hours for the superheated metal fragments to cool down, and until then, the air would reek of roasting carrion.

"You know how to piss off the wrong people, Augie," he whispered to himself, surveying the carnage. He stepped gingerly, and drew a nickel-plated 1911 from its holster. He wasn't sure how many intruders had assaulted his fortress, but he wasn't going to take chances with a guard left behind on rear security to keep anyone from leaving the battle.

Hammersmith looked down at the shining, mirror-surfaced handgun and sighed. He should have grabbed a rifle when he'd had the chance. From the roar of explosions and autofire that emanated from inside of the fortress, he doubted that he would have been sufficiently armed with a machine gun in each hand.

"This way, sir!" one of his bodyguards called out. "The helicopter's through that archway."

Hammersmith enviously spied the Heckler & Koch rifle in his protector's fist, but knew that the weapon was in better hands for now. Besides, he had the ultimate firearm in his pocket, the detonation control for a two-megaton nuclear bomb buried on the ULMA grounds. One press of the button and he'd turn this section of Tennessee into a steaming, fused crater, and the resultant fallout would spread up the coast on prevailing winds, bringing a cloud of radioactive contamination that would kill painfully or render entire cities uninhabitable. He mused, tempted by the thought of pressing the button now, because it was on a timer once he activated the bomb, but he pushed that impulse aside.

If there were problems with the helicopter and he was forced to land, he'd be caught within the blast zone. He'd imagined himself as a god, but even the burning fires of a nuclear detonation would be too much for him to endure.

Trying to hide his nausea over the stench and sight of corpses, he charged to his bodyguard's side, feeling the comfort of a guiding hand ushering him away from the slaughterhouse that had become his fortress.

"Just a few more minutes and you'll be on your way to safety," the bodyguard told him, his voice firm but soothing. Hammersmith heard a sudden roar behind him, small explosions pounding out a rapid drumbeat. Gunmen screamed as they were torn asunder by a monstrous, unseen weapon and Hammersmith's feet froze to the ground in shock.

"Come on, sir!" the bodyguard urged. "We have to leave now!"

"My men," Hammersmith whispered. It wasn't concern; he'd given up his compassion for his fallen warriors the moment he saw the burned, twisted corpses in the courtyard. He was paralyzed by the shocking realization that he no longer enjoyed the protection of an army of elite troopers.

The bodyguard yanked hard on Hammersmith's shoulder, dragging him to the end of the corridor that led to the helipad. For a brief instant the Fist of Heaven mastermind caught a glimpse of one of the enemy. He was six feet tall, built like a football player and carrying one of the biggest black guns he'd ever seen in his life. The weapon was fed by a fat drum and the intruder pivoted that horrible gun at him before the bodyguard whisked him behind cover.

Thunderbolts spit through the archway, sizzling through the air until they struck the side of the hangar. When they connected, they hammered fist-size dents in the corrugated steel of the building with explosive power. Suddenly the ULMA commander realized that these were no earthly enemies descended upon the righteous army of white purity.

No one could have wielded such weapons. Hammersmith tried to push the thought away, but the appearance of the cannon-wielding giant brought to mind his worst fear.

The blond hair. The blue eyes. The remarkable physique. And a weapon that struck like thunder.

Hammersmith had brought down the wrath of angels upon himself. The helicopter must have been some sort of illusion to conceal their holy presence on the earth.

"No. No, I believe!" Hammersmith shouted at his bodyguard as he was dragged to the helicopter. "They cannot want to bring me harm. I am their servant!"

"Sir! Get on the damned helicopter before…"

Hammersmith pushed the muzzle of his .45 up and under the bodyguard's chin. One did not blaspheme in the presence of the Heavenly Host. A pull of the trigger and the sinner's head snapped back, geysering a fountain of brains and blood that fanned out under the rotorwash of the helicopter.

"I'll pray for thy eternal soul," Hammersmith said, looking down at the corpse.

Perhaps the bodyguard wasn't wrong about the state

of the aircraft he stood next to now. The pilot behind the stick shouted through the cockpit door, motioning wildly for Hammersmith to climb aboard. Rather than risk his afterlife, Hammersmith turned away from the aircraft and strode toward the fortress.

Carl Lyons burst into view and saw his quarry walking slowly toward him, handgun hanging forgotten at his side.

"Hammersmith! Drop your weapon!" Lyons bellowed, his tone stentorian in manner to be heard over the engine of the idling helicopter.

The roar of the Able Team commander, so amplified, had the desired effect on Hammersmith, as the nickel-plated .45 clattered on the ground.

"Please, I did not understand the message you had given me all these years," the dazed mastermind said numbly. "I repent."

Lyons was confused by the sudden supplication of his opponent, but his attention was caught by movement by the helicopter. The pilot and the hangar crew had rushed out into the open, handguns at the ready.

Lyons opened fire on the men before they could shoot him, getting off the last two of his FRAG-12 rounds before the AA-12 clunked on an empty breech. The special-purpose shotgun grenades struck the pilot as he leveled an Uzi machine pistol at the Able Team commander, its densely packed explosive core slamming a massive chunk out of the gunner's rib cage so large, his lungs and heart slid out through the gap.

The second AA-12 missile missed the hangar crew but smashed into the side of the helicopter, right at the engine. It was a throwaway shot as Lyons was already drawing his Smith & Wesson .357 auto from its holster in a swift movement. That hasty round struck the aircraft's turboshaft and detonated, shattering the mast that balanced the rotors atop the craft.

Even as Lyons opened fire, punching high-velocity bullets into the last of Hammersmith's defenders, the whirling disc formed by the rotor blades tilted toward the ground. Two of the hangar crew literally exploded as the spinning aluminum wing planes struck them, their bodies popping like balloons filled with tomato sauce.

Hammersmith turned, dazedly, watching the carnage as the avenging angel before him unleashed his lightning-swift punishment on those who dared to call themselves the Fist of Heaven. He looked back at Lyons, jaw slack.

"What is thy name?" he asked Lyons.

"Christ," Lyons cursed, noticing that Hammersmith's brain had snapped, reality having long since abandoned him.

As soon as he said that, Lyons thought he'd made a horrible mistake, but tears welled up in the madman's eyes.

"I waited for your return," he sobbed. "It is me, Augie Hansen. Your devoted servant." Hammersmith collapsed to his knees, head bowed, hands held up.

"Stand up," Lyons growled. "You've got a message to send before I let you die."

Hammersmith looked up, swallowing hard. "Yes… as you command, light of the world."

Lyons rolled his eyes and shoved him back toward the fortress.

BLANCANALES HAD LOCATED mission control and solved the problem of prosecuting the computer staff of the Fist of Heaven with a 40 mm high-explosive shell through the door. The blast inside ripped technicians apart with violent efficiency, and the eldest member of Able Team reminded himself that those men were not only barricaded and armed, but they were also interfering with the shutdown of the orbital weapons platforms poised to destroy cities.

He thought about the thousands they'd already killed or crippled over the past few days, and knew that while it wasn't specifically solved to the letter of the law, Blancanales had made those murderers pay for the blood they had spilled with their lives.

As he walked back to the improvised television studio, he saw Lyons walking along, escorting a man in a black-and-red uniform. The dark-clad person looked as if he had been reduced to tears, eyes red-rimmed and sunken, cheeks glistening with sorrow.

"Is that…?" Blancanales began.

"Hammersmith. Or Augie Hansen," Lyons said.

"He came quietly?" Blancanales asked.

Hammersmith looked up and saw the white-haired, veteran Stony Man warrior and reached out gently as if to touch his silvered tresses. "Silver and gold. Gold for the light of the world, and a halo of silver for the commander of his armies, Michael Archangel."

Blancanales turned to Lyons with some surprise. Lyons spun a circle in the air around his ear, then shrugged. Hammersmith entered the ULMA television studio and stood in front of the camera.

"May I?" Hammersmith asked.

"Barb, the main bad guy's gone koo-koo for coco-nuts," Schwarz said into his com link to the Farm. "He wants to say a few words for the audience at home."

Hammersmith smiled, then reached into his pocket. "My Lord, take this. I would trade it for the coin I have earned today."

Lyons accepted the radio detonator in the palm of his hand. On a hunch, he plucked his Smith & Wesson .357 Magnum Centennial from its pocket holster, then pressed it into the broken mastermind's hand. Hammersmith felt the weight of the weapon in his palm. "You would almost believe that this was a true handgun."

Schwarz and Blancanales bracketed Lyons as Hammersmith turned to the camera and began to speak, retracting his sins. He claimed the presence of angels, and pointed to them, but since the Able Team warriors were out of the view of the lens, the Fist of Heaven commander appeared to be simply hallucinating.

It still made Blancanales, a religious man at heart, uncomfortable to be referred to as part of the Heavenly Host. However, the madman's confession and apparent repentance were exactly what Lyons had intended to beat out of the mass murderer.

"Know that God smiles upon you all, and that a time of joy is coming for us all," Hammersmith concluded his speech.

He aimed the snub-nosed Magnum under his chin and pulled the trigger, collapsing out of the frame.

Blancanales grimaced at the aftereffects of madness splattered all over the green-screen tarp behind him. "It'd have been a little more convenient if he'd done all this shit before we showed up and expended more ammunition than Operation Desert Storm."

Lyons looked at the corpse on the floor. "It wouldn't have happened. He was so convinced that he was doing some higher power's will that he would have never given up. But when we kicked down his door and tore apart his plot, he realized the only thing that could have usurped his plan was nothing less than the hand of his god, proving him wrong."

Schwarz shook his head in disgust. "So are we going to buy in to that hype?"

Lyons sneered. "They say the Lord works in mysterious ways. But if that's so, you two wise-asses are my penance for whatever sins I committed before."

It was a bad joke, but it was meant to dismiss the grimness of Hammersmith's suicide.

It didn't work, but the three men of Able Team didn't shed any tears for the dead man on the floor.

Whatever his fate, it had been earned in terror and dispensed with blood and thunder.

EPILOGUE

Earth Orbit

The last of the Scorpions expended its final dregs of compressed air, giving it sufficient thrust to angle toward deep space. The task of throwing itself at the Earth and missing was put to the extreme. As it accelerated through the gravity well, it was too high and moving too fast to be dragged down into the atmosphere. Sheer momentum was sufficient for the orbital weapons platform to spiral off into the solar system on a course that would only intersect with the third planet from the Sun two million years in the future.

If the human race was still present on the tiny blue pearl in the depths of space, then, Aaron Kurtzman had hoped, they would have a defense against the object.

If not, the odds were strong that it would land in the seventy percent of surface area that composed Earth's oceans or land in unincorporated countryside.

Two million years and with a ninety percent chance of never landing on a human being, the satellite was as safely disposed of as humanly possible.

Back in the War Room, Kurtzman poured himself another cup of coffee, but thought the better of taking a sip.

"Can you guys hold down the fort while I go catch a nap?" Kurtzman asked.

"We'll be here, Bear," Delahunt told him. "Sleep well."

Kurtzman poured the sludge coffee back into the pot, then turned his wheelchair to the hallway.

A little downtime was what he needed, and he hoped that the forces of hatred and chaos would remain quiet, at least for a few hours.

Arlington National Cemetery

JOHN CARMICHAEL LOOKED at the Presidential Medal of Honor that he'd received for risking his life above and beyond the call of duty. David Arcado's sister had held a small glass-and-wood case carrying his posthumous reward during the ceremony. He'd stayed long after the other mourners had left, alone with his thoughts and the little piece of metal dangling from a decorative ribbon. It was such a small thing, and though he'd been personally handed the medal by the President, somehow he didn't feel right with it. Carmichael couldn't help but feel a pang of regret over his dead partner.

Belay that, he thought. *This isn't a pang—this is a full-blown knife through my heart.*

A good soldier had sacrificed his life to get the word out about a dangerous conspiracy, and all that his family could be provided with was a carefully constructed lie.

Carmichael wished that he could have given credit to the four mystery men who had encountered him in the jungle and who had risked everything to bring the war to a small army of slave traders and maniacs who hurled weapons into the skies above an unsuspecting world. He missed his friend, but he didn't like the fact that Arcado's recorded "final acts" were a fabrication of what David, Gary, Rafe and T.J. had done.

He looked up and saw the Englishman who'd been called David, standing somberly looking at the freshly dug grave for Arcado. Carmichael turned and walked to him.

"You and your team, you've earned this," Carmichael said, extending the ribbon and its medal toward the Phoenix Force commander.

"Feh, we've probably earned three hundred of those bloody things. My apartment's too damn small to put them anywhere except a rubbish bin," McCarter answered. "I just wanted to extend an invitation. Two in fact."

A small business card was pressed into Carmichael's hand.

"What's this for?" Carmichael asked.

"A part-time job for the people I work for. Ever try your luck at being a ranch hand?"

Carmichael smirked. "I'm not the cowboy type."

"And at night, you get to fire machine guns and learn all the latest kung fu moves," McCarter added.

"I'm more a Krav Maga man myself," Carmichael answered, but his tone indicated an increased interest.

"Kung fu. Krav Maga. Moo goo gai pan. Cream of sum yoong gai. It's all the same to me," McCarter said.

Carmichael tried to suppress a grin at the Briton's silliness. "What's the other invitation?"

"Me and my mates showed up with six six-packs of

beer, and there's only five of us. Gary wanted to divide it up equally using this fancy stuff called math, but I said why not give John a ring and we can suck down some Brittney's with a friend of the family?"

"Just as long as we don't have to listen to her music, I'm up for tapping that keg," Carmichael answered.

McCarter chuckled. "Lad, I can see I've got a lot to teach you about cockney rhyming slang."

Carmichael's heart ached for his lost partner, but an offered hand of friendship was a powerful, healing salve.

The two men went to join the rest of Phoenix Force as they pulled drinks from the cooler in the bed of their truck.

Carmichael glanced back to the grave.

"Rest in peace, brother."

TAKE 'EM FREE

2 action-packed novels plus a mystery bonus

NO RISK
NO OBLIGATION TO BUY

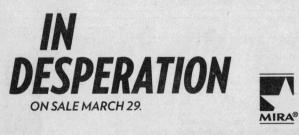